Coordinación editorial: M.ª Carmen Díaz-Villarejo
Diseño de colección: Gerardo Domínguez
Maquetación: Silvia Pasteris

© Del texto y las ilustraciones: Mikel Valverde, 2009
© Macmillan Iberia, S. A., 2009
    c/ Príncipe de Vergara, 36 - 6º dcha. 28001 Madrid (ESPAÑA)
    Teléfono: (+34) 91 524 94 20

www.macmillan-lij.es

ISBN: 978-84-7942-499-2
Impreso en China / Printed in China

GRUPO MACMILLAN: www.grupomacmillan.com

Este libro pertenece a:
....
....

Mikel Valverde

Rita tieNe NoVio

MACMILLAN
Infantil y Juvenil

Rita y Berta. Berta y Rita.

El apellido de Rita es Bengoa y el de Berta, Bengasi. Cuentan que el tatarabuelo de Berta había llegado a ser un importante ministro de un Rajá de Cachemira, al norte de la India, lugar de donde proviene una rama del apellido.

En segundo curso, la señorita Coliflor, que ese año fue su tutora, había colocado a los alumnos en clase por parejas y en orden alfabético y las dos niñas habían coincidido la una al lado de la otra. A lo largo de aquel curso, codo con codo y mesa con mesa, compartieron muchas horas de clase así como libros, bolis, reglas y unos cuantos secretos. Desde entonces, se habían convertido en grandes amigas y, en el siguiente curso, intentaron que sus profesores las colocaran juntas en clase. Y lo cierto es que lo consiguieron y su amistad y complicidad creció con el paso de las semanas y los meses.

Ya estaban en cuarto y, un año más, las dos compañeras se sentaban una al lado de la otra. También se ponían juntas en el comedor y compartían el mismo grupo de amigos en el colegio.

Sus compañeros, los profesores y algunos padres y madres, se quedaban admirados al ver el cariño y la camaradería que unía a aquellas dos grandes amigas.

Tanto Rita como Berta, pensaban que nunca podrían encontrar en toda la galaxia a alguien que fuera mejor amiga que su compañera de pupitre.

Hasta que ocurrió aquello.

Todo comenzó un miércoles, en clase de Plástica; aunque en realidad, el asunto había comenzado a germinar tiempo antes.

—¿Tú qué vas a dibujar, Rita? –le preguntó su compañera de pupitre.

—No sé…–respondió ella antes de llevarse la parte posterior del lápiz a los labios y mirar hacia el techo intentando imaginarse algo–. ¡Ya lo tengo…! –exclamó después de pensarlo unos instantes –voy a dibujar un paisa…

—Yo voy a dibujar una pareja de novios –dijo Berta sin dejar que terminara la frase.

—Pues yo voy a hacer un paisaje donde…

—Voy a dibujar a dos novios que se quieren mucho –le interrumpió de nuevo Berta.

—Oh, seguro que te queda muy bien. Yo voy a hacer un paisa…

—¿Sabes por qué voy a dibujar a dos novios? –le preguntó su compañera dejándola de nuevo con la palabra en la boca.

—Pue… –intentó decir Rita.

—Porque tener novio está muy bien –dijo Berta respondiendo a su propia pregunta. Estaba claro que tenía ganas de hablar y no tenía ninguna duda sobre el tema–. Todo el mundo tiene novio o novia. Esta semana he visto en una revista que ha comprado mi madre, que todas las chicas de las fotos tenían novio. No había ninguna que no lo tuviera. Y agarrados de la mano parecían muy felices –añadió la niña mientras comenzaba a pintar el fondo de una hoja en blanco de color rosa chicle.

Rita se daba cuenta de que aquello no era una conversación. Su compañera quería hablar y cuando se ponía así, lo mejor era dejarla contar lo que tuviera en la cabeza. Rita sabía que apenas le iba a dar opción a intervenir.

—Vaya —asintió ella a la vez que esbozaba el tronco de un árbol con una pintura de color marrón.

—Además, ¿no te has dado cuenta de que en las películas que terminan bien todo el mundo acaba con novio y contento?

—La verdad es que…

—Debe de ser maravilloso tener novio —suspiró Berta entrecerrando los ojos y poniendo cara de pan bimbo.

Alex, el profesor de dibujo, que caminaba entre las filas de pupitres ofreciendo su ayuda a los alumnos, hacía un rato que se había fijado en ellas.

—Chicas, si tenéis alguna duda acerca del dibujo, podéis comentarla entre vosotras o preguntarme a mí —les dijo con discreción cuando pasó junto a ellas—. Pero la clase de Plástica no es para hablar de cotilleos —añadió dando un ligero tono de reproche a las últimas palabras.

—Oh, profesor, nosotras no cotilleamos. Justo ahora mismo Berta ha dicho que debía de ser maravilloso saber hacer el color *robio* —excusó Rita a su amiga.

—Ya, color *robio* —murmuró el profesor.

—Sí, es un color que he inventado yo

mezclando el amarillo, el marrón, el anaranjado
y el gris. ¿Sabe por qué lo he llamado color *robio*?

    —Rita, no seas cuentista. Seguid trabajando
en el dibujo y dejad vuestras cosas para la hora del
recreo. Entonces podréis hablar de lo que queráis,
de colores *robios* o de novios –soltó en voz baja
el profesor antes de alejarse en dirección al pupitre
que ocupaba Héctor, quien había levantado la mano.

    Al darse cuenta de que su profesor había
escuchado al menos parte de lo que había dicho,
Berta se puso roja como el interior de una sandía
y se quedó callada tres minutos.

    Para Rita fue un alivio, y pudo terminar de
pintar el tronco y comenzar con las hojas de un árbol
del paisaje alpino que había decidido dibujar.

Sin embargo, cuando habían pasado aquellos 180 segundos, Berta volvió a la carga:

—No me explico por qué hay gente mayor que no tiene novio. Deben de ser tontos.

—Bueno, mi tío…

—Mi madre dice que las personas que no tienen novio o novia son raros –aseveró Berta haciendo un movimiento con la pintura que tenía en la mano.

—Creo que Álex nos está mirando –le avisó Rita mientras pintaba y miraba de reojo buscando a su profesor.

—¿Tú quieres tener novio? –le preguntó sin rodeos su compañera haciendo caso omiso a su advertencia.

Rita dio un bote de sorpresa en el sitio, lo que hizo que golpeara con las piernas en la mesa.

—¿Pero qué dices? –preguntó con algo de incredulidad, un poco de reproche y mucho de vergüenza.

—Pues eso, que si quieres tener novio.

—No. Y, de momento, solo me apetece terminar el dibujo –dijo Rita intentando dar por zanjado el tema.

Pero su compañera no quería dejarlo ahí, sobre todo ahora que estaba a punto de confesar a su mejor amiga aquello para lo que había iniciado la charla.

—Pues yo sí quiero tener novio –dijo Berta con toda la seguridad que pudo aplicar a cada una de sus palabras.

—Vale –admitió Rita mientras buscaba la goma en el estuche. Se había equivocado al dibujar con el lápiz la cumbre de un monte.

—Lo he decidido –insistió.

—Bien –Rita borraba con cuidado.

—Y al que he elegido de novio está en esta clase –soltó Berta, que hacía rato que se había olvidado del encargo del profesor.

Dentro de Rita se estaba produciendo una lucha feroz. Por una parte, le encantaba dibujar y quería hacer aquel paisaje, al que pensaba darle un aire misterioso; pero por otro lado, las últimas palabras de su compañera habían despertado su curiosidad.

Además, Álex les había advertido que no debían hablar en clase.

Pero la curiosidad de Rita es algo parecido a un monstruo grande y pesado al que, una vez que se ha despertado, es muy difícil volver a controlar.

—¿Quién es?

—¿Quieres saberlo?

—Sí –la cumbre de la montaña se había quedado a medio hacer, a pesar de que Rita no abandonaba el lápiz de su mano. La curiosidad la dominaba por completo.

—De acuerdo, te lo diré –casi le susurró en voz baja Berta, poniendo cara de que iba a contar un secreto muy gordo–. Y si lo hago es porque soy tu mejor amiga y siempre lo seré.

—Vale, ¿quién?

Berta miró a un lado y otro para asegurarse de que nadie la oía antes de decir:

—Edu

—¿Edu ?

—Sí.

—¿Eduardo Sánchez Abasolo?

—Solo hay un Eduardo en esta clase.

—Sí, pero es que Edu…

—¿Qué?

—Es un poco raro… le gusta que le llamen Carlos Eduardo.

—Eso es porque es muy original.

—Ya, pero... –Rita se lo pensó antes de continuar–. Edu siempre viene a clase con la cara manchada de nocilla. No se lava la cara.

—No son manchas de nocilla, son lunares que tiene en la cara.

—No, es nocilla.

—No te metas con él, va a ser mi novio.

—Vaya, ¿otra vez con el color *robio*? –las interrumpió su profesor, quien se había acercado hasta su sitio sin que ellas se dieran cuenta, inmersas como estaban en la charla.

—Oh, claro, es que no sé si sabe que el color *robio* es un color muy difícil de hacer –intentó disimular Rita.

Sin embargo, Álex no tenía el mismo punto de vista, ni cromático ni dialéctico, que sus dos alumnas.

—Lo que sé es que habéis pasado la hora de clase hablando y que apenas habéis hecho nada de lo que os he dicho. No quiero volver a oíros en lo que queda de hora y espero que mañana me entreguéis terminado el dibujo –les dijo muy serio el profesor.

—Pero es que no sé si vamos a poder terminarlo en clase –musitó Berta.

—Pues aprovechad el poco tiempo que queda y acabadlo en casa. Mañana quiero verlos terminados —sentenció Álex antes de girarse para dar otra vuelta por el aula.

Así era, en apenas cinco minutos sonaría la sirena que marcaba el final de la clase.

Rita se concentró y se puso a dibujar lo más rápido que pudo.

Pero, al cabo de unos segundos, vio cómo Berta le pasaba un papel y lo dejaba delante de sus narices. El papel tenía escrito:

¿Me ayudarás a que Edu sea mi novio?

Rita escribió una respuesta y se la pasó a su amiga.

No sé.

Leyó Berta.

"Por favor, eres mi mejor amiga".

Escribió esta en otro papelito.

Vale,
te ayudaré.

Puso Rita en el papel.

Solo entonces, Berta la dejó tranquila.

Pero por mucha prisa que se dieron, ni Rita
ni Berta pudieron terminar el dibujo en clase y
tuvieron que llevarse la tarea para terminarla en casa.

Por la tarde, después del entrenamiento
y de haber terminado los deberes, Rita se sentó en
la mesa de la cocina con sus estuches para terminar
el dichoso dibujo.

—¡Qué bonito! –exclamó su madre al verlo.

—Gracias –respondió ella.

—Sí, está muy bien, sobre todo el color con
el que has pintado las montañas –intervino su padre,
que había hecho una pausa mientras cocinaba una
tortilla de patata.

—Es color novio, digo *robio*... quiero decir,
que es un color marrón claro –le salió a Rita, que ya
estaba muy cansada a esas horas.

Martín, su padre, se le quedó mirando con
una mueca que parecía una sonrisa.

—Vaya, parece que nuestra hija confunde
las palabras. Eso suele pasar cuando una se enamora
o tiene novio... –dijo dirigiéndose a Mónica,
su mujer, pero sin quitar ojo a su hija.

—¡Yo no tengo novio! –exclamó Rita.

—Sí, ya, ya. Je –dijo por respuesta su padre
mientras no paraba de sonreír.

—¡¡Te digo que no tengo novio!! –insistió ella
de mal humor.

—Bueno, hija, no te enfades —intervino su madre haciendo una seña a Martín para que siguiera con lo suyo —ya sabes que tu padre es un bromista, no le hagas caso.

—Sí, pero que sepas que no tengo novio y no pienso tenerlo nunca. Los novios no dan más que problemas —repitió la niña mientras recogía sus cosas de la mesa.

—De acuerdo, hija.

A Rita le costó abandonar el mal humor. Quería haber preguntado a sus padres durante

la cena por qué había gente que pensaba que las personas que no tenían novio eran raras; pero vistas las burlas, se olvidó del tema.

Cuando se terminó el yogur y recuperó el ánimo, deseó con todas sus fuerzas que aquella noche su amiga se olvidara para siempre de Edu y de la promesa que ella le había hecho.

Al día siguiente, en el patio del colegio, poco antes de entrar a clase, Rita comprobó que Berta no se había olvidado del tema, si no todo lo contrario.

—¡¡Rita, Rita, Rita!! ¿sabes qué película vi ayer con toda mi familia? —le preguntó emocionada su compañera sin poder contener los nervios.

—Ni idea.

—La de Wall·e. Es preciossssa —dijo seseando con mucho empalago Berta.

—Ah sí, la de un robot de limpieza.

—La de un robot que se enamora de una robot y se hacen noviosssss —le corrigió—. ¿Te das cuenta? Hasta los robots tienen novio.

—Psí —respondió sin mucho entusiasmo Rita.

—Prometiste que me ayudarías, recuerda.

—Bueno...

—No te preocupes, lo tengo todo pensado —dijo Berta mientras subían a clase—. Escribiré una nota anónima y en ella le preguntaré a Edu si quiere ser mi novio.

—Pero si es un anónimo, ¿cómo va a saber él quién quiere ser su novia? —razonó Rita

—Es verdad. Pero es que tampoco quiero poner mi nombre en la nota. Si otra persona lo leyera, me daría mucha vergüenza.

—Pues no le digas quién eres, pero dale alguna pista.

—¡Claro! —exclamó Berta radiante como una novia el día de su boda. Al instante sacó un papel y un lápiz de la mochila y se puso a escribir.

Poco después leía a su compañera la nota:

¿Quieres ser mi novio?
Firmado: una chica que se sienta en la segunda
hilera de mesas empezando por la ventana.
En una de las dos primeras mesas de la fila..

—¿Qué te parece?

—Pues que has sido muy clara, tal vez demasiado –respondió Rita.

—No, tú tenías razón. Es mejor dejarlo todo bien claro, para que Edu no se confunda. Quiero que sea mi novio y el de nadie más. Si otra niña me lo quitara, sería capaz de aplastarla como a un gusano –gruño Berta con voz ronca y amenazadora a la vez que agitaba un puño cerrado.

Rita no se había fijado hasta entonces en lo gordas y fuertes que eran las manos de Berta.

—Bueno, vale, no te pongas así –le dijo un poco asustada al ver en la cara de su amiga aquella expresión que causaba pavor. Yo ya te he ayudado, tal como te prometí, ahora te deseo mucha suerte y que seáis muy novios.

—No Rita, lo que quería pedirte es que tú dejaras la nota en la mesa de Edu a la hora del recreo.

Rita se quedó paralizada, cortocircuitada, como un robot al que se le hubiera fundido el fusible principal.

—¿Pero por qué yo? –preguntó.

—Porque la que pide ser novia no puede hacerlo.

—¿Y eso?

—Es que me da mucha vergüenza.

Rita se dio cuenta de que el resto de sus compañeros ya habían subido al aula y que las clases iban a comenzar en breve.

—Por favor Rita –le rogó Berta– eres mi mejor, mi gran amiga… por favor...

—Vale –aceptó ella–. Pero ahora vamos a clase; si no, volverán a regañarnos.

Las dos compañeras subieron de dos en dos las escaleras y, corriendo por el pasillo, llegaron justo antes de que entrara en clase Ana, la profesora. Era primera hora, tenían clase de Matemáticas.

Después de que Ana abandonara la clase, llegó Miguel Amorebieta, el profesor de Lengua, que era un poco quisquilloso. Cuando este terminó con los artículos demostrativos, comenzó el recreo.

Todos los niños y niñas se levantaron montando un ligero barullo para dirigirse al patio. Las dos amigas fueron las últimas en levantarse de su sitio. Con disimulo, Berta, le dio la nota.

—Toma, déjala en su mesa, bajo el estuche. Así, mi novio la verá cuando regrese –le susurró antes de unirse a un grupo de niños que abandonaba el aula.

Rita miró alrededor. Casi todos sus compañeros habían salido del aula e iban charlando por el pasillo. Ella se quedó mirando el calendario que colgaba de la pared, haciendo que se interesaba mucho por los domingos y días pintados de rojo.

La clase parecía vacía. Echó una ojeada a su espalda y vio a Natalia Alonso, que revolvía en su mochila buscando el bocadillo. Rita disimuló y llegó hasta la puerta de clase para luego regresar a su sitio como si de repente hubiera recordado algo.

—Je, qué tonta, se me había olvidado coger el capuchón del boli. ¡Qué despiste, je, je! ¡Qué haría sin mi capuchón de boli favorito…! –dijo mientras comprobaba que Natalia abandonaba la clase.

Por fin sola. Había llegado el momento.

Quería terminar cuanto antes con aquello. Contuvo la respiración y se acercó a la mesa de Edu con cuidado, sin tocar nada para no dejar pistas que la delatasen.

Estiró la manga del jersey y con ella cubrió su mano para no dejar huellas.

Tomó la nota que había guardado en un bolsillo trasero del pantalón, levantó el estuche y la puso con cuidado sobre la mesa.

Cuando colocó de nuevo el estuche sobre el papel, le vio. Estaba agachado, muy cerca de la mesa de Edu, por eso no había advertido antes su presencia.

—¿Qué haces ahí? –gritó.

—Estaba atándome un zapato –se excusó él.

—¿Y por qué tardas tanto en atarte un zapato?
Y además, ¿por qué no te lo atas en el pasillo?
–le riñó.

—Porque si salgo con los cordones sin atar,
me puedo caer; y he tardado tanto porque no
llevo las gafas puestas –se excusó el niño, un poco
cohibido por aquella repentina regañina de una de
sus compañeras.

Rita se dio cuenta que se estaba excediendo y
y de que eso podría delatarla.

—Ah, no te preocupes, eso suele pasar: Yo me
he quedado la última porque se me había olvidado
el capuchón de un boli y me había entretenido
mirando de lejos un estuche que es igual que el mío
–se excusó–. Solo miraba, je. Ha sido una cuestión
de curiosidad. Soy muy curiosa ¿sabes?

—Ah no lo sabía.

—Sííí, soy curiosísima y por eso me he acercado, para ver el estuche de cerca, pero ni lo he tocado.

Se estaba poniendo nerviosa y hablaba de una forma exagerada.

—Porque yo no tengo ningún motivo para tocar un estuche y menos ese. Fíjate, ni siquiera sé quién se sienta en este pupitre. ¿Por qué iba a querer yo tocar un estuche parecido al mío? —estaba perdiendo de nuevo el control—. ¿Eh?, dime, ¿ por qué? —le inquirió de forma intimidatoria.

—No lo sé —respondió el chaval antes de salir corriendo de clase sin despedirse.

Era Guillermo Ruiz de Azúa. Rita se quedó preocupada. Guille no era un mal chico, eso decía su amiga Berta, y ella pensaba que, agachado como estaba, era imposible que la hubiera visto dejar la nota. Pero entonces le vino a su cabeza una frase que alguna vez había oído decir a su abuela:

"En estos tiempos, una no se puede fiar de los hombres".

Rita pensó que tal vez su abuela tuviera razón, pero estaba segura de que los tiempos habían cambiado desde entonces y se dirigió a paso ligero al patio para juntarse con sus amigos.

Berta la esperaba con mirada expectante.

Al llegar junto al grupo, Rita guiñó un ojo a su

compañera de pupitre y le dijo disimuladamente en tono de confianza:

—Tranquila, todo ha salido bien, date por ennoviada.

Sin embargo, Rita no las tenía todas consigo. ¿Le habría visto Guille dejar la nota? Se suponía que aquel niño en esos momentos estaba jugando un partido de fútbol, pero el chico permanecía en medio del patio mirándola sin hacer caso del balón que pasaba a su lado.

—¿Ocurre algo? –le preguntó Miren.

—No, nada –respondió ella.

—¿Seguro, Rita? –intervino Sonia.

—Hoy estás un poco rara –añadió Rafa.

—Estoy bien, en serio… aunque tengo un ligero dolor de cabeza. ¿Por qué no nos alejamos del campo de fútbol? Aquí hay mucho ruido.

Y el grupo de amigos se fue al otro extremo del patio para pasar el resto del recreo: Rita, sin poder quitarse de la cabeza a Guille y Berta, a Edu.

La primera deseaba que el recreo se alargara hasta la eternidad. Así no tendría que regresar a clase y enfrentarse a la realidad. Y es que Rita tenía la sensación de que algo en el plan que había diseñado su amiga había fallado. Era de nuevo aquella intuición que aparecía de vez en cuando dentro de ella y que casi siempre acertaba.

Por otro lado, Berta tenía muchas ganas de regresar a clase y confirmar a Edu, con una mirada de novia, que ella era su pretendiente y que sería una pareja fiel.

Pero por mucho que cada una de las dos amigas lo deseara, el recreo duró la misma media hora de todos los días, y cuando la sirena sonó, todos los alumnos, incluidos los cinco amigos, subieron a sus aulas.

Tenían Conocimiento del medio con Pilar, su tutora. Era la última hora de la mañana. La clase comenzó bien. Abrieron el libro y, con un mapa, la profesora les explicó cómo se distribuyen los países por el norte de África, cosa que Rita conocía muy bien tras su aventura por aquellas tierras.

Sin embargo, Rita notaba algo. No lo veía, pero sentía que alguien la estaba mirando.

Cuando Pilar les encargó que dibujaran un mapa, ella dirigió su mirada disimuladamente hacia el lugar donde se sentaba Edu y...

¡¡No podía ser!!¡La estaba mirando! ¡A ella!

Rita se puso un poco nerviosa. Miró de nuevo y allí estaba él, con las manchas de chocolate decorando su cara de plátano y sus ojos clavados en ella.

Intentó calmarse y comenzó a pensar.

—Mmmm, claro —se dijo—. Este besugo ha leído la nota y está intentando mirar a Berta; pero como yo estoy en medio, es inevitable que su mirada se tope conmigo. Bien, le facilitaré las cosas para que pueda ver a su chica. Rita se estiró hacia atrás lo más que pudo en el pupitre para dejar un espacio abierto entre su compañera y el zampador de nocilla.

Miró de reojo, y... ¡Edu la seguía mirando a ella! No entendía.

Se tumbó cuanto pudo sobre la mesa para
dejar claramente a su compañera a la vista de Edu.
Estaba muy cerca del papel, lo tocaba con la nariz.
Le dolía la espalda, pero a ella le daba igual, todo
fuera por los novios. Echó un vistazo a su derecha
y... y....

¡¡Seguía con la mirada fija en ella!!
¿Por qué? Rita no entendía, pero allí estaba Edu
con cara de pánfilo, mirándola, apoyado en la mesa,
pasando olímpicamente del Sáhara, Marruecos,
Libia, Egipto y Túnez.

Un temor apareció en la mente de Rita.
Era algo horrible, pavoroso. Sin embargo, ella tenía
que comprobarlo.

Se armó de valor y se giró hacia aquel Romeo
goloso y le miró de frente. Era espantoso, Edu la
observaba con un gesto más empalagoso que un
helado de mermelada de ciruela azucarado. Ella no
perdió la calma y, muy tiesa, le aguantó la mirada
hasta que, de repente, con un gesto rápido, Rita se

giró a la derecha y Edu… también, siguiéndola con la mirada.

Una finta, y Rita se movió con agilidad felina a la izquierda; pero aquel chalado hizo lo mismo que ella sin dejar de clavar sus ojos merengosos en ella.

—¿Rita, Edu, puede saberse qué estáis haciendo? –les dijo Pilar, la profesora–. Por favor, haced el mapa, y dejad vuestros jueguecitos para después de clase.

Su tutora lo dijo así en voz alta, delante de todos. Los había reñido y había dicho sus dos nombres… ¡juntos!

Rita notó cómo le subían los colores y se giró y se puso cerca, muy cerca de la página en la que estaba dibujando, intentando ocultar su cara, haciendo caso omiso de algunas risitas y, sobre todo, procurando evitar la mirada de Berta. Su compañera había estado enfrascada en el dibujo del mapa y se había extrañado al oír decir aquello a la profesora.

Sin embargo, al cabo de unos segundos, su gran amiga le pasó una nota escrita en un papel.

> Estás convenciendo a Edu de que voy a ser una novia guay, ¿verdad? Gracias por seguir ayudándome para tener novio.

Leyó Rita.

Con disimulo, ella escribió a su vez:

> De nada. Somos muy amigas y nada nos separará nunca ¿verdad?

Leyó Berta.

> Claro que no.

Escribió esta en un nuevo papel que le entregó a su compañera.

Los alumnos terminaron los mapas, así como el tiempo de la clase se fue agotando poco a poco.

Todos recogieron sus cosas, las guardaron en las mochilas y salieron del aula. Mientras guardaba el estuche, Rita se concentraba para no mirar hacia el pupitre de Edu. Pero cuando lo hizo, de soslayo, se dio cuenta de que él había salido de los primeros.

"Uf, menos mal", pensó.

Las dos amigas abandonaron la clase, y cuando estaban a punto de bajar las escaleras, alguien salió como un rayo tras ellas.

La sorpresa superó al susto.

Allí, con una rodilla en el suelo y una mano en el corazón estaba él, Eduardo Sánchez Abasolo, con expresión de flan de huevo poco hecho en la cara.

—Ejem, yo os dejo solos –se disculpó Rita dando un paso hacia atrás para dejar a su amiga a solas con aquel Juan Tenorio nocillero.

—No, no te vayas Rita, amor mío. Lo sé todo –dijo Edu con voz empalagosa.

Los ojos de Berta parecían que iban a salirse de las órbitas. Los de Rita eran como dos canicas que se alejaban, fugaces.

—Sí, sé lo que has hecho a escondidas para que sea tu novio. He leído tu nota –afirmó aquel Romeo.

Berta miró a su compañera de pupitre. En su mirada había fuego.

—Je, mira lo que dice este mequetrefe… este chico, uy perdón Berta, no quiero molestar a tu… tu… amigo especial –intentaba disculparse Rita como podía.

—¡Y quiero decirte que sí, que yo también quiero ser tu novio, Rita! –estalló Edu poniéndose en pie y cantando su noviazgo a los cuatro vientos por el pasillo del colegio.

Berta, también explotó:

—Así que tú, que decías que eras mi mejor amiga, has cambiado la nota y le has pedido a escondidas a Edu que sea tu novio…!

—¡No, no…! –intentó excusarse Rita.

—¡Sí, Sí! –dijo pletórico el Don Juan.

—No quiero saber nada más de ti NUNCA –bramó Berta mirando con ojos de fiera a su súbitamente ex amiga– no me hables NUNCA más. ¡Y tú! –añadió dirigiéndose a Edu–. A ver si te limpias la cara, que siempre vienes a clase con manchas de nocilla, ¡eres un guarro! –y dicho esto se alejó de allí a todo correr.

Él ni se inmutó ante las palabras de Berta y permaneció con aquella sonrisa bobalicona mirando a Rita. Ella, sin embargo, no sabía qué hacer, se había quedado paralizada.

La voz de Edu la sacó de aquel estado de conmoción.

—¿Vamos juntos al comedor?

Ahora los ojos de Rita echaban chispas.

—¡Deja de decir tonterías y olvídate de mí! –respondió remarcando sus palabras con unos golpecitos con el dedo índice en el pecho de su pretendiente.

—No son tonterías, ahora somos novios,
y los novios van juntos a los sitios.

—¡Yo no soy tu novia!

—Sí lo eres, me lo has pedido y yo he
aceptado.

—Estás equivocado, merluzo.

—No lo estoy, merlucita.

La cosa se estaba poniendo cada vez peor.
No había imaginado que ese niño que siempre
iba despeinado, algo descuidado en el vestir y al
que adornaban la cara aquellas manchas de dulce,
fuera como el personaje enamoradizo de una
telenovela. No había otro remedio, tenía que decir
la verdad para quitarse de encima a aquel pesado y
reconciliarse con su amiga.

—Mira, Edu, la que quiere ser tu novia es
Berta. Yo solo he intentado ayudarla, ¿vale? –le dijo
con toda la amabilidad que pudo.

—Entonces ¿por qué me mirabas en clase?
–respondió él sin abandonar aquella expresión
azucarada.

Ahí la había pillado, no sabía qué responder.

—Eehhh… eso era porque quería saber si tú ya sabías que ella quería que tú supieras que ella quería ser tu novia

—¿Qué?

—¡Que Berta es la que tiene que ser tu novia y que yo quiero que te olvides de mí! –otra vez comenzaba a perder el control.

—No puedo hacerlo, tú y yo somos novios –insistió Edu.

Rita creía que le iba a dar un ataque.

—Brrrrrrrr. ¡Déjame en paz!! –exclamó Rita antes de darle la espalda y alejarse de allí.

Edu se quedó inmóvil mirándola, viendo cómo se alejaba con la misma cara de embobado que había mantenido durante todo el rato.

—¡Y no me mires! –le gritó ella deteniéndose y girándose para luego seguir su camino.

"Qué forma de andar tan bonita", pensó él.

"Tengo que hablar con Berta y aclararlo todo". Eso era lo que pasaba por la cabeza de Rita mientras andaba por los pasillos en dirección al comedor.

Cuando entró vio que sus amigos ya estaban sentados en el sitio habitual que ocupaba el grupo. Cogió su bandeja y, tras elegir los platos, se dirigió hacia uno de los sitios que quedaba libre en la mesa. Fue a sentarse junto a Berta, como siempre, pero cuando estaba a punto de hacerlo, esta dijo al resto de amigos en tono arisco:

—Por favor, decidle a la niña que se va a sentar a mi lado que el sitio está ocupado.

Rita se quedó en vilo, a medio sentar y sorprendida.

Ninguno de sus amigos dijo nada.

—Berta, tenemos que hablar —le dijo Rita.

—Y también le decís que no tengo nada que hablar con ella.

—Edu se ha confundido, todo tiene una explicación.

Berta mantenía una mirada de acero fija en el plato de lentejas, y se dirigió a Miren, Rafa y Sonia.

—Aún sigo escuchando a una niña hablar. ¿Vosotros, que sois mi amigos y que no quitáis el novio a nadie, me haríais el favor de decirle que se calle?

Los amigos permanecieron en silencio con la mirada ausente. La tensión era insoportable y Rita se colocó junto a Rafa lo más lejos que pudo de su compañera de pupitre.

Berta se estaba equivocando, estaba interpretando mal algo que había ocurrido por accidente y que ella misma había planeado. Y en unos minutos había pasado de considerarla su mejor amiga a una enemiga irreconciliable.

Por la tarde, todo siguió igual. A pesar de que solo las separaban unos centímetros, Berta no le dirigió la palabra, ni siquiera miró a su compañera.

Todo lo contrario que Edu, que seguía allí, a dos filas, mirando a Rita con mirada embelesada.

No lo soportaba a él, y no la entendía a ella, pues no dejaba que le explicara lo que había pasado. Decidió intentarlo una vez más y esta vez emplearía los métodos de su compañera.

Cuando el profesor no miraba, escribió una nota en un papel y con disimulo la dobló y la dejó delante del cuaderno abierto de su compañera.

Sin embargo, para su sorpresa, Berta reaccionó de una forma que no esperaba. Había levantado la mano.

—Sí, Berta, ¿tienes alguna duda acerca de lo que he explicado?

—No, señor profesor, pero quiero denunciar que la niña que se sienta a mi lado ha escrito una nota en un papel y la ha dejado delante de mí. Y por eso no puedo atender en clase, me está molestando.

Aquello fue como un golpe. El primero.

El segundo vino luego.

—Vaya, vaya, así que hay una alumna que va dejando notitas en clase de Inglés –dijo con un tono de humor, más de Sicilia que de Oxford, Antonio, el profesor, aunque a él le gustaba que le llamaran Anthony–. Sabéis que si hay algo que no me gusta, son las notitas.

Sí, lo sabían; lo había dicho un montón de veces; nadie sabía por qué, debía de ser una manía. Con Anthony aprendían mucho, pero era una persona especialmente maniática y supersticiosa. El profesor, con cuidado de no pisar las baldosas de color oscuro, se acercó al pupitre de las dos ex amigas y tomó el papel.

—Rita, ¿has escrito y has pasado tú esta nota? –le preguntó con aire de juez.

No había escapatoria.

—Sí.

—*Yes*, querrás decir —rebatió el profesor hablando como un magistrado.

—Sí, *yes*.

—Al resto de la clase nos gustaría saber qué has escrito en este papel, ¿sabes?

—No, *please*, no la lea, *don't read it*.

—El inglés no te salvará —dijo Anthony por respuesta a su súplica mientras desdoblaba el papel—. Sabes que no me gustan las notitas, es algo muy poco británico.

Edu y yo no somos novios.
Luego te cuento lo que ha ocurrido.

Leyó en voz alta el profesor.

Un clamor de risas resonó en toda la clase.

Un griterío que Rita apenas escuchaba, ya que estaba intentando con todas sus fuerzas convertirse en invisible. Sin embargo, no lo consiguió y todas las miradas se clavaron en ella y en Edu, quien, lejos de esconderse, levantaba las manos haciendo la señal de victoria y gestos afirmativos con la cabeza.

—Ya está bien, *children* —calmó los ánimos el profesor—. Dejemos este asunto y sigamos con la clase. Y advirtamos al Romeo de este curso que tenga paciencia, pues su Julieta va a estar hoy ocupada. Rita, quiero que hagas para mañana los ejercicios de la página 54. Así no olvidarás que en clase de Inglés no se pasan notitas –sentenció.

No lo había pasado peor en su vida.

En cuanto terminó la clase salió corriendo en dirección a casa, no quería saber nada de Berta ni del resto de los compañeros de su clase, y menos de Eduardo Sánchez Abasolo. Los odiaba a todos.

No era verdad, pero por unos momentos, eso era lo que creía sentir.

En casa se encontró protegida, a salvo de todos ellos, aunque lo cierto es que le costaba abstraerse de lo sucedido aquel día.

—Últimamente parece que te mandan mucha tarea... ¿O es que esto que estás haciendo es un castigo? –le preguntó su madre mientras ella hacía los ejercicios en la mesa de la cocina.

—Bueno... je.

—¿Eso qué significa?

—Que sí, es un pequeño castigo. Ha sido el profesor de Inglés.

—¿Ah, sí? ¿Y por qué? –intervino Martín su padre.

—Por darle un papel a Berta.

—¿Y para qué le dabas un papel? –continuó.

—Pues para decirle una cosa.

—Bien, dejadlo –intervino su madre, que estaba viendo cómo Rita comenzaba a perder la paciencia–. Ella debe cumplir su castigo y hacer caso al profesor.

—Estoy de acuerdo, pero solo quería saber por qué Rita escribe notas.

—Porque sí –contestó ella.

—Tú nunca escribías notas –insistió su padre.

—Pues hoy he escrito una.

—No será que…

—¡¡NO TENGO NOVIO!! –gritó ella.

Y dicho esto, cerró el cuaderno y se fue a su cuarto sin hacer caso a su hermano pequeño, que quería que jugara con él.

Los ánimos se tranquilizaron a la hora de la cena, y, luego, mientras leía en la cama absorta un libro de aventuras, Rita llegó a olvidarse de todo lo ocurrido. Esa noche soñó que era una valiente capitana de barco que se dirigía sin miedo a la conquista de nuevos e inexplorados mares sorteando gigantescos témpanos de hielo. Y deseó, desde lo más profundo, que el día que había vivido no hubiera existido jamás y que en realidad todo hubiera sido un mal sueño.

Pero lo peor estaba por llegar.

Cuando al día siguiente llegó al patio del colegio, lo vio. Aunque no lo reconoció al principio.

"¿Quién será ese chaval que está junto a los demás de clase?", se preguntó.

Estaba repeinado, con el pelo mojado, la cara relimpia, vestía un jersey de pico con una camisa de color chillón y corbata, y calzaba zapatos que brillaban. Además de la mochila, llevaba en una mano una gran bolsa de plástico, mientras mantenía la otra oculta en la espalda.

Parecía fuera de lugar.

Sin embargo, los demás alumnos no le miraban a él, sino a Rita, que no entendía nada. En cuanto se percató de su presencia, la miró.

Cuando ella le reconoció quiso huir, pero su cuerpo había sufrido tal impresión que no la obedeció y se quedo allí plantada mientras él se le acercaba.

—Rita, ejem, toma —le dijo dándole un ramo de flores que guardaba oculto.

—Pe...pero Edu... —llegó a balbucir ella.

—Llámame Carlos Eduardo, ahora que eres mi novia.

El resto de niños que asistía a la escena comenzó a aplaudir y Rita recobró la compostura.

—¡¡Eduardo, Carlos o como te llames: déjame en paz, no soy tu novia!! —bramó blandiendo las flores como si fuera una espada.

—¡Qué flores más bonitas! —exclamó Yuli, la profesora de ciencias que pasaba por allí.

—Se las ha regalado su novio —intervino Mari Paz Serrano.

—¡No es mi novio! —protestó Rita.

Pero sus palabras eran como gotas de agua dulce que se perdían en un mar de risas cómplices de los que la miraban. Sí, todos los que la rodeaban sonreían; todos menos una persona.

Al llegar a clase, huyendo de Edu, se llevó una segunda sorpresa.

—Rita –le llamó Pilar, su tutora, cuando
se dirigía a su pupitre–. Estos días vas a sentarte
al fondo de la clase –dijo señalando un lugar que
quedaba vacío muy cerca del sitio de Edu.

—Pero… ¿por qué…? –preguntó ella
desconsolada.

Su tutora en voz baja le comentó:

—Berta me ha dicho que tiene una
enfermedad desconocida, pero muy contagiosa; y
por precaución prefiero que te pongas allí. No te
preocupes yo cuidaré de tu amiga, no te pongas
triste por ella.

Sentada en su sitio, Berta miraba la escena poniendo cara de niña enferma, dolida por la separación.

Rita se sentó, resignada, en la esquina de la clase.

Edu no dejaba de mirarla cuando los profesores no vigilaban. Era una pesadilla.

A la hora del recreo todo el colegio sabía que Rita tenía novio y que el elegido era Edu o Carlos Eduardo, como a él le gustaba que le llamaran.

Ella fue a juntarse con sus amigos, pero el grupo de clase no estaba al lado de la puerta donde acostumbraban a juntarse.

Allí solo se encontraba Rafa.

—Hola Rafa –saludó Rita–. ¿Y los demás?

—Están con Berta; dicen que la has traicionado, que le has quitado el novio.

—¿Y tú?

—Yo no sé, no estoy seguro; así que, si quieres, damos una vuelta y jugamos a algo.

—Vale, gracias, Rafa.

—…Edu nos sigue –indicó su amigo señalando al enamorado, que se movía tras ellos a algunos metros de distancia.

—¡Lárgate! –le gritó Rita. Y Carlos Eduardo desapreció entre los niños y niñas que jugaban al fútbol.

Rita había llegado tarde al patio, ya que había tenido que buscar un jarrón para dejar las flores y había pensado ir a hablar con Javi, otro de los amigos de su barrio que también estudiaba en el colegio pero iba a otro curso. Su padre tenía una frutería y se enteraba de muchos cotilleos. Tal vez pudiera darle alguna información valiosa para ayudarla a deshacerse de su pretendiente.

—Hola, Javi –le saludó.

—Hola, Rita, je, je.

—¿A qué viene ese je, je? –preguntó ella algo mosca.

— Me han dicho que tienes…

—No es mi novio –le cortó.

—Bueno no te enfades. Hola, Rafa –dijo saludando.

—Javi, ¿sabes algo de Edu? –le preguntó Rita.

—Mmm… así que se llama Edu.

—Sí.

—No será Eduardo Sánchez Abasolo, uno al que le gusta que le llamen Carlos Eduardo… –comentó Javi poniendo cara de detective privado.

Rita sintió un escalofrío.

—El mismo ¿por qué lo dices?

—Ufffff –exclamó Javi con un gesto nada tranquilizador–. ¿Sabéis por qué le gusta que le llamen así?

—Ni idea –respondieron los dos a coro.

—He oído que se pasa los fines de semana con sus padres viendo telenovelas de amor y comiendo bollicaos. No sale a jugar a la calle con el resto de los niños, ni lee, ni juega con la consola. ni nada, solo ve teleseries románticas.

—¿En serio?

—Sus amigos me lo han contado. Se pasa el día viendo telenovelas.

—¡Pero si son muy aburridas! –se le escapó a Rafa.

—Sí, pero a él deben de gustarle –comentó Javi mientras se encogía de hombros. Luego añadió dirigiéndose a Rita:

—Lo que no entiendo es cómo tú…

—Te he dicho que no es mi novio, ha sido un malentendido.

—Pues has escogido para malentenderte a un chalado romántico.

—Ya lo sé –dijo ella desanimada.

Cuando regresó a clase comprobó que la chaladura de Carlos Eduardo era de primera división. Sobre la mesa de su pupitre encontró varios regalos envueltos con lazos rojos y una tarjeta que decía:

> Como te gusta viajar
> y también la geografía,
> mi amor siempre tendrás
> por la noche y por el día.
> Para Rita de su novio:
> Carlos Eduardo.

Ella intentó esconder los regalos, pero era demasiado tarde.

El resto de sus compañeros y Ana, la profesora, ya los habían visto.

—A ver, Rita, por favor: recoge los regalos que te han hecho, vamos a empezar la clase.

Las risitas del resto de sus compañeros recorrían las hileras de los pupitres. Las risas de todos, menos de una.

Rita intentaba hacer entrar en razón a Edu, pero él no la hacía caso.

—Edu, escucha –le decía a veces al salir de clase, cuando la seguía con su sonrisa de enamorado para darle un nuevo regalo.

—Llámame Carlos Eduardo.

—Vale, Carlos Eduardo; verás, te has confundido de chica.

—No, estoy seguro de que mi novia eres tú, recuerda que me lo propusiste, dejaste la nota bajo mi estuche, *mi amol*.

—¡No me llames así!

—Lo que tú digas.

Era eso, claro. Guille la había visto dejar el papel y se lo había dicho a Edu y ahora el galán no la dejaba en paz. Rita intentó hablar con Guille, pero este se escabullía en cuanto terminaban las clases.

Pasaban los días y las muestras y declaraciones de amor de Edu se multiplicaban.

Seguía recibiendo regalos que eran cosas pequeñas y sencillas como tebeos o pinturas, envueltos en paquetes muy aparatosos y acompañados de sus correspondientes notas.

En una ocasión escuchó que, al pasar, algún profesor decía a otro:

—Mira es Rita, la novia de Edu, hacen una pareja muy bonita.

—¡Oiga, yo no soy la novia de nadie! –le respondió ella con un bufido.

—Pe... perdona –se disculpó el profesor.

Cuando vio en una pared su nombre escrito
a lápiz junto al de Carlos Eduardo, unidos por
un corazón, casi le da un patatús. A partir de ese
día Rita siempre llevaba una goma para borrar su
nombre
y los corazones que iba poniendo su enamorado
por todas partes.

    —Rita, últimamente me pides que te compre
muchas gomas, ¿ocurre algo? —le preguntó un día
su madre.

    —No, es que últimamente me confundo
mucho cuando dibujo.

    —¿En serio? ¿Va todo bien?

—Todo va de maravilla, no podría ir mejor. Me asombro todos los días de lo bien que va, mamá —respondió Rita.

Su madre enseguida se dio cuenta de que, si no lo estaba ya, Rita estaba a punto de meterse en un lío.

Una tarde, tras salir del entrenamiento de taekwondo, emprendió el regreso a casa tras comprobar que Edu no la estaba esperando. Entonces vio a un niño a lo lejos que le resultó familiar.

—Es Guille, ahí lo tengo —se dijo.

Corrió hacia él a toda velocidad pero con sigilo, para cogerlo por sorpresa.

Estaba con dos amigos, sentado en un banco del parque bebiendo agua de una botella después de haber jugado un partido de baloncesto. Agazapada, como un explorador del ejército, se aproximó a ellos camuflándose entre unos arbustos.

—¡Clac!

Había pisado una rama, y Guille, de un brinco, saltó del banco al percatarse de su presencia.

—¿Qué ...qué quieres? –le preguntó asustado.

—Quiero hablar contigo. Por tu culpa, Edu se ha empeñado en que sea su novia y no me deja en paz. Ahora tienes que ayudarme a convencerlo.

—Pe.. pe... si yo no he hecho nada —se excusó él.

—¡No seas mentiroso! ¡Tú me viste dejar la nota en su mesa y se lo has dicho!

—Yo no le he dicho nada, porque no te vi.

—¡No digas mentiras! –exclamó en tono amenazante Rita.

—Es cierto –respondió Guille antes de echar a correr.

—¡No huyas! ¡Te atraparé y me las pagarás! ¡Me vengaré de ti! –le amenazó Rita gesticulando. Pero lo cierto es que no se le ocurría qué podía hacerle a Guille y no tenía ganas de pensar en ello. La venganza daba mucho trabajo, y aquella tarde, después de las horas de clase y de haber aguantado a Edu, Rita estaba agotada.

Los días se sucedieron y Edu seguía con sus regalitos. Rita los guardaba en el trastero de casa, sin que sus padres los vieran, pues le daba mucha vergüenza. Hasta que un día, cuando regresó del colegio, comprobó que su galán había dado un paso más: había comenzado a enviar también regalos a su casa.

—Rita, ¿me puedes explicar qué significa esto? –le preguntó su madre mientras señalaba cuatro cajas de zapatos envueltas en papel de regalo que contenían varias poesías de amor.

—¿Y esto? –añadió su padre ante otro montón de regalos de su pretendiente que salían de la puerta del trastero.

—Je, cuántos regalos, ¿eh? —acertó a decir ella.

En conocimiento del medio
he visto tus ojos de refilón.
No tengo otro remedio,
que entregarte mi corazón.

Firmado: Carlos Eduardo

Leyó su madre.

Martín, su padre, ya no tenía la expresión burlona de los días anteriores.

—Esto es muy raro, cuéntanos qué sucede —le dijo.

Ella les contó que Edu la asediaba con regalos e insistía en que fuera su novia, pero que ella estaba harta de él.

Así que, tras ponerse en contacto con los responsables del colegio y conseguir el teléfono de los padres de Edu, su madre los llamó esa misma noche y habló con ellos muy seria pero con mucha amabilidad.

Cuando Mónica, su madre, colgó el teléfono, miró a Rita con gesto grave.

—Rita, no me dijiste que tú le habías dejado una notita diciéndole que querías ser su novia.

—No, mamá es que la nota no era mía —se excusó ella.

—A mí me han dicho que tienen pruebas de que sí.

—En realidad, la que quería ser su novia era mi amiga Berta.

—Vaya, así que fuiste tú la que le invitaste a empezar con todo esto, ¡esta sí que es buena! —intervino su padre.

—¡No soy su novia, estoy harta de él y no pienso tener novio nunca, odio a los novios! —protestó Rita antes de desaparecer por el pasillo camino de su cuarto.

Sus padres se quedaron allí plantados, sin saber qué hacer, rodeados de una pequeña montaña de regalos y de poesías de amor.

—¿Y ahora qué hacemos con todo esto? —preguntó Martín.

—Será mejor que lo guardemos, por si Rita cambia de opinión. Con esta niña nunca se sabe. De todas maneras, creo que un día de esta semana debemos ir a hablar con la tutora de la clase.

Rita también decidió que tenía que hablar con alguien:

"Tengo que ir a consultar con las ranas sabias del parque, ellas son las únicas que pueden ayudarme. Claro, que hay un problema… mmm… he de idear un plan", se dijo mientras analizaba la situación aquella noche en la cama.

Al día siguiente se dirigió al colegio con una nueva goma de borrar con la cual fue eliminando los corazones y las confirmaciones de su noviazgo con Edu. Las había por todas partes, desde la parada de autobús en que se bajaba Edu, hasta las esquinas del colegio. El muy pillo escribía en lápiz en paredes viejas o sobre papeles que pegaba con celo, para que nadie se quejara de sus grafitis amorosos. Era un romántico enfermizo, pero no tonto.

Rita recibió más regalos ese día y un nuevo puñado de poesías e intentó esquivar sin éxito a Edu, que no dejaba de seguirla. Por suerte, Rafa continuaba acompañándola fielmente, mientras el resto de las amigas compartía el tiempo libre con Berta, que seguía sin hablarle.

—Después de clase voy a ir al parque, para hablar con las ranas sabias de todo lo que ha pasado, y no quiero que Edu me siga. Él no es del barrio y no conoce el secreto. Necesito que me ayudes –propuso a su amigo durante la comida.

—No te preocupes, tú solo dime lo que hay que hacer –contestó él.

Al terminar la última clase de la tarde, Rita y Rafa se dirigieron juntos, lo más rápido que pudieron, hacia la salida del colegio. Una vez fuera, junto al patio y en una esquina que quedaba un poco oculta, ella sacó de la mochila una peluca de mujer de un disfraz que había utilizado su padre en carnavales y un bote de laca. Rafa se la puso y Rita moldeó un peinado similar al suyo.

—Toma, ponte mi cazadora y quédate aquí de espaldas. Ya me la devolverás –le indicó a su amigo sacando la prenda de su mochila–. Así, Edu te confundirá conmigo sin problemas.

Dicho esto, Rita se puso un gorro de lana que también había llevado y se mezcló entre la multitud de alumnos que en ese momento abandonaban el edificio.

De un vistazo, vio a Rafa apoyado en una pared y a Edu acercándose a él con un paquete de regalo en la mano. El besugo había picado el anzuelo.

Rita se movió con paso rápido entre los niños y padres que abarrotaban la salida del colegio y, en cuanto se vio a salvo de miradas, comenzó a correr. De vez en cuando se paraba en seco y se ocultaba en alguna esquina para asegurarse de que nadie la siguiera.

Todo parecía ir bien. Cuando se acercó al parque, se quitó el gorro y se dirigió directamente hacia el estanque.

Allí, en la zona más húmeda y apartada, en un lugar oculto por unos grandes árboles y altísimas hierbas, viven unas ranas ancianas que son muy sabias. Ellas aconsejan y ayudan a los niños cuando tienen algún problema o se meten en líos. Es un lugar secreto que solo los chavales de ese barrio conocen y ellos son a los únicos que escuchan, pues solamente ellos conocen la existencia de aquellos seres tan extraordinarios.

—Crrroaacccc, hola Rita, veo que vienes de nuevo a pedirnos consejo —le dijo una de las ranas en cuanto la vio sentada ante ellas en un tronco.

—Sí, crrroac, y debe de ser su cumpleaños, porrrrque lleva una bolsa con varios regalos —añadió otra de las ranas.

—¡Felicidades, crroac! —exclamó una tercera.

—Hola, ranas sabias. No es mi cumpleaños, son los regalos que me ha hecho un chico... —dijo ella.

—Crrrroac, ¿ha sido tu novio… croac? —preguntó la cuarta de las ranas.

—¡No es mi novio! —reaccionó Rita.

—Crrroac, perdona, no quería ofenderte —se disculpó la rana.

—Bueno… perdóname tú a mí, estoy un poco nerviosa por todo lo que me está pasando —dijo ella.

—Crrro, crrroo —cuéntanos lo que te ocurre y procuraremos ayudarte —le animó la rana que la había saludado en primer lugar.

Rita contó a las ranas sabias todo lo ocurrido desde el día en que Berta le pidió que le ayudara a entregar aquella notita a Edu, y estas escucharon atentamente la historia.

—Crrroacc, veo que estás metida en un buen problema –comentó una de las ranas.

—Sí, crrroacccccc, tanto tu amiga Berta como Edu son muy cabezotas –añadió otra rana.

—Cro, cro, croacccc, pero para todo hay solución –agregó la tercera de ellas.

—Requetecrrroac, si no quieren escuchar, tal vez haya que buscar otro modo de decirles las cosas.

—Sí, pero ¿cuál? –preguntó Rita un poco despistada.

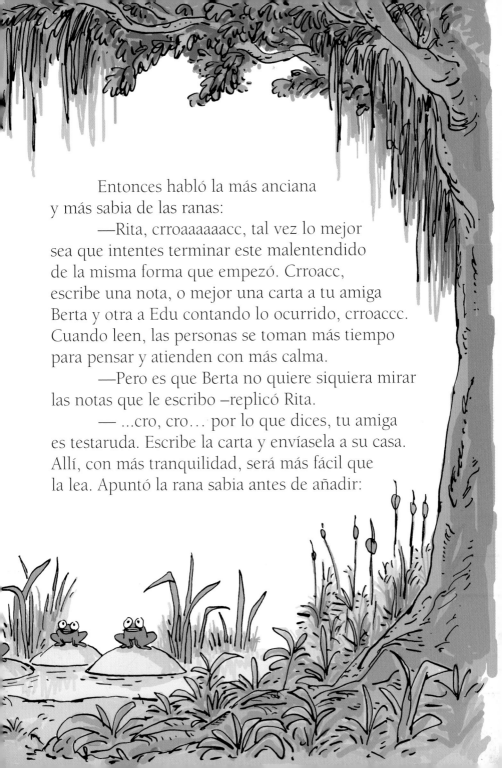

Entonces habló la más anciana
y más sabia de las ranas:

—Rita, crroaaaaaacc, tal vez lo mejor
sea que intentes terminar este malentendido
de la misma forma que empezó. Crroacc,
escribe una nota, o mejor una carta a tu amiga
Berta y otra a Edu contando lo ocurrido, crroaccc.
Cuando leen, las personas se toman más tiempo
para pensar y atienden con más calma.

—Pero es que Berta no quiere siquiera mirar
las notas que le escribo –replicó Rita.

— ...cro, cro… por lo que dices, tu amiga
es testaruda. Escribe la carta y envíasela a su casa.
Allí, con más tranquilidad, será más fácil que
la lea. Apuntó la rana sabia antes de añadir:

—Y te aconsejo que también escribas una más explicándole todo a la tutora de vuestra clase, ella te ayudará, croac.

—¿Tú crees?

—Croac, estoy segura de ello —respondió la rana sabia.

—Vale, muchas gracias de nuevo, ranas sabias —dijo Rita antes de levantarse y abandonar el lugar.

Cuando atravesó la zona de las canchas deportivas, en el otro extremo del parque, Rita percibió que una sombra se movía tras unos árboles que había junto a la pista de baloncesto. Siguió andando por la calle en dirección a su casa dando un pequeño rodeo. Lo había visto: era un chico y la estaba siguiendo.

Comenzó a andar más rápido y el chaval hizo lo mismo. Se imaginaba de quién se trataba, por lo que no pidió ayuda, sino que se escondió en un callejón para sorprenderlo.

Cuando su perseguidor, despistado, pasó junto a su escondite, Rita se colocó a su espalda.

—¡Ya está bien de seguirme, estoy harta de ti! —le gritó.

Pero cuando el niño se dio la vuelta, Rita se llevó una sorpresa.

—¡Guille! —¿tú?

—Ah, ho…hola, sí, je.

—¿Por qué me estabas siguiendo?

—Es que… quería hablar contigo –respondió
él un poco asustado. Sabía que ella era cinturón rojo
fosforito de taekwondo y tenía muy mal genio.

—Y yo también quería hablar contigo, quiero
que me digas por qué le dijiste a Edu lo de la nota.

—Yo no se lo dije.

—¿Ah no? Entonces ¿cómo supo que yo dejé
el mensajito en su mesa?

—Cometiste un fallo.

—¡Imposible!

—Sí, lo cometiste. Al hablar conmigo vi que
estabas nerviosa y no dejabas de mover el capuchón
de un boli que tenías en la mano. Mientras me
contabas lo del estuche, dejaste el capuchón en la
mesa de Edu.

Rita rememoró la escena… era cierto. Cuando
descubrió a Guille tenía el capuchón en la mano
y cuando salió de la clase tras dejar la nota ya no
lo llevaba.

—…Y creo que tienes la manía de poner tu inicial en casi todas tus cosas, incluso en los capuchones de los bolis. Lo sé porque una vez que se me habían olvidado las pinturas, me dejaste tu estuche y lo vi –continuó el chaval.

Rita escuchaba estupefacta. Todo lo que decía Guille era verdad punto por punto.

—Solo quería decírtelo para que no estés enfadada conmigo.

Así que había sido eso. Había cometido un error en la "operación notita de amor" y Edu había pensado que era ella la que quería ser su novia.

Ella también tenía parte de culpa en aquella situación, y tal vez debiera ser más comprensiva con los otros. Aunque era muy difícil serlo con Edu. Lo intentaría y, desde luego, seguiría el consejo de las ranas sabias.

—Perdona por no haberte escuchado antes Guille –se disculpó Rita.

—No te preocupes, sé que Edu es un pesado y que lo estás pasando mal. Si quieres, puedo ayudarte.

—Vale, tengo que hacer una cosa y me vendría muy bien que me echaras una mano. ¿Podrás juntarte con Rafa y conmigo a la hora del recreo?

—No hay problema.

—Gracias, hasta mañana –se despidió Rita de Guille.

—Adiós.

—Ah, una cosa –recordó ella antes de abandonar el lugar–. ¿Has visto algo...?

—¿Te refieres a antes, en el parque?

—Sí.

—Yo también soy del barrio, Rita, y también conozco el secreto. Y sé que si alguna persona mayor se entera, el hechizo se romperá y las ranas sabias desaparecerán. No te preocupes.

—Vale

Al día siguiente, cuando Anthony dijo a los alumnos que podían salir al recreo, Carlos Eduardo, que había llevado un anillo de compromiso de plástico para formalizar el noviazgo, se llevó una sorpresa.

Guille estaba esperando a Rita en el pasillo para bajar al recreo.

Lo de Rafa lo aceptaba, pues sabía que eran buenos amigos, pero aquello hizo que se borrara de golpe de su cara aquella sonrisa de enamorado que había permanecido inalterable durante varios días.

Mientras los tres se alejaban por el pasillo, el novio tiró el anillo a la papelera y luego, cabizbajo, se dirigió al rincón más sombrío del patio.

Rita pretendía que tanto Guille como Rafa la ayudaran a escribir las cartas a Berta y a Edu, pero aquellos dos chorlitos en realidad tenían ganas de pasarlo bien.

—Yo nunca había escrito una carta ni una notita de amor, je, je, mira lo que he puesto —decía Guille.

> Te quiero mucho, como la trucha al trucho.
> Soy uno al que le gusta nadar y tengo
> una bañador rojo.

—Ja, ja —le seguía la broma Rafa—. Pues mirad esto:

> Me gustas un montón,
> llevo toda la vida esperándote.
> Una que te ve todos los días
> en la parada del autobús.

Había escrito el chaval en otra nota.
—Esta sí que es buena, escuchad:

> Me muero por conocerte.
> Llevo una falda y cazadora negra
> y me gustan las películas de miedo.

Habían bajado varias hojas de papel para hacer borradores, y aunque ella intentaba poner un poco de orden, Guille y Rafa no atendían y no paraban de escribir mensajitos en broma y comentarlos.

¿Te gustaría quedar conmigo?
Uno que se ha quedado contigo.
Estoy todos los días a tu lado, quieto.

Quisiera perderme contigo.
Una que está cinco pasos a tu izquierda,
luego siete a la derecha, veinticinco hacia detrás,
dos metros a la derecha
y tres en diagonal izquierda.

Cada vez que te veo, me enamoro.
Uso gafas y trabajo en la óptica.

Me gustaría enrollarme.
¿Me das cuerda?
Una que lleva un cordel en el pelo.

Estoy por ti. Súmate conmigo
o mi vida se dividirá.

Quiero restar el tiempo contigo.
Uno al que le gustan los números

Guille y Rafa lo estaba pasando en grande.

—¡Os he pedido que me ayudéis, no que escribáis notitas de amor en broma! –dijo Rita intentando ponerse seria: ella también lo estaba pasando bien y no podía evitar reírse con sus amigos.

> Conservo mi amor por ti desde que te vi.
> Trabajo en los congelados
> del supermercado de tu barrio.

Leyó Guille.

> Estás más rico que el dónuts recién hecho.
> La panadera.

> Me gustas más que la tarta de queso.
> Para mí, tú eres la guinda del pastel.
> El pastelero.

> Has abierto la puerta de corazón, amorcito. Te quiero más que al candado de mi bici.
> Trabajo de cerrajero.

—¡Ja, ja, ja! –rieron los otros dos.

Rita decidió dejar las cartas de Berta y de Edu para otro día y se sumó a escribir notas con sus amigos.

El sonido de la sirena que indicaba el fin del recreo los sorprendió cuando tenían acumulados un montón de mensajes,

—¡Vamos, tenemos que ir a clase, los demás ya han subido! –les avisó Guille al ver el patio casi vacío.

—¿Y qué hacemos con las notas? Son un montón y es mejor no subirlas a clase, por si acaso. Pero podemos guardarlas para leerlas otra vez, son muy divertidas...

—Dejémoslas aquí, escondidas. Luego, cuando salgamos de clase, las recogemos –propuso Rafa.

Doblaron los papeles ligeramente, los escondieron junto a una ventana que tenía una verja y entraron en clase justo antes de que Ana cerrara la puerta.

El patio del colegio quedó vacío, azotado por un viento cálido y extraño que se había levantado de repente, sin avisar, como una mirada furtiva en una fiesta.

Cuando, una vez terminadas las clases, los tres amigos pasaron por el mismo lugar para recogerlas, se llevaron una sorpresa: las notas habían desaparecido.

—Vaya –exclamó decepcionada Rita.

—¡Alguien nos las ha quitado! –protestó Guille.

—Sí, seguramente –aceptó Rafa antes
de añadir–: Debo irme, tengo entrenamiento
de balonmano.

—¿Pero vais a entrenar con el viento que
hace? –se extrañó Rita.

—Creo que sí, y si no podemos, iremos
al polideportivo –respondió su amigo antes de
alejarse camino de los vestuarios.

Guille y Rita también se marcharon, pues
igualmente tenían cosas que hacer.

Los alumnos y los profesores fueron
abandonando el colegio, y en la esquina donde Rita
y sus amigos habían guardado los mensajes de
amor, el viento se seguía filtrando por entre los
barrotes y parecía silbar una especie de melodía.

Unos puntos blancos, casi diminutos, se
movían en el cielo al compás de aquel sonido.

Ninguno de los tres amigos se fijó en aquellas
manchas claras que parecían flotar en el aire.
Ni tampoco lo hicieron el resto de los viandantes
que paseaban a esas horas por las calles y los
parques, absortos como estaban en sus quehaceres.

Ni siquiera las vieron las personas que estaban en las terrazas de sus casas, ocupadas en alguna labor, sin mirar al cielo para ver el atardecer.

Por eso, nadie se percató de que una multitud de mensajes de amor estaban volando por toda la ciudad y que, poco a poco, aquellos pedazos de frágil papel se separaban y se iban repartiendo por diversos lugares.

Y es que había sido aquella ventisca la que había provocado que una de las notas de amor se volara y que, luego, el resto de notitas se movieran y fueran arrastradas también por la corriente de aire.

Así, los mensajes de amor escritos por los tres amigos volaron en todas las direcciones; y el viento, caprichoso y juguetón, hizo que cada uno de aquellos mensajitos llegara a una persona distinta de la ciudad en las últimas horas del día.

Aquella noche, un montón de dulces y amorosos sueños flotaron como una nube de algodón invisible por todas las calles, plazas y avenidas.

Cuando al día siguiente Rita se dirigió al colegio, tuvo una sensación extraña. Había algo diferente esa mañana en la mirada de algunas personas con las que se había cruzado, algo que le resultaba extrañamente familiar y a la vez perturbador.

Al ver la expresión de natilla en la cara
de Anthony, el profesor de inglés, lo recordó:
era la misma cara de enamorado que había gastado
Edu desde el funesto día en que ella dejó la nota
en su mesa.

Y aquel gesto, aquella especie de mueca de
amor, se repetía en varios de sus compañeros.

¿Qué estaba pasando? ¿Se estaban
enamorando todos de repente? Se preguntó Rita.

Para su sorpresa, el profesor le indicó que
se sentara junto a Berta, en el lugar que había

ocupado desde el principio de curso hasta su separación por la "presunta" enfermedad de su compañera.

—Hola, querida amiga, veo que tu goma de borrar está a punto de gastarse, ¿Quieres que te deje la mía? –le sorprendió la voz de su compañera de pupitre al verla sacar sus cosas del estuche.

—Eeeh, sí, gracias –reaccionó ella.

—Perdona por haberme enfadado así estos días y no haberte hablado, me he portado muy mal contigo –se disculpó Berta hablando con una amabilidad inmensa.

—Vale, todo fue un error, yo no… –intentó decir ella.

—Fue un malentendido, lo sé, no quise escucharte, lo siento.

—Ya lo he olvidado todo –dijo Rita a la vez que sonreía con los ojos.

—*Childreeen* –advirtió Anthony en un tono inhabitualmente alegre y cantarín–. Hoy es un día maravilloso, así que vamos a empezar la clase en una jornada esplendorosa y llena de luz como esta.

El tono acaramelado de aquellas palabras llenó la clase y avisaba de que iba a comenzar a dar la lección en aquel día gris y nublado.

Rafa esperaba a Rita a la hora del recreo.

—Rita, prometo que hoy te voy a ayudar a escribir las notitas para Berta y Edu –le dijo.

—Creo que ya no necesito escribir la nota a Berta…

Entonces se dio cuenta:

Esa mañana Edu no le había llevado ningún regalo, ni le había sonreído, ni siquiera la había mirado. Todo parecía haber cambiado de repente.

—…Y, de momento, tampoco voy a escribir nada a Edu –dijo por fin mientras bajaban las escaleras.

De nuevo se juntaron el grupo de amigos: Miren, Berta, Sonia, Rafa y Rita, y volvieron a pasear, a jugar y a charlar durante el recreo. A veces, Guille se juntaba con ellos.

Berta contó que estaba muy contenta, había recibido una notita de un chico de la clase de al lado proponiéndole ser novios.

Y lo mismo le había ocurrido a una chica de otro curso, quien le había preguntado a Guille si quería ser su novio.

Y él había aceptado.

Poco a poco, en los días sucesivos, los cinco amigos se fueron enterando de la gran cantidad de parejas de novios que se habían formado por todas partes. Los cartelitos y los nombres de parejas llenaban los rincones del colegio y las calles y las plazas de la ciudad.

Todo el mundo parecía haberse enamorado de repente.

También Sonia y Miren tenían novio.

Pero ¿y Edu?

Eduardo Sánchez Abasolo sufrió el proceso contrario.

Todo comenzó por la frustración que le produjo al ver a Rita con Guille aquella mañana en el pasillo. Pensó que Guille, a quien consideraba su amigo, quería quitarle la novia y aquello le provocó una especie de *shock*. Desde ese momento, sufrió una transformación.

Una mirada audaz y decidida sustituyó a la sonrisita enamoradiza, y, aunque no dejó de vestirse como un repollo, las manchas de nocilla no volvieron a aparecer en su cara.

Pidió disculpas a Rita por su comportamiento y en pocos días comenzó a convertir en musculatura sus carnes flácidas y se convirtió en un niño muy atractivo. Y es que Edu había decidido cambiar de vida y olvidarse de las telenovelas.

Comenzó a jugar con los demás niños y a hacer deporte, y decidió, con una lucidez asombrosa, no seguir viviendo en el mundo irreal que mostraba la televisión.

Los profesores se quedaron admirados del cambio y las niñas del colegio estaban perdidamente enamoradas de él.

—Carlos Eduardo, ¿no quieres que seamos novios? –le propusieron en varias ocasiones algunas niñas.

Y él, con una amabilidad y unas maneras de actor de cine, respondía:

—Por favor, prefiero que me llames Eduardo. No puedo ser tu novio, ya que creo que somos demasiado jóvenes para tener una relación de

ese tipo, aún somos unos niños. Pero, si quieres, podemos ser buenos amigos –decía el adonis.

Y las niñas quedaban aún más perdidamente enamoradas después de escuchar aquellas palabras.

Así fue: Edu se convirtió en el novio más deseado del colegio y el amor se adueñó de la

ciudad. Multitud de personas que se veían día
a día, y no se habían atrevido a demostrar sus
sentimientos por timidez o vergüenza, paseaban
ahora de la mano con sus amados o amadas en un
torbellino de felicidad. Y es que el viento misterioso
que aquel día se había llevado las notas escritas

por los tres amigos, había trasladado los papeles
a las personas indicadas. La casualidad, el amor
y la naturaleza se habían aliado de una forma
prodigiosa.

Después del episodio del "noviazgo",
Rita se quedó muy contenta por haber recuperado
la amistad de Berta y también la de Edu.

Sin embargo, una vez que pasaron
las semanas y aquellas jornadas llenas de regalos
exagerados y constantes miraditas comenzaron
a borrarse de su memoria, empezó ver a las parejas
de novios con un poco de envidia.

¡Se les veía a todos tan felices, parecían tan invencibles! Las declaraciones de amor llenaban las paredes y en ellas aparecían escritos muchos, multitud de nombres, todos... menos el suyo.

Por eso, una mañana, cuando salían al recreo, le hizo un gesto a su fiel amigo y lo atrajo hacia un rincón. Allí, en voz baja, para que nadie la oyera, le propuso con una sonrisa pícara:

—Oye, ¿me ayudas a escribir una notita?

—Oh, Rita no empieces otra vez —le respondió Rafa.

TO LOIS WALLACE

If a man is going to California, he announces it with hesitation; because it is a confession that he has failed at home.

—Ralph Waldo Emerson
Journals, XI

The air quality tomorrow will be unhealthful for sensitive persons.

—Weather Forecast
W-KNXT
Los Angeles

Unhealthful Air

Chapter 1

ONCE UPON A time in Hollywood, people got pushed into
swimming pools and Errol Flynn let loose a bunch of
white mice at a party and an actress shot a producer in
the worst possible place. The guy who was shot is still
around, and still walking very slowly, but Flynn is long-
dead and anybody who dunks anybody these days gets
slapped with a lawsuit. The entertainment capital of the
world just ain't what it used to be.

The last few years, for instance, the bottom line in the
industry has been timing. After all the hype and hys-
teria and splendiferous superlatives, it's come down to
this: timing—the ultimate shrug, the unqualified concession to a Universal that never made a musical, the
star-fucking genuflection to the sun.

Oh, for the old days when Beauty reigned over the
backlots—a Goddess with too many Hungarian disci-
ples, maybe, but the budgets then could absorb them. I
never detract from the Hollywood pioneers. These con-
summate chiselers knew a finely chiseled profile when

they saw one. True beauty was the shikseh in the kosher dream.

No more. After money comes meaning. Most of the latest Oscar winners have more depth and significance than *The Great Train Robbery*. So though somewhere in space the filmed story still has its rendezvous with the slowly throbbing public brain, making the connection has become tougher. That's where perfect timing, planned or serendipitous, comes in. As an incurable romantic, I find the split-second a poor substitute for such old standbys as love and destiny. But, like all good whores, I keep one eye on the clock.

All of which has nothing to do with Fortunata and what happened, except that a minute either way and I never would have run into Otto Preminger at the Beverly Wilshire, and that's how it all started. Of course, if I'd put my car in the hotel garage, I'd have also missed him. But the parking valets in Beverly Hills are bigger snobs than the maître d's and my TR-6 had been getting pitying looks from the cleaning women coming to work on the buses from Watts. So sensitivity, still one of the dirtiest words in town, also gets a screen credit. As for my being there at all, my motive was the world's oldest.

I did a quick tour of the El Padrino bar, but couldn't spot anyone who might be good for a fifty, let alone the five hundred I needed. Then, because I was parked north of Wilshire, the hotel lobby was a shortcut. And there was Otto at the reception desk.

I waited until he finished autographing the registration form. He took a long time writing his last name, as if he wasn't sure if it had one or two M's.

"Hello, Otto," I said.

He turned to me and beamed. Everybody has seen pictures of Preminger in his prime and he never aged a day after he directed *Laura,* so there's no need to describe him. As for his beam, it was indescribable.

"Who says it isn't a small world?" He threw his arms wide, then wrapped them around me in a Viennese hug, the kind of hug Franz Werfel must have given Thomas Mann when they met for coffee.

"You remember me, Otto?"

"How could I forget you?"

"Dan Dailey," I reminded him.

"You really think I don't know who you are?" His beam turned into an injured pout.

"Then you must have taken a memory course."

"Did you hear that?" He appealed to the waiting bell-hop for sympathy. "I fly all the way from New York to get insulted." He faced me wearily. "All right. I have to prove my memory? You name any agent in this phony town and I'll name all his wives."

"Swifty Lieberman," I said.

"Esther, Patricia, Hilary and Michiko."

"Four for four," I admitted and he beamed again. The bellhop started jingling the room key, impatient to unload the one suitcase and get his tip.

"Otto," I said. "Can you give me ten minutes?"

"Now?" He was too generous to refuse, but he looked tired from his trip. Desperate as I was, I couldn't press him.

"How about tomorrow?"

"Of course. Let's see." He searched his pockets for his appointment diary. "I've got a talk show in the morning. 'Why Don't You Wake Up, Los Angeles?' With the Chiclet teeth and stupid questions."

" 'Good Morning, Los Angeles.' " My correction was offhand.

"Then I've got lunch with the so-called executives at Paramount." He found his diary and peered at a scribbled-on page. " 'Good Morning, Los Angeles.' "

"I liked what you said better."

"What did I say?"

"Get Your Ass Out of Bed, Los Angeles."

"I never said that. I never use such words." He turned to the bellhop for corroboration. "Did I say such a thing?" The bellhop shook his head and jingled the room key.

"Maybe in the afternoon, Otto?"

"Why not?" He automatically looked at his watch, probably still on New York time. "I should be back here by three. Come to my suite at five after."

"Thanks," I said. "Get some sleep."

"You, too."

His bear hug when we parted was less Viennese, more *Ich bin ein Berliner*.

I was on the corner of Rodeo, waiting for the light to change, when the Chicano who'd signed in Otto came running out of the hotel.

"*Señor!* Wait!"

His tails flapped as he hurried toward me. He straightened his boutonniere and adjusted his cravat.

" 'Scuse me, *señor*," he said. "But please could I have your card?"

"What card?" All I'm carrying is an American Express which was voided six months ago.

"Your business card, please."

"I don't have one."

"None at all?" Nobody can go from obsequious to suspicious faster than a room clerk.

"I'm a writer," I said. "Writers like to pretend that writing isn't a business."

"I see, *señor*." He kept nodding without conviction.

"Now tell me why you wanted it."

"It is not for me, *señor*. For one of our guests."

"Which one?"

"I am not allowed to say, *señor*. Hotel rules."

"Doesn't the hotel have any rules against your running around the street asking people for their cards?"

"I only ask for yours, *señor*"—I was getting sick of the *señor*—"because this guest ask me to."

"He or she?"

"One of our guests, *señor*."

"And why would one of your guests want my card?"

"I don't know, *señor*." He looked genuinely puzzled. "Unless he or she wish to get in touch with you."

One of my favorite feelings comes from being topped by an overdressed peon.

"Give me one of yours," I said.

He fished it out expertly. *Alfredo Gomez, Assistant Reservations Manager*. I scribbled my name and phone number and the address of the North Sweetzer Arms on the back.

"Just in case you haven't got the wrong guy."

Driving back to the North Sweetzer Arms, the subject was mostly business cards. This hadn't been the first time I'd been caught without one. I wondered if other writers carried them and played around with their thermographed wording. For Mailer, in Bordoni Bold: *Journalism, Pseudo-Poetry and Great Novels*. Vidal used a delicate italic: *Histories Veritas and Political Acumen*. Roth, Malamud and Bashevis Singer had the same seraphic typeface: *Talmudic Suffering: With Plots, Yet*.

As for myself: *Corey Burdick, Screenplays Rewritten*. I rewrote the job definition. *Lousy Screenplays Made Less Lousy . . . Slightly Less Lousy . . . A Little Literate*. All were too coyly self-deprecating. A simple *Hack* in the lower left corner would say it all.

Bitch session over, I gave a few seconds to the mystery guest at the hotel. Short odds somebody had thought I was somebody else. The El Padrino Bar had twenty-watt bulbs out of deference to the older hookers. In its semidarkness I'd twice been taken for dead actors, namely Jeff Chandler and John Hodiak. But celebrity-chasers don't ask for business cards. The decision went to some shlock operator who'd seen me talking to Preminger and wanted to use me as a contact.

The North Sweetzer Arms was one of the last of a dying breed. Between my divorce and the condominium explosion, Los Angeles's chief attraction for me was its abundance of residential hotels, their apartments so identical that I could move every other month without feeling uprooted. Each had a minimum of wooden pieces, all painted cream with coffee-colored surfaces. Tarnished bronzed lamp bases always flanked a lumpy three-cushioned sofa and there was usually a big painting of some distant Chinese junks on a yellow sea. The walls were solid and the floors heavily carpeted. The rooms defied any impulse to settle in and the maids cleaned them accordingly.

I'd developed a fondness for these places. Their transitory nature kept things in perspective. They were constant reminders of how uncluttered life could be. After seven years in them, I still existed on a typewriter, dictionary, telephone-answering machine and not enough clothes to fill two suitcases.

Now most of these places were gone and the women who managed the few survivors were increasingly selective. Mrs. Fogarty, who ran the North Sweetzer Arms, only took me in because I mentioned I was a writer. Not that the trade name works magic. Half the deadbeats in the unemployment insurance lines use it. Mrs. Fogarty wanted credits and she had a personal reason for asking.

Luckily, she'd seen a Charlton Heston picture I rewrote.

Mrs. Fogarty had been one of the bleached beauties floating by in some of the Busby Berkely musicals and had one of the world's largest collections of Dick Powell records. Her apartment could absorb them. It was twice the size of the rented ones and she had her own furniture and effects—a blend of Sloane showroom and Warner Brothers prop room. In my three months' residence, I'd been an increasingly regular visitor for that personal reason of hers: like every other landlady, waiter and cabdriver in Los Angeles, Mrs. Fogarty had a story idea that would make a great motion picture. And like all the others, she just needed a writer to put her thoughts down on paper. So far I'd been encouraging enough not to be asked for any rent since my initial deposit.

She'd pushed one of her folded notes under my door. As always, it was to C. B. and signed E. F. and asked me to drop in if I didn't get home too late. In parentheses, "I've had some exciting new thoughts." Her notes were rarely without parenthetical promises like this. So far, any excitement had failed to materialize. But when she enacted potential scenes with full ex-chorus-girl vigor, I always managed to fake some enthusiasm.

Her story had to do with the first woman President who happened to be madly in love with her Secretary of State. We hadn't decided yet whether his appointment should follow or precede what she called their first physical union. The kicker was that because he screwed up on a delicate crisis in Latin America or someplace, he had to go. True Love versus the Popular Vote. Needless to say, big pictures have been built on less.

My answering machine yielded two messages.

"It's Janet." Since our divorce, she always said her name as if I might have trouble placing it. "Zachary came home last night. I think it would be productive for you to talk with him."

Zachary was home. Our only child had discovered, after much soul-searching in the Himalayas, that one could go home again. "Productive" was one of the words in the current top ten.

The other call was from Demetrious. He didn't bother giving his name after the bleep. Maybe he knew that nobody else sounded like him. Or left such succinct messages.

"Hey! What the fuck's goin' on?"

Simple translation: I owed him five hundred and should have paid him yesterday.

I went down to Mrs. Fogarty's apartment. During the usual Sara Lee cheesecake and Napa Valley Chianti, we listened to "I've Got My Love to Keep Me Warm," "By a Waterfall" and "With Plenty of Money and You." Then to work. Her exciting new thought was that our heroine should have an emergency red phone on her bedside table and that it should ring at (her words) "an inopportune moment." She seemed to want to discuss the details of that moment, but I suggested we leave that until the script stage and reminded her that one scene did not a movie make.

"I see it as a modern version of Elizabeth and Essex," she said.

"Elizabeth had Essex beheaded."

"I know. We've got to come up with something equivalent for Alexander." She'd already christened her Secretary of State.

"How about a vasectomy before a joint session of Congress?"

Darryl Zanuck never appreciated my sense of humor. So why should Mrs. Fogarty? The script conference was over and when I was leaving she reminded me that my rent was overdue.

It was almost one-thirty when my phone woke me up. I managed to take it before the answering machine could.

"Mr. Burdick," she said. "I hope I didn't wake you up."

"So much for hope."

"I didn't call you earlier 'cause I thought you might be writin'."

"I just finished."

"Mr. Gomez told me you're a writer."

"Gomez?" I reached groggily for a cigarette. A conditioned reflex: I'd given up smoking in 1972.

"You know. You put your phone number on the back of his card."

"Oh. *That* Mr. Gomez."

"I suppose you're wondering why I'm callin'."

"It's your dime." It had sounded better when three minutes cost a nickel.

"Mr. Burdick," she said. "Are you writin' a movie for Mr. Preminger?"

"It's been known to happen." I instinctively skirted direct questions about what I was doing.

"Is he a homosexual?"

"Otto?" I couldn't help snorting. "Hell, no."

"Are you?"

"Not that I know of." I was dimly aware of having defended Otto's manhood more vehemently than my own.

"You sure were doing a lot of huggin'."

"He hugged me," I corrected. "And those were very heterosexual hugs. You've obviously never been to Vienna."

"No," she said. "Not the one in Europe."

I'd never heard of any other. But there was a Paris in

Texas and a Warsaw, Indiana and a Smyrna, Tennessee.
So why not a Vienna just down the road a piece from her
hometown? I had trouble locating this. Her accent was
riding a cross-country bus somewhere between our Paris
and Warsaw and Smyrna. A drama major playing dumb
or an Ozark's urchin in a luxury hotel. Both were possibilities.

"I only asked," she said, " 'cause you wouldn't be interested if you were that way."

"Interested in what?"

"You know."

"Remind me."

"Mr. Burdick, did you ever hear the joke about the
girl who was so dumb she thought she could get to be a
movie star by going to bed with a writer?"

"Not lately," I said.

"Well, I guess I'm just about as dumb as you can get."
Either she'd studied with Lee Strasberg or Smyrna, Tennessee was a good bet. "Mr. Burdick?"

"I'm still here."

"Can you hear me blushin'?"

"Loud and clear."

"And are you interested?"

"Intrigue is better than interest."

"Huh?"

"Forget it. I was just quoting Sam Goldwyn."

"Don't you ever just say yes or no?"

"Now you're quoting my ex-wife."

"Mr. Burdick, are you makin' fun of me?"

"If it has to be yes or no, it's yes."

"Well, you just remember that someday."

"You'd better tell me your name, so I'll recognize it in
lights."

"Fortunata," she said. "F-o-r-t-u-n-a-t-a." She recited

it like a finalist in a spelling bee. "And if the dialogue you write is as barfy as what you talk, I don't know why Mr. Preminger was huggin' you."

"Maybe he likes barfy dialogue."

"Maybe you're a couple of old queers."

With that, she hung up. I lay in the dark stillness of the North Sweetzer Arms, doing a playback of the whole conversation. My dialogue had been insulted by experts over the years, but no one had ever called it barfy.

Chapter 2

IF YOU CAN'T trust your bookie, who can you trust? So I trusted Demetrious. If my horse won, I knew he'd pay up. And if I welched on a bet, I knew he'd have my legs broken.

Demetrious operated out of a room behind a pizza parlor about a furlong and a half from Hollywood Park. It was a small operation. He didn't have a chalk man. He didn't even have a board. He just sat at a table with two phones and made all his entries on a yellow ruled pad. The place wasn't a hangout. You paid or picked up your money, and unless Demetrious told you to sit down, you left. The only fixtures in the room were the two apes who were his collectors. Either one could have played left tackle for the Rams without going to practice.

"Don't explain to me," I once heard Demetrious say into one of the phones. "Explain to Damon when you see him."

The shorter of the apes had grinned in anticipation. He had two upper teeth and nothing below. The other collector, who I immediately dubbed Pythias, looked at him with envy.

I'd never seen Demetrious anywhere but in the stuffed chair behind his table. So I didn't know how tall he was. Unless his legs were out of proportion, I'd have guessed five-seven or eight. I knew he weighed over three hundred pounds because he complained about it in hot weather.

It was hard to separate his features from his fat. If the blubber could have been peeled away and whatever was bloating him drained off, his face might have had handsome proportions. He had the thick, wavy black hair that Greeks specialize in. His forehead showed he hadn't been stinted on brain space. His nose, even with the fleshiness, had a centurion slant.

Demetrious never worked in his shirtsleeves and he never changed his navy, pin-striped suit, summer or whatever goes for the other seasons in Southern California. His collar was always open because shirts didn't come in his neck size, but he always wore a loose and loud tie.

There are all kinds of magnetic currents involved in horse racing. Bettors who use the same bookie tend to coalesce at the track. It's just one of the many phenomena about the game for which there's no explanation. You break a cardinal rule by comparing your selection with the guy's ahead of you in the window line, you drown some of your sorrow in a drink with him between races and, playing cat and mouse, you gradually find out you're both making your off-track bets in the same place.

So, I've met a few other degenerates who bet with Demetrious. All of them told the same story, that Demetrious was an illegitimate son of Aristotle Onassis and that the old man had paid him to stay far away from Greece. One guy's version was that the banishment was to make him go on a diet and that Demetrious wouldn't be allowed back into his homeland until he got his poundage below two-fifty. Another version was that it was Jackie O. who'd originally caused the expulsion because she couldn't stand obesity.

The only thing I knew for sure about Demetrious was that he'd once made book in London. He'd mentioned it several times—once in a table-pounding tirade about his having to pay off the cops and hide in a back room with stinking Dago pizza fumes that made him sick, while the bookies in England were legal and made fucking fortunes and even got knighthoods from the Queen.

"It's all part of Erewhon," I said.

"Fuck him too," he said.

Of course, he had a valid gripe. We can trust our bookies because, except in Nevada, they operate outside the law. Most of the races are legitimate, so we who bet are betting against each other. In places like England, where bookmaking has become a respectable business, the horseplayer bets against the bookie. It's no mystery, when the big money's down, who decides which animal crosses the finish line first.

Another quote from Demetrious: "Three times when I was over there, they fixed the English Derby. Can anybody fix the Kentucky Derby? The Preakness? The Belmont?"

I shook my head sadly after each classic was named.

"But someday . . ." he promised.

I was tempted to ask him why he'd left England and given up a possible knighthood for a back room with Dago fumes. Just as well I didn't. One of his customers I got to know later at the track told me that Demetrious had tangled with one of the big bookmaking operations in England. The reason he wore the loose tie was to cover the scar. Anyone with less fat around his throat wouldn't still be able to holler. Horse racing isn't called the sport of kings for nothing.

Begging your bookie for a little more time isn't exactly the best way to start the day, so I returned Janet's call first. I was relieved when her answering machine clicked on. One-way conversations are the best kind, especially in the morning, especially with former wives. She'd made a new recording since the last time I'd phoned. This one was less sugary and her instructions brisk. I waited for the beep, as told, then said I'd received her message, was very anxious to see Zachary, but had a tough script deadline to meet. I promised to come over as soon as I'd met it.

Demetrious picked up his phone on the first ring.

"Five nine seven," I said. That was my account number. Names were never mentioned in case the line was tapped.

"What's the matter?" he said. "You like photo finishes?"

"Is it that close?"

"Any closer, it's a dead heat." I tried to think he hadn't stressed the *dead*.

"I'll have the five hundred tomorrow."

"What's wrong with today?"

"I won't be getting it until this afternoon." As I explained that it would be a check and I probably wouldn't be able to get to my bank before it closed, I tried to believe everything I was saying. I visualized Preminger writing out the check. I saw myself cashing it.

"You going to the trotters tonight?" He cut off my fantasy.

This was the middle of September. The Oak Tree meeting at Santa Anita wouldn't start for another week.

But they had harness racing at Hollywood Park at night.

"I don't like the trotters," I said.

"Try."

"Give me a reason." I'd picked up his manner of speech—one of the bad habits that comes from a writer's ear.

"You got a hundred on you now?" he asked.

"Sure," I lied.

"Three things," he said. "You don't bet more than the hundred. You don't tell nobody. And you bring me half the take tomorrow morning, *plus* the five you owe me."

"You mean I'm finally going to have a winner?"

"Sunday's Guest in the third. It should go off nine-to-one."

Half of nine hundred—four hundred and fifty dollars—just for going to the track and making a bet. Almost enough to square me with Demetrious, and if Preminger came through, more than enough to keep Mrs. Fogarty happy. There was always the unexpected, but a gift from Demetrious had never been in the miracle department. The uninformed would be suspicious. The uninformed always question blessings. Why would Demetrious practically hand me four hundred and fifty bucks? Why half the winnings? Why not a third, or twenty-five percent. Anybody in his pocket would do it for that or even less. But he wanted me to stick to the three things he'd spelled out. He didn't want me tempted to make a little side bet on my own. He wanted me satisfied with my share. Then why me? Why had I been chosen? Again the answer was obvious. I wasn't that special. There'd be ten other clients of his on the same errand. We'd each get four-fifty, his take would be forty-five hundred and we'd all be too grateful to consider changing bookies during our worst losing streak.

The uninformed still wouldn't be satisfied. Deme-trious could have sent Damon and Pythias to the track with a bundle or made the bet himself. But any paddock bum knows the folly of that. Playing the horses is a follow-the-leader game and a sudden drop in the tote-board odds starts a stampede. Ten guys plunking down a hundred each at different windows and times bring the odds down slowly. If one or two guys laid out the same total, Sunday's Guest would never trot in at anything like nine to one.

"It's a deal," I said.

"Ten o'clock tomorrow morning," said Demetrious and hung up.

Maybe the uninformed have a point. The amount I had to come up with, or else, had almost doubled.

Chapter 3

IT HAD BEEN ten years since I'd worked for Otto Preminger, and all downhill. He'd paid me five thousand a week then and it took me eight or nine weeks to patch up the script he was shooting. I don't know what his was about any more than the others I've rewritten. The only thing I remember was a character called God who had something to do with the Mafia. This is not to be confused with *The Godfather,* which was a big hit. I've never worked on big hits.

The only reason I remember the God character is because of the casting problem. Otto's first choice to play the part was Frank Sinatra. He'd directed Sinatra in *The Man With the Golden Arm* and claimed they'd come out of it inseparable for life. But Sinatra wasn't taking his calls and the office messenger who kept trying to deliver a copy of the script to his house couldn't get past the four mastiffs in the driveway.

Otto's second choice was Senator Everett Dirksen of Illinois. This wasn't as dumb as it sounds. Most people assume that God is a basso, and Dirksen could have handled Verdi's lowest notes. Besides, he'd hammed it up good in the Army-McCarthy hearings. Preminger used the lawyer, Joseph C. Welch, from that same hit show in *Anatomy of a Murder*. So while I was still sweating over the ending, the script marked THIRD REVISION: FINAL: FINAL: was dispatched to Washington by courier, followed by one or two daily telegrams. Dirksen never answered them and the script came back in a postage-free government envelope without any accompanying letter.

Otto was driving me to The Bistro for lunch when he sprang his third brainstorm.

"Alfred Hitchcock," he said.

"Where?" I looked around at who was inside the cars we were passing. Otto always drove fast.

"For God," he said.

"Perfect." At anything over twenty-five hundred a week, I've never argued.

What followed could be used to substantiate the industry's obeisance to timing. Except The Bistro happened to be one of Hitchcock's favorite restaurants and he lunched there practically every day.

"Alfred!" Otto spotted him as soon as we came in.

Hitchcock was at the front corner table with three other people who looked like sycophants. He was hunched over a plate of lamb stew, so when he rolled his guppy eyes toward Otto, they seemed to peer out of his jowls.

"Alfred," said Otto. "I have a part for you in my new film." I always liked the way Preminger said "film." He made it sound like an infection.

"Aow?" said Hitchcock. He finally took his nose out of his stew. "What's the character?"

"He's called God," said Otto.

"I'm bored already," said Hitchcock and went back to eating.

"I'll send you the script." Otto promised it over his shoulder on the way to our table.

The Bistro at lunchtime isn't a celebrity hangout, but this particular day there were a number of recognizable faces. I spotted Milton Berle and Burt Bacharach and one of the Gabors. I didn't see Dan Dailey until he stepped in front of Otto.

Dailey got the Viennese bear hug, but being a dancer he managed to slip the brunt of it. Otto asked him about his wife and children and his own state of health, awarding each of Dailey's smiling "just fines" a beaming "that's good." Then Dailey went back to his table and Otto sat down next to me.

"Who was that?" he whispered.

"Who? With Hitchcock?"

"Not with Hitchcock. Who was I just talking to?"

"You mean you don't know?"

"Will you stop avoiding my question?" This was an appeal, not a reprimand. "Who is he?"

"Dan Dailey," I said.

"Oh my God," he said.

"I thought you wanted Hitchcock for God."

"Save your jokes for the script," he said. He held both cheeks like he had matching toothaches. "How could I forget Dan Dailey? He's a star!"

"Because you never remember anybody."

"Who doesn't?"

"Otto," I said gently, "you have a form of autism common to great directors. D. W. Griffith couldn't even remember the last name of the Gish sisters. It's your withdrawal from unreality."

"All right," he said. "Name any top agent in this phony town."

This was Otto's party piece whenever his bad memory

was exposed. Somehow he'd managed to memorize the names of the wives of all the leading agents in the business. Considering both the divorce and agency mortality rate in Hollywood, this was no small accomplishment.

"Go ahead," he insisted. He'd pulled this routine on me several times by then, but obviously didn't remember it.

"Mitchell Bloom," I said.

"He's been married to Gilda, Kathleen, Vanessa and Nori."

"Okay. I'm impressed."

"Ask me another one."

"Lee Radnitz."

"Shirley, Bernadette, Beryl and Tikio."

"One more." He was as near to gloating as I'd ever seen him.

"Phil Popkin."

"Sylvia, Moira, Daphne and Ming Toy."

I don't want to diminish Otto's feat. But sequential memory is aided by definite patterns and there was a definite one involved here. Not only is an agent usually on his fourth wife by the time he reaches the top, but the religious and ethnic progression of his mates seldom varies. From the girl of his own faith, to one who proves his agnosticism, to one foreign to his guilt feelings, to one who's foreign to all his feelings. In other words, from Jewish to Catholic to English to someplace west of Krakatoa.

"Imagine forgetting him." Otto tilted his head toward Dan Dailey's table. "And he's such a good dancer."

The fact that Otto chose the wives of agents to prove his memory was characteristic of him. In the Hollywood hierarchy, these ladies are the bottom of the pile. Whatever the social function, their husbands desert them immediately upon arrival and get down to business with other guests. Nobody talks to agents' wives. They don't even talk to each other. But Otto had—at least enough to find out their names. And he would have done this out of kindness, not condescension. How Ming Toy Popkin must have *qvelled* when Otto Preminger greeted her by name.

"Do you think Dan Dailey could play God?" whispered Otto.

"With one foot."

"Ummmmmmmmmm."

Far as I know, Dailey was never offered the part, nor was Hitchcock sent the script. The picture was made and God was portrayed by Groucho Marx who read every fatuous line I'd written from a cue card. I believe this was Groucho's last movie. From *A Night at the Opera* and *The Big Store,* to God off a cue card. There should be something both sad and typical in this. But in all honesty, I never found Groucho very funny except when he was ad-libbing.

During my script job, I kept kidding Otto about the Dan Dailey incident, which was why I'd used Dailey's name when I ran into him in the hotel lobby. From that moment on I wasn't as panicky about the five hundred I owed Demetrious. Otto was the kindest and most generous person I'd ever known, so I couldn't imagine him refusing to help me out of a tight spot. What I could imagine, and my big worry, was that he'd forget our appointment.

This was unfounded. I knocked on the door of his suite at exactly five after three and he opened it immediately, as if he'd been waiting on the other side. I got half a hug on the way in.

"First, I get you something to drink." He went to the

imitation antique phone on the desk. "What would you like?"

"Dewars, water, no ice."

He dialed room service and carefully enunciated my order, then asked for a vodka and tonic with a twist for himself. Not being provincial, he didn't accuse me of being pseudo-British about the no ice.

"So." He hung up the phone. "How is Betty Grable?"

"She's been dead for years."

"Of course." He gave himself the double-cheek slap. "Such a wonderful girl. You must miss her."

"Very much." I'd never met Betty Grable, but I associated her with World War II and I'd developed a perverse nostalgia for that.

"I can imagine," he said. "You were marvelous together in *Mother Wore Tights*."

"Otto," I said, "you still don't know who I am."

"What do you want me to do," he said, "sing *Shine On Harvest Moon*?"

"Dan Dailey sang that," I said. "And he's dead, too."

He stared at me, just stared. There wasn't even the grimace which news of anyone's death always produced on his face.

"Then who are you?" he said.

"I'm Corey Burdick."

He didn't even blink. I had to go through the whole story about Hitchcock and Groucho Marx before my name rang a tiny bell. But he was still hazy about the film. Even directors with good memories have trouble recalling their flops.

I switched to small talk.

"How was 'Rise and Shine, Los Angeles'?"

"The same stupid questions," he said. "What was Marilyn Monroe really like? How did I discover Jean Seberg? Always the same questions."

"Great men are often known less for their achievements than for the company they've kept."

"I think that line was in *Exodus* and I threw it out."

"Maybe you should have saved the line and thrown out the picture."

"Why do you insult me?" he said. "Do I say anything about those terrible scenes you wrote for Harpo Marx?"

"You're absolutely right," I said.

"So why do you insult me?"

"Because I want something from you and I hate myself for asking. You're getting the rebound."

"Those lines I threw out of *The Moon Is Blue.*"

"Good riddance."

"I don't understand." His sigh was truly bewildered. "Everybody insults me."

"Show me a maligned person in this business," I said, "and I'll show you an honest man."

"That line, maybe I could use." He smiled to show that all was forgiven. "Now then, what's the something you want?"

"A favor and a half."

"Favors are easy. Halves, I'm not so good with." He beamed at his own humor and waited. "So?"

"Money," I said. "What else?"

"Is that all?" He looked disappointed, but immediately took out his wallet and began emptying it. "Only I never carry much cash." The bills he laid on the coffee table came to six hundred and fifty dollars.

"Five hundred saves my life," I said.

"What's cheap is cheap." His smile this time was to assure me he was kidding. "If you need more, I'll write a check."

"Five hundred is fine."

"Better take six."

I was tempted. Anyone else, I would have accepted. But then, nobody else would have made the offer.

"I only need five hundred," I insisted. "Honest."

"All right." He finally accepted it. "Now, what's the half of a favor?"

Before I could tell him, the waiter arrived with our drinks. It got a little confusing. He started to put his tray down on the money that was spread out on the coffee table. I scooped it out of the way just in time and Otto somehow thought I was trying to pick up the check.

"No! No! Absolutely not!"

He snatched it from the waiter who then was only interested in seeing what Otto was adding for his tip. As usual, Otto took a long time signing his name.

"Preminger has only one M," I said.

"I know that," he said. "But how many T's are in Otto?"

The waiter looked mildly satisfied with his tip, which meant it was about fifty percent. Then the phone rang. Otto apologized to me for answering it before picking up the receiver.

"From Washington," he said, cupping the mouthpiece.

I only half-listened to his end of the conversation because the waiter had left and my drink, as usual, was all wrong. Otto's presented no problem. The vodka was in the right-shaped glass and the small bottle of tonic water was open and waiting. But mine took some figuring out. There were two tumblers. One held a piece of lemon peel and five ice cubes. The other was filled with Scotch. It not only had no water, but no room for water.

"I believe you, Eddie," Otto said into the imitation antique phone. "Yes, I'm sure she's beautiful. Of course she's talented. But did I ever tell *you* who to put on the Foreign Relations Committee?"

I'd figured it out. I picked up the two tumblers and headed for the bathroom.

"Eddie," pleaded Otto, "did I say she *wasn't* your niece? But in my films there is no nepotism."

I dumped all the ice cubes into the john and salvaged the lemon peel. This stayed in the now-empty glass which I then filled about halfway with the Scotch from the other one. After that, it was only a matter of adding the right amount of water. I also had the rest of the Scotch for another round in case I hung around that long.

"Any time, Eddie," said Otto. "You know I always enjoy talking with you." He was putting the phone in its cradle when I came back.

"Muskie or Kennedy?" I asked.

"Who?"

"On the phone."

"I was talking to Senator Javits."

"Then why did you call him Eddie?"

"Who called him Eddie?" He'd poured the tonic water into his glass of vodka and was peering around the room. "Where's my ice?"

"I'm sorry," I said. "It's in the bathroom."

"What's it doing in the bathroom?"

"I put it down the toilet."

"Oh." He managed to shrug it off. Something else was bothering him more. "Why would I call Jacob Javits 'Eddie'? I don't even think it's his middle name."

"I'll phone down for some more ice," I said.

"No, no. It doesn't matter." He sipped his drink and made a face and turned to the tray on the coffee table. "The waiter forgot my lemon peel."

"No, he didn't." I pointed to it floating in my drink. "Here." I tried to fish it out with a stirrer.

"Leave it. It's soaked with Scotch."

"Let me call down for another twist."

"Don't bother." He went back to his chair. "I didn't really call him Eddie." He was trying to ride a joke he didn't quite get. "Did I?"

"Many times."

"Oh my God!" He picked up the phone and found Javits's number in his address book and asked the operator to place the call.

"So?" He hung up the phone. "You still haven't told me the half of a favor."

"You've been generous enough for one day," I said. "I'll take a rain check."

"Now I'm really curious."

"Okay." I tried to look appropriately silly. "A young lady has offered to go to bed with me if she gets a part in your next picture."

"Daniel." He shook his bald head disapprovingly.

"I don't know who she is or what she looks like. But ten to one she's got more talent than Jacob Javits's niece."

"Daniel." He said it mournfully this time. "Why do you want to make me feel guilty about your sex life?"

"I don't," I said. "I just want you to say no to this so I won't feel so guilty about taking your money."

"All right. No. Absolutely not. I wouldn't give even a walk-on to this girl."

"Thanks," I said. "And have a good trip back to New York."

We shook hands in the way that has its advantages over hugging and he was showing me to the door when the phone rang again. It was his call to Washington.

"Jacob?" Otto began humbly. "What must you be thinking of me?"

I waved good-bye from the doorway, but he was too intent on his apology to notice.

"How could I call you Eddie? It must be from the warm vodka with no lemon peel."

Chapter 4

SUNDAY'S GUEST was ten-to-one in the morning line. When
the riders came out, the tote board was showing it at
nine. The odds held steady through the warm-up time
and I thought Demetrious had hit it right on the nose. I
waited until two minutes before the start before getting
into a betting line. By the time I got to the window, Sunday's Guest was down to seven-to-two and still dropping.
One of Demetrious's errand-boys had broken the rules.

It hurt double when Sunday's Guest breezed in by a
dozen lengths. Instead of four hundred and fifty bucks,
my half of the win came to a hundred and thirty-nine
plus change. Demetrious's half went into my wallet, next
to the five hundred I owed him. I knew I should have
packed it in right then. But give me a stake and anything on four legs, sulkies or no sulkies, and I don't leave
the track until they close the gates. I hit the seventh
race Exacta and was over three hundred ahead. Then
my usual luck came back. But I still had fifty or sixty
more than I came with after the last race and I hadn't
touched my wallet or Demetrious's dough.

It was about midnight when I finally got out of the parking lot. I drove up the San Diego Freeway and across Sunset in a more detached state than I normally have after the races. The money I'd won and given back wasn't enough to cause anguish or second-guessing. And harness racing still didn't hold any kick for me. But it was better than Napa Valley Chianti and Mrs. Fogarty.

There was also a good feeling that I traced to having been given the tip by Demetrious. I figured he'd been testing me. It was possible that bigger and better sure things lay ahead. His vague promise of "someday . . ." gave me a little something to look forward to. If three Derbys in England had been fixed, why not a cheap Claimer at Santa Anita? The fictioneer in me took over the idea, and I began to consider its possibilities as a film story. I reminded myself that, though life often imitated bad movies, it never imitated mine. I should have added a "yet."

The parking bays at the North Sweetzer Arms were synchronized to the apartments. So mine was number twelve. I backed into it and was half out of my car when I saw him coming toward me. If he hadn't been all in white, I might have been more wary. That and his ten-gallon hat and the octagonal glasses with silver frames and his friendly country-road greeting.

"How ya doin'?" he said.

He was big, but soft, with the kind of pink skin that meant he didn't have to shave every day. His smile would have been more disarming with bigger teeth. There was a sixteenth of an inch between his front ones.

"Not too bad," I said.

"I guess you're Mr. Burdick."

"I've been called worse," I said.

My answer wasn't definite enough for him. He stopped

in front of me and stood waiting, like a delivery man who wouldn't turn over a parcel until he saw some identification.

"I'm Corey Burdick," I said.

Just that. I'd only been slugged twice in my life and both punches had followed argument, threats, name-calling and a certain amount of pushing and shoving. I'd never been hit just for saying my name. And I'd never been hit that hard.

He caught me square on my left eye and I bounced off the Buick Skylark in bay eleven before going down. The cement garage floor didn't feel as hard as his fist had. My face was in a spread of grease and I didn't like the taste. His first kick flipped me over. I saw the second one coming. I even saw the thistle design on his shiny boot before it thudded into my ribs. He kicked me four more times, but that one hurt the most. Then he was leaning right over me. Fat faces are grotesque hanging down. His cheeks were buttocks, his mouth an obscene hole.

"You pay attention now," he said.

He did the expected. He slid my wallet from my inside coat pocket and took the money out of it. I was going by touch then. The eye he'd hit had gone out completely and my brain wasn't focusing the other one. I felt the wallet hit my chest, but only just. Either I was getting numb or it had been dropped gently or there wasn't anything left in it to give it weight.

"You keep far away from Bambi," he said. "Or next time I won't be so easy."

Last thoughts from a garage floor. Names are crucial to me. I sweat over christening my characters. I don't believe roses would smell like roses if called anything else. I've always steered clear of women called Bertha, Dorothy or Pearl. I have always hated Disney animal names. Bambi was high on the list. If only spaced-teeth had said "my girl" or "my wife" or just plain "her," there might have been a chance that I had earned my pain. If he'd said any other name but Bambi, it wouldn't have hurt so much.

I heard the car engine start up and my right eye dimly saw a Mustang driving out of the garage. It was white— what else? Its whiteness made its Avis sticker stand out. The background blue of the license plate was watery, but its yellow numbers and letters registered.

902 EJC. I committed them to memory before blacking out.

Chapter 5

IT WOULD HAVE been nice if one of the other tenants had found me, especially the long-legged blonde who kept her Toyota in bay sixteen, and I'd come to in her bed with an ice pack on my eye. But I always take these kind of dissolves out of the scripts I rewrite and there's a vengeance embodied in every cliché. So when I woke up I was still on the garage floor and nothing had changed. The first thing I did was check my wallet. Everything was there but the money.

I managed the yardage to my apartment, then assessed the rest of the damage. My pants and jacket had sopped up enough grease to be written off by a dry cleaner. My side and kidney area were turning purple. But my face was the big disaster. My left cheekbone was a doorknob. The eye above it was in the wrong place and it didn't look like I'd ever get the blood out of it. When gentle swabbing with wet cotton eventually did, I was amazed to see the pupil still there. But the lid was closing fast.

During all this, I was planning what to say to the cops.

Assault, theft of six hundred and forty dollars and 902
EJC. The Los Angeles Police Department would wel-
come such concise details from an articulate victim. As
soon as I finished working on my eye, I dug out the phone
directory. It was in the drawer of the table that held my
answering machine. While looking for the number, I automatically switched this on.

A beep and a click. Whoever had called hadn't wanted
to leave a name. I'd developed a hatred for that combination of sounds. It always left the lousy feeling that I'd
missed out on something important by not being there.
After a gap in the tape it happened again. That made it
worse. A third beep was followed by my agent's voice.

"Corey. Perry. Call me."

Another beep and another hanging up. But this time
there was a longer pause between. The caller had almost
said something. For no reason at all, I thought of a star-
let I'd once had in the sack when the phone rang. It was
my phone in my bedroom and nobody knew she was there.
After about the fifth ring she asked me to answer it in
case it was for her. It takes that kind of hope to keep
going in show business.

The machine beeped again and this time she spoke.

"Ain't you ever home, Mr. Burdick?"

The rest of the tape was blank and I turned off the
machine. I was still thumbing pages of the phone book,
gradually realizing that, like almost everybody else, I
didn't know how to call the police. The precinct numbers
covered most of a page. I finally found a number for Hollywood, but there was another one for West Hollywood
and while trying to decide between them I mentally rehearsed what I'd say. Open and shut as it was, it didn't
come out that way. My eye was evidence enough of assault, but how did I prove I'd been robbed? If there'd been

over seven hundred dollars in my wallet, how come I didn't pay my rent? Who was my employer? Which bank manager could I give as a reference? All questions I couldn't answer. I envisioned the facial expressions of the two young cops making out their report. Police reports were beginning to use bigger words than the *Antioch Review*. They'd probably sum up the whole thing as an intersection imbroglio.

Then I had a better idea. More accurately, I remembered the idea because I'd used it in rewriting a script that Steve McQueen was supposed to do, but didn't. I'd defended it to a skeptical producer and it had stood up. Calling the police probably wouldn't get Demetrious's money back. But this could.

The Avis woman I was put through to sounded friendly and efficient and I had no trouble sounding indignant.

"You have a white Mustang, license number 902 EJC."

"Just a moment, sir." Thanks to computers, it didn't take much longer. "Yes, we do, sir, but I'm afraid it's out on rental right now. However . . ."

"However, right now I've got it."

"Are you having some trouble with it, sir?" She started giving me the number of their breakdown service. I had to talk over her.

"Wait a minute, honey. It ain't that easy." Just raising my voice hurt my face and ribs. "There were two white Mustangs in a parking lot tonight. Yours and mine. And the idiot attendant gave mine to the idiot who's renting yours."

"Oh." This one wasn't in the manual. "Now, let's see how to straighten this out."

"I'll tell you how!" In spite of my rib cage, I managed to yell. "You call the idiot who's renting yours and tell him to get in my car and drive it over here and we swap."

"But it's almost two o'clock, sir."

"Okay. If you don't want to wake him up, give me the jerk's number and I'll do it."

"I'm not allowed to, sir." She was sounding efficient again.

"You got any better suggestions?"

"Perhaps if you call back after ten o'clock when our manager's here."

"Look," I said, "my white Mustang is a year older than your Mustang. It's got eighteen thousand more miles on it. It needs a new transmission. You want to forget the whole thing, that's fine with me."

That did it. She went off to consult a superior and came back with his consent.

"The leasee is Mr. Q. Dookes," she said. If she hadn't spelled it, I would have used a *U* for the two *O*'s. The address was on Pico and she also had the phone number. I thanked her and dialed it.

"Bolero Motel." A Steppin Fetchit voice. I hung up.

The police again reared their close-cropped heads. Any more delay in contacting them would cancel the law as an option. I made my decision and took two Valium. Every time they were about to work, I must have moved and the pain counteracted them. I had to take three more to get some sleep.

Chapter 6

DEMETRIOUS started taking bets at nine-thirty. I got there a quarter after, but he was already in his chair giving a customer some bad news on the phone.

"To cut a short story," he said, "you lost."

He wasn't alone. Pythias was sweeping the floor and the Kid was sprawled on the beaten-up leather couch against the wall. I'd never seen him before, but he gave me a bucktoothed grin. It didn't come out just right, because at the same time he was trying to bite off a hangnail.

I'll always call him the Kid. I might as well, since, in spite of everything that happened later, I never found out his name. And not being a client of Demetrious, he didn't have a code number. The Kid was a client of nobody, a servant of no one, a slave to nothing except his fixation. It's a fixation that escapes me, just as my obsessions elude others. His had to do with wires and engines and energy and what makes things work. His dishevelment went with that. Not that he was messy. But his hair hadn't been combed since kindergarten and if his

socks matched it was a fluke. He just couldn't be bothered with such things. He probably felt the same way
about sex and politics.

The buckteeth gave him a cocky look. But he wasn't.
Confident, yes. But only about what he did, and there it
was a hundred and ten percent. It's a look I like to see
in certain places. In the middle of the desert, for instance, on the way to Vegas, when my car breaks down.
Then I want a pickup truck to stop and somebody who
looks like the Kid to step out and ask me what seems to
be the trouble. At times like these, the buckteeth and
unkempt sandy hair and freckles and maybe a tattoo on
one arm make me feel secure. Give their owner a mon-
key wrench and he can reconstruct the world. He doesn't
need people or love or money. All he needs is to hear the
motor that won't turn over start turning over. And he
looks hurt if you try to pay him for saving your life. People with this mentality are the truly fortunate.

Except in this case, he was in Demetrious's place, same
as me. But not for long. As soon as Demetrious hung up
the phone, he turned to him.

"We'll talk about it some more."

The Kid took the hint and was off the couch and out
the door like he had a hundred important things to do.
Demetrious waited until the door was closed before ex-
ploding.

"Big mouths! They get a sure thing, they got to give
it to every broad they ever laid."

"I didn't."

"Maybe yes and maybe no."

"I didn't." I repeated it firmly.

"Fuckin' second favorite when it shoulda been nine-
to-one!" His fist hitting the table made both phones jump.
"But someday . . ."

"Someday," I agreed.

"Your eye looks like a cunt," he said.

"Wait till you see the other guy."

"I know him?"

"No. But you're going to want to."

"Why should I?"

"Because he's got your six hundred and forty bucks."

He gave me the long stare he used on deadbeats. I took out my wallet and showed its empty money flap.

"I got rolled." I pointed to my eye to back it up.

"How do I know?"

"I had your money last night. Otto Preminger will verify that."

"Who the fuck's Otto Preminger?"

"He's a very eminent director and producer."

"I ain't impressed." He looked from my wallet to my eye. One of his phones rang. "Okay," he said. "You got to five o'clock to come up with my money."

"Loan me Pythias," I said, "and you'll have it in an hour."

"Pythias? Who the fuck's Pythias?"

I pointed to the ape who was putting the broom back into a closet. Demetrious reached for the phone that was still ringing.

"Gus," he said. "Go with this guy."

When we got outside, Gus took one look at my car and said we'd go in his. It was a Volvo—black, naturally. The speedometer showed over thirty thousand miles, but he'd kept it spotless. I sneaked looks at him with my good eye as he drove, enjoying thoughts of what he was going to do to the pink flab of Mr. Q. Dookes. I looked forward to the blood on the white suit, not movie ketch-up but real son-of-a-bitch blood. The ten-gallon hat was going to be force-fed and eaten piece by piece by the lit-

tle teeth with the gap in front. Gus would do the holding
and I'd do the feeding. The six hundred and forty dollars
had become incidental.

The Bolero Motel lived up to its name. For some reason, maybe to do with the climate, cheap motels in L.A.
are painted a diarrheic brown. This one needed a new
coat.

Gus parked on the side street. The motel was two-
storied and there were some service steps at the back.

"What's his room?"

"I don't know." I added a "sorry." I felt dumber than
he looked.

"Always find out the room." I'd had my first lesson in
collection tactics.

We walked around to the entrance. The clerk was
moonlighting his social security. He was wizened and
black and almost a hunchback, but when he saw my face
he clucked sympathy. I asked him which room Mr. Dookes
was in and he asked me what I wanted. Then he saw
Gus and he couldn't look it up fast enough.

"Two sixteen." He took the key out of its slot and
handed it to Gus. "Upstairs, on the left."

I glanced back from the foot of the steps, but he had
no intention of reaching for the phone. Gus motioned me
to go on ahead.

"The bastard's big, but pulpy," I said quietly. He
couldn't have cared less.

Before we got to it, I knew the open door down the
hall would have a two and a one and a six on it. A fat
Mexican maid with a cart of linens was trying to figure
out why it wasn't on her check-out list. There was nothing in the closets or drawers.

"God damn." The old room clerk just wagged his head

when I reported back to him. "But I'm glad to see the dust from that one."

"Driving a white Mustang?" I thought it a good idea to make sure.

"That's him."

"Let's go," said Gus.

I stalled him long enough to use the pay phone in the motel lobby and call Avis. As I expected, 902 EJC had been returned. I did some nervous talking on the drive back to Inglewood, dropping names of stars even he'd be sure to recognize, pretending any one of them would loan me the money I'd been robbed of. But Gus gave me the silent treatment. He didn't say anything to Demetrious, either, when we walked in. He just turned both thumbs down.

"You still got to five o'clock," said Demetrious.

"I'll need a couple days," I said.

He gave me a look that would make a plate umpire reverse a decision.

"Tomorrow noon. Right here." He tapped the exact spot on his desk where he expected to see the money.

Chapter 7

A DIGITAL SIGN in front of a bank showed the time 11:46 and the temperature already eighty-nine degrees. The sun was what I always described in my screenplays as a dirty smudge in the smog. It was going to be a rough day for asthmatics, the kind of day when Los Angeles looks its lousiest.

Whatever the disclaimers, L.A. is a product of its own minority industry. The simplest answer to the simplest question has a screen-test delivery. Everybody is constantly auditioning. Life is a series of re-takes, which is as good an explanation as any for the insane resistance to aging in a desert climate which prematurely ages everything.

A big city is supposed to have a heartbeat and this one hasn't. The only thing that sustains it is its obvious impermanence. It was never supposed to be and it is certain to stop being. But meanwhile, it needs a clear sky and high-key lighting from a bright sun to sustain its image. It wasn't getting any today.

Perry Lutz had asked me to meet him for coffee in a

deli on Fairfax. According to his secretary who'd relayed this when I returned his call it was important.

Delicatessen coffee always tastes like it was made last week. The dishwasher hasn't been invented that can get the lipstick off the chipped brown cups they all use. The sugar won't pour out of the sticky glass containers. The rags the waitresses mop up the tables with smell like jockstrap pouches from the Tokyo Olympics. Fairfax Avenue delicatessens are agents' favorite meeting places before they hit it big.

Perry Lutz hadn't yet, as evidenced by his representing me, as also evidenced by his only being on his third marriage. Operators like Perry had two kinds of clients: those possibly on the way up and those definitely on the way down. I was a definite. Perry obviously thought I had a season or two left in the minors. Like all agents, he used a lot of baseball analogies. The minors, in this case, was television.

"You're a hold-out," he'd said many times. "The network boys can't stand hold-outs. They want everybody in the shit with them."

Another time he'd tried a highbrow approach.

"Arthur Miller's written for the tube. Bernstein's conducted on the tube. What makes you so special?"

"Each man," I said, "should have one thing he refuses to do."

"So don't climb Mount Everest."

I liked Perry. I liked the way he introduced himself. "Perry Lutz—rhymes with klutz." I envied his energy and eternal optimism. His obsequiousness would have been an occupational deformity if it wasn't so all-inclusive. Perry opened doors for everybody, stepped aside for everybody, refused to leave elevators until he was the last person to get off on that floor. More than one bucket-carrying cleaning woman had been motioned on ahead by his courtly hand.

"Today a cleaning woman, tomorrow she's got a three-picture deal."

Long before they make it big, agents have to keep up appearances. Somehow, Perry managed to. He drove a Bentley, he always picked up the tab and he had a house in Pacific Palisades.

"Three bedrooms, a sauna and six boutiques."

The boutiques crack had to do with his third wife, Gillian. She was another rock singer from Liverpool who'd tried to cash in on Beatlemania and sleep her way up the charts. She gave up somewhere in the bottom twenty and married Perry. Since then she'd been on a buying spree. I got the latest installment as soon as he sat down opposite me in the booth at the deli.

"Twelve hundred bucks yesterday," he said. "For cloth luggage with somebody else's initials all over it."

"Planning a trip?"

"To Vegas, overnight. Twelve hundred bucks to carry a douche and a toothbrush."

"And I only need a little over six hundred." I sneaked it in, but he ignored it.

"I wouldn't mind so much if she spent it in Saks or Neiman-Marcus. But no. She's got to give it to the Arab gyp joints on Rodeo. You think that isn't deliberate?"

"Still," I said, "the Arabs probably own Saks by now."

He looked at me as if I'd denounced Israel.

"Her psychiatrist told her that excessive buying is a sign of frigidity."

"He could be right."

"He *is* right. So I'm paying him to tell her what *I* could have told him." He drank his coffee, oblivious to the taste, and sneaked a look at my swollen eye. "What did you say about six hundred?"

"Six hundred and forty to be exact. And I need it by tomorrow noon."

"Bookie trouble?" He waited for me to nod. "My first wife's analyst said gambling is a death wish."

"It's more complicated than that," I said.

"With writers, everything's complicated."

"I really need it, Perry."

"Six hundred and forty!" He made the amount sheer agony. "Some drunk ran into my mailbox last night. You know what a new mailbox costs?" Another furtive look at my eye. "And what the hell happened to your face?"

"The same thing that happened to your mailbox."

"It's that *shmattie* you're driving. It attracts hostility."

"Your secretary told me this get-together was important."

"It is. It could be very important."

My eye was obviously bothering him, so I averted that side of my face.

"I've been talking up that Scott Fitzgerald thing," he said. "A couple of network *shtunks* are interested."

"But I'm not."

"It's going to contaminate you to take a goddam meeting?"

He drummed his fingers nervously on the table. I'd never before noticed how stubby they were. The ring on the middle finger of his right hand had a big zircon star. More wealth dangled from his neck, two Krugerrands on a thick gold chain. Perry always wore dark turtleneck sweaters under pale sports jackets. They and the gold coins and chain and ring and perfect tan and thin mustache and deep frown all spelled agent. Even when he smiled, his forehead frowned. I shouldn't have been surprised by his stubby fingers. They were proportionate to his build. His heel-lifts were a good two inches.

"There must be some script that needs a rewrite," I said. It was the first time I'd complained about his not coming up with anything.

"Sure there are," he countered. "Dozens of them." He started listing them on his sawed-off fingers. " 'Hotel' . . . 'T. J. Hooker' . . . 'Dynasty' . . ."

"You're ruining my lunch."

"We're not having lunch. I got a date at La Scala." He checked his watch. More gold. "In twenty minutes."

"I need a movie job, Perry."

"No way."

"Even a cheapie. Anything."

"You know how many pictures this town is turning out?" He didn't wait for an answer. "Ten, twelve a year."

"And every one of them is rewritten at least twice."

"You're finished in features." He threw it in fast.

"What're you talking about?"

"I can't get you on a feature."

"I've done six that made money and only three real bombs." My writer's ear had picked up his phrasing. "MGM should have my batting average."

"It's got nothing to do with that. You've got the worst reputation anybody can have in this town."

"Like?"

He fiddled with his Krugerrands.

"Like . . . anti-Semite."

"Then what am I doing in a kosher deli?"

"I mean it, Corey."

"Who used the smear brush?" As if I didn't know.

"The Raskins."

"You mean Shirley Raskin. Sam only holds the ladder."

"You had to tell her what she is. Everybody *knows* what she is! But *you* had to tell her."

"Somebody had to."

"Nobody had to. Did anybody tell Harry Cohn what he was?"

Perry was right, of course. Today's independent producers were poor imitations of yesterday's moguls. But put them all together they spelled power. In the case of the Raskins, I'd had motivation and I'd been right. On the screen those stand for something. But not in a story conference around a marble-topped table on chrome legs with two original Chagalls on the walls.

The film I was rewriting for them was about the Holocaust. The Raskins had already made five pictures dealing directly or indirectly with the Holocaust. They'd won Anti-Defamation League awards and National Council of Christians and Jews awards and two Academy Award nominations for best picture. And Shirley Raskin kept saying that this picture was going to be the best of all. She kept saying this and talking about the Holocaust and concentration camps and she kept eating. We'd just come back from lunch and there was a huge bowl of cashew nuts on the marble-topped table and she kept scooping them up with both her fat hands and shoving them into her big mouth and only stopped occasionally to wash them down with some Tab right out of its can while she talked about the Holocaust. And I kept trying not to watch or listen. But I couldn't look away any more than I could stop thinking about a camp near Ohrdruf that my outfit had got to first. The official report that came later said about four thousand of its inmates had died or been murdered, a lot of the murders just before we arrived. That explained some of the stench.

I can still smell it and I can still see the old horse in the field with the twenty-five or thirty screaming skeletons chasing it. The horse was too old to break into a real gallop and they were hemming it in, wobbling more than running as they converged on it and finally catching it, grabbing its tail and mane. Then some of them threw themselves across its low-scooped back and others tackled its legs or pulled at its heavy, shaggy hooves until they managed to tumble it over. They had nothing to kill it with and were too starved to wait. They used anything sharp they could find, flat sides of stones and broken branches and pieces of glass. Then another inmate arrived with a knife and was applauded and cheered as he managed to slit the horse's side while the others held it down. I can still hear the noises that the horse made and see the skeletons trying to chew the raw meat and the blood oozing onto their chins and filthy prison-camp clothes. And I heard and saw them that day during the story conference. And I thought that if Shirley Raskin reached into the bowl for one more fistful of cashew nuts, I had to do something. Or if she said "the Holocaust" one more time, I had to do something. Then she did both.

I don't remember exactly what I said. I'm sure it sounded manic and incoherent. But I remember pieces. I know I called her a walking vindication of Hitler. I know I said that she cheapened the suffering of millions, that her main interest in the Holocaust was making money out of it and that if she kept up the combination of cashew nuts and Tab, her body would be even more of an obscenity than it already was.

I remember her husband's words more clearly than my own. Sam Raskin yelled that if he hadn't recently had open-heart surgery, he would've broken every bone in my fucking Nazi body with his bare hands. So they'd resorted to killing me the slow way. The Raskin episode had been over a year ago. It takes a lot of Beverly Hills dinner parties to achieve the final solution.

"That's how it is," said Perry.

"Don't you know any goy producers?"

"There are Jewish producers and there are Jewish producers with goysheh names and once there was Cecil B. DeMille. At your age, I have to teach you balls and strikes?"

"I don't need the lecture," I said. "If I don't come up with the six forty by tomorrow noon, I won't have any fingers to write with."

He took one more look at my eye and it softened him.

"I made us a nine o'clock date at the network." He said which one. "I'll have the dough with me."

"Do I get it for showing up, or only if we make the deal?"

"I've invested a lot of time in you, Corey." It was a line I'd heard from every agent I'd ever had. It was a leverage line. I'd parted company with enough of them to know we'd come to the crossroads.

"You didn't answer my question," I said.

"If they offer you a deal and you take it, I'll bail you out. Otherwise . . ." He shrugged and pulled a dollar from a gold money clip to pay for our coffee. "Be there by ten to nine."

"I'll think about it," I said.

"Be there," he repeated. "And bring some dark glasses."

He hurried off on his built-up heels. The waitress came over to pick up her tip and asked me if I wanted a menu. She was heavy and uncorseted and probably could have told me exactly how many miles she'd already walked that day. I said I'd be leaving in a minute. The place was filling up for lunch and I knew she'd be clocking me.

Each man should have many things he refuses to do. That I was down to one, and that this was refusing to write for television, were good grounds for self-pity. I wouldn't be hard-pressed to name six martyrs who've been canonized for less. But I'd long ago given up comparing my lousy luck with other people's windfalls. My final defiance, for what it was worth, had something to do with words and the craft I'd labored at most of my life. Considering the sins of my screenplays, the line I'd drawn was a fine one. But, when pushed hard enough, I can always defend one cesspool against another.

The theatrical motion picture has been essentially harmless. During its short, garish life, it's traveled the well-worn path from novelty to placebo to a pretension to art. And callow and insipid as movies are, they're probably less so than most daily existence. During the medium's infancy, in a more puritan time, it had definite possibilities. There was a stag-party expectancy in the world then and hidden pornography in most aspects of life. But the camera failed to catch any of this and the audience gradually went home. Unfortunately, television cornered it there. The rest is history.

Janet always called my refusing to write for television a cop-out. During those years when the cinema-versus-TV debate went with dessert, she took the television side. She found movie producers "gross" and television executives "bright and informed." I still can't argue much against her generalities. Motion pictures are made by vulgarians. Their armadillo hides feel no pain, but they manage to fake it, loudly and crudely, to justify their ruthlessness. Their saving characteristic, though, is that they sometimes believe what they're saying about what they're doing.

Television executives are something else. If they be-

lieve in anything, it's escaped me. They front for audience ratings and the advertising buck while talking
ecology and Bartók. I guess they are bright, Book-of-the-
Month-Club speaking. Everyone of them seems to have
a degree in something or other, and most of them look
like they played in the marching band at Dartmouth or
Nebraska State. Most of them also look like they played
the glockenspiel.

Whatever Shirley and Sam Raskin were, they never
went near a glockenspiel.

Chapter 8

I DROVE BACK to my place to get something to eat. There were three pairs of beeps and clicks on my answering machine with no sounds of disappointment in between. I made myself a ham on rye. The bread was stale, but not yet fatal. Packaged loaves are too big for the single parent. By the time you're halfway through them the mold spots start showing up.

I improvised an ice bag with a towel and held it on my eye. At intervals, I examined the damage like an ophthalmic surgeon. The skin had gone charcoal-black with a sickly yellow fringe. A streak of deeper black marked the broken tear duct. The lump on my cheekbone was down some, but still hurt to touch. I could see why people found me hard to look at. Perry was right about the dark glasses. The pair I had concealed most of the mess.

I took out my address book, made myself comfortable on the bed and prepared to make some last-ditch calls. The first was to the Beverly Wilshire. But as I expected, Preminger had checked out. One down, maybe three or four possibilities to go. Before I could try the next one, the phone rang.

"Mr. Burdick?"

"Hello, Bambi."

The pause told me I'd guessed right.

"How did you find out my name?"

"Let's say a mutual acquaintance told me."

"I hope you mean Mr. Gomez."

"I don't mean Mr. Gomez."

"Darn," she said. "Quentin got to you first."

"If you mean Quentin Dookes with the spaced teeth, you get an unqualified yes."

"I've been tryin' to warn you. I kept callin' you and all I got was that dumb recording."

"You could have left a message," I said. "Beware of a pink gorilla in a white hat or something."

"Did he hurt you bad?"

"Now what makes you think that?"

"I know Quentin." She sighed as she said it. "He only gets like that 'cause he's so homosexual."

"I think you'd better fill me in," I said.

"Maybe we could meet somewhere."

"I'll be here later today."

"What if Quentin shows up again?"

I suggested Wally's Bar on Third Street, partly because it had low visibility, mostly because I could still sign for the tab there. I started to give her detailed directions.

"It's only a street and number." She went huffy. "We have those in Venables, too."

"Venables, Tennessee?"

"Now what would Venables be doin' in Tennessee?"

"Five-thirty sharp," I said.

"I think I remember what you look like," she said.

I told her I'd changed a little.

Back to the last-ditch calls. Making a movie is like a sea voyage. You spend a lot of time with the same people over a short period and become pretty close. Then it's over and you go your different ways. You promise to keep in touch, but usually don't. Of all the actors and directors and producers I'd worked with, there were only a few I could call out of the blue who might loan me money.

My luck was consistent. George Roy Hill was scouting locations in Morocco. Martin Manulis was in Philadelphia trying out a play. Jack Lemmon was in a celebrity golf tournament in Florida. I called Preminger's New York office and his secretary said she wasn't expecting him until late the next afternoon. Late the next afternoon would be too late.

That left me only one other possibility.

Chapter 9

BEING DIVORCED seven years, I felt next to nothing about the house. About our once sharing it, that is. What's happened to real estate prices since gives me definite twinges.

We bought the house in Brentwood for eighty-five thousand. At the time we split up, the prices hadn't gone up all that much and I was working. So I waived my community property rights. This particular day, we could have put the place on the market for half a million and had a dozen takers. So much for noble gestures.

Janet's new husband, a securities analyst (née stockbroker), hadn't even acknowledged my generosity with an inside tip on the market. His name was Charles Howard. I don't know what his last name was before some linguistic lawyer tinkered with it. The Charles part was a fit. It's a name I often use in scripts for shnooky characters.

I parked my TR-6 alongside Janet's Mercedes to emphasize my destitution. She'd put a new knocker on the front door. The mask of comedy was gone, replaced by a

Tibetan monk in some kind of agony. Zachary hadn't come home empty-handed.

I clattered the brass monk twice, then strolled out to the pool. It was a ritual we'd adopted after our divorce. I never went inside the house unless invited. The invitations added up to one or two a year, providing it was raining hard when I came around. I thought a curtain had twitched in an upstairs room after I'd parked. But it was hard to tell through dark glasses.

I'm not going to do a job on Janet. We never played the game of "Blame the Partner." Instead, we resorted to flippancies. It's been reported to me that she's often said she could compete with two-legged fillies, but not the four-legged kind. I've chosen a self-demeaning pose. My fictional creations couldn't live up to her; things like that.

In truth, it was the customary clash of derangements. Our insanities diverged. The specifics are unimportant. Money was one, melancholy another. We possessed several impossible combinations, all undetectable before middle age. Unfortunately, our marriage had one tangible result. I watched it come out of the house.

"Corey."

He walked toward me as if he had bowel trouble. He was too tall for the postures of Asian humility.

"Zachary."

He touched his forehead with his fingertips instead of offering to shake hands. I took a deck lounge. He lowered himself gingerly into the butterfly position. All he had on was a pair of washed-out denims that a shark must have chewed. He'd grown a full beard and the tufts of hair on his shoulders looked like its excess droppings. But the main difference in him was a detergent cleanliness. I mentioned that.

"Inside as well, I hope." According to his humble smile, it was more than a hope.

"How's the Great Wall of China?"

"Great," he said.

"And Hong Kong?"

"Crowded."

"The Himalayas?"

"Vast."

"Calcutta?"

"Filthy."

It had become a word-association game.

"Was it all worthwhile?"

"Infinitely."

"Why?"

"Because I found myself," he said. And then, as if it followed naturally, "What happened to your eye?" So much for dark glasses.

"It's a long story."

"Speaking of stories," he said. "I read some of yours."

"Only some?"

"Three to be exact." My one book of short stories contained twelve. "I may try one of your novels."

"The stories are safer," I said. "You can just say which one you liked best without compromising your integrity. With a novel, it's all or nothing."

"I found parts of each of the three interesting."

"That's most generous of you, Zachary." My sarcastic tone earned me a spiritual smile.

"What do you want, Corey?" he said. "Approval?"

"For one thing, I want not to be called Corey."

"What would you suggest? Father has such metaphysical implications. Pa sounds so log-cabinish. Not Daddy, I hope."

"Forget it." I know when I've been topped. "Tell me

more about Calcutta. I hear it's got some great cat-
houses."

"I'd rather talk about your writing," he said. "Why do
you write screenplays?"

"I don't," I said. "I rewrite them."

"Is there a difference?"

"Vast as the fucking Himalayas." My sacrilege got me
nowhere.

"Was it materialism that seduced you?"

"Materialism is a lousy lay."

"That's three slang sexual terms you've used in your
last four sentences."

"I know a few more," I said.

"Did anyone ever tell you that your conversation has
a sound-track quality?" He'd inherited *his* sarcastic tone
from his mother. It was better than mine.

"Why not?" There was no way I could keep from
sounding defensive. "Life's been imitating movies for a
long time."

"Especially fatuous movies."

"Are there any other kind?"

"Definitely," he said. "I saw some beautiful films in
India and China. The kind that never come here."

"But they meant something to you."

"Definitely."

"Much more than my stories."

"Yes." At least he put a little reluctance into it.

"Okay," I said. "I doubt if I can make this as profound
as some smelly mystic wailing from the top of Dalaghuri.
But if you think all the DNA has leaked out your navel,
you'd better take another look. Half your fingernails and
that crappy beard and every other goddam thing you've
got comes from me. And those stories and my novels come
from the same place. So maybe you could have found

yourself in the public library and saved that round-trip fare."

I thought it was pretty good for an off-the-cuff speech. I didn't think it had a sound-track quality. I waited for it to unnerve him.

"I have a feeling," he said, "that Mother married you partly because of your stories and books. That isn't a very good advertisement, is it?"

"Are you gay?" I said.

"What?"

"Gay," I repeated. "Can't you handle it?"

I think he started to blush, but he managed to control it with yoga.

"We are more than our sexual preferences," he said.

"*Sri Oribindo*. Volume Four."

"As a matter of fact, I was quoting a Sherpa I met."

"A Sherpa's sex life is kind of limited."

"How little you know, Corey."

"Are you gay, Zachary?"

"Are you developing paternal feelings about my ass?"

"I'm trying to find out if the new faggots are into mugging and ten-gallon hats."

"I trust the obscurity is meaningful."

The words in the top ten always left me with nothing to say and "meaningful" was number four that week. We sat in silence. He seemed entranced by his long toes and picked at some scaly skin between two of them. I looked at some dead bees floating in the pool and defined my options.

He probably kept his money in a goatskin pouch. And he probably had more than I needed. I had a hunch he'd give me whatever amount I asked him for. And a saintly smile would come with it. Janet might even write me a check if I went to the door and begged a little. Her smile wouldn't exactly be saintly.

Or I could not show up at Demetrious's place at noon and look forward to traction. Or I could do the one thing in life that I had so far refused to do.

Zachary stayed in his butterfly fold when I got up. It was going to take him awhile to unravel.

"It's been productive talking to you, son," I said.

"I'm glad of that, friend," he said.

Chapter 10

NOT HAVING TOO much imagination, I've never squandered it, especially on anticipating what people will look like. Disappointments outnumber pleasant surprises about six-to-one in that department. But with my face in the mess it was and my rib pain cutting my breath intake in half, it was hard not to think about the cause of it all.

So I thought about Bambi. And that meant envisioning her. Our conversations, if they could be called that, eliminated a lot of images, most of them regal. She also had to be a fit with Quentin Dookes. I canceled his boots and white suit. The days when clothes were a guide to character were long-gone. Dookes's punch and kicks and laconic threat were more reliable. I tossed them into the pot and Bambi came out a cheerleader.

She'd be solid and bouncy. She'd have learned to walk with a book balanced on her head and could twirl a baton before she could read. She'd have thirty-two white, strong, even teeth, each making a gleaming contribution to her permanent smile. She would enter Wally's Bar

with invisible pom-poms and streamers, her skin de-
pilatoried and beige, and her first word to me would be
"Hi." She was already twenty minutes late.

Having gone this far, it was hard to stop the projector.
Gridirons kept floating by, reprising all the games I'd
ever seen. I'd forgotten the scores and most of the players. Only the beseeching girl cheerleaders remained, an
endless stream of cartwheeling, somersaulting, inacces-
sible vitality, perfect limbs splayed in midair or angled
into a dozen consonants, spelling out such difficult words
as "fight" and "team." Thirty rows up in the bleacher
seats, nothing I yelled could faintly affect the outcome.
But they made me try, exhorting me to go hoarse on
monosyllables, to sway and wave and sing and care about
the final score. And I did care, every time. Their faces
were wired to the scoreboard. So for the duration of their
strutting and leaping and half-assed dancing, my sole
concern was for the final numbers that would appear on
it. Winning was the magic button inside their snug satin
shorts and I wanted them to go on smiling, to keep
bouncing and jiggling until my desire could penetrate
them, until each syncopated, screaming one of them
emitted a last ear-shattering "Siss-boom-bah" and collapsed into something pliant and subdued and feminine.

My vision of her had become so definite, I couldn't accept a substitute. So I didn't pay much attention to the
girl who'd come in. She stood just inside the door, scan-
ning the nearest occupied tables, then moved slowly past
the crowded bar. One of the men there looked her over
and put his hand on her arm, but she pulled away. She
said something to the bartender and he pointed toward
the rear booth where I was waiting.

"Hi."

She seemed taller than the five-foot-seven she'd someday prove with a tape measure, partly because I was looking up at her, but mostly because she was so thin. It was the kind of thinness that a loose blouse couldn't hide. Hers tried, a size too big and worn outside her jeans. But no pom-poms or streamers. I felt like telling her to go outside and make another entrance, this time acrobatically.

"Hi," I said.

She sat down facing me. Her dark glasses were twice the circumference of mine, but I wasn't ready for her face yet. I was stuck on her hair. The cheerleaders I'd seen had all kinds of hair: long and short, and every shade. Except pink. Even allowing for the bar's lighting, her hair was pink, short and fluffed like candy floss and naturally pink.

"What am I keeping these fool things on for?" She took off her dark glasses and laid them carefully on the table as if they were expensive.

It was a clown face. All the parts were in the right place. Taken singly, each was nicely shaped. But put together, they were hard to take seriously. Not that she was smiling, toothily or otherwise. Clown faces rarely do. I should add that I've always found clowns sad. Bambi had that quality, too. She was a cheerleader whose team was forty points behind with less than a minute to go. She was too vulnerable for nature's elements, for any elements. She was the most desirable female I'd ever seen.

"You keepin' *your* glasses on?"

She made it something of a challenge, so I took them off. I upstaged the bad side of my face for a moment, then gave her the full view. She whimpered slightly as she took it in. Then she reached across the table and her fingertips touched the most swollen part of the swelling. Any other fingertips would have hurt. Hers were healing. I was about to say so when she began to cry.

"Hey. None of that."

I made a warning gesture toward the waitress who was on her way. But this made Bambi cry more. She wasn't auditioning. The sobs were real.

"All because of me," she said.

The waitress seemed used to young ladies crying in the rear booth. But I didn't want to get on her shit list while I still had credit in the place.

"Don't worry," I said to Bambi. "He probably didn't suffer. And Chihuahuas can go to heaven, too."

The look I got from the blowzy waitress made her shit list preferable. She asked us what we wanted to drink. I ordered another Scotch and water. Since the bar didn't stock Dr. Pepper, Bambi sniffed back her tears and settled for a Seven-Up.

"It's a three-fifty minimum," said the waitress.

"Well," I said, after she left, "where do we begin?"

"How's your script comin'?"

"Never mind my script."

"What did Mr. Preminger say about what Quentin did to you?"

"He doesn't know. He's gone back to New York."

"What's the movie gonna be about?"

"What's this thing between Quentin and you about?"

"Maybe you could use it in your script."

"I'll tell you after I hear it."

"It's a long story."

"So you said."

The waitress brought her Seven-Up and my Scotch and water. Bambi took a sip to wet her throat and began her long story. Like all amateur storytellers, she started in the middle.

Chapter 11

VENABLES TURNED out to be about a hundred and ten miles from Fayetteville, which has the university. I made the mistake of asking her which university.

"Now how could anybody not know where the Razorbacks come from?"

The Dookes were fourth- or fifth-generation Venables. Bambi wasn't sure which. But Grandpa Dookes had been in the trenches and regaled her with tales of Belleau Wood and still put on his uniform every Armistice Day, even though it was way too big since he'd started shriveling. His wife had died giving birth to James Madison Dookes, who was Bambi's father and the Venables town drunk. Bambi figured that trouble having babies ran in her family. Her parents had been married eleven years before she came along and they thought she never would, which was why they'd adopted Quentin, who was six at the time and already showing signs of mayhem to come.

Bambi didn't begin it this way, establishing the locale and leading characters. She started in the middle, which was the day the talent scout came through Venables and stopped for lunch at Smitty's, where she worked. News that the talent scout had disappeared from the Hollywood scene (about the same time that Clark Gable did) hadn't yet reached Razorback country. So when she served him a Smitty's Special and he told her that she emanated the same quality as some of the big stars he'd discovered, he didn't have to ask her twice to make her start packing.

Yes, she'd been a cheerleader. And she'd mastered the art of twirling and joined "Knees Up," the baton marching team of Venables High that got honorable mention in the state contest two years running. Her theatrical roots, though, went much deeper. Her mother had subcribed to *Photoplay* and *Modern Screen* for her beauty shop, which was in their parlor, and baby Bambi had memorized the pictures in the back issues long before she'd learned to read.

"Mom was the spittin' image of Ella Raines, only prettier."

Ella Raines was one of those names I had trouble affixing to a face. It was all mixed up with Debra Paget and Andrea Leeds and the girl who married Howard Hughes. I made the mistake of saying so.

"Now how could anybody not remember Ella Raines?"

Her scathing questions of disbelief kept interrupting the plot. I faked around this one, pretending I'd suddenly placed Ella and that she was indeed a great beauty. She probably was and might still be, which meant that Bambi's looks came mostly from the town drunk.

I was more interested in hearing about her stepbrother. Quentin Dookes was the greatest athlete in the history of Venables High and had been protecting her since the day she was born, sometimes too much so. He was "real strong" and his temper was "real bad" and, as she'd already mentioned, he was a homosexual.

"He'd be with the Cowboys or Oilers now if he'd gone to the U. of A." She'd made this a sad afterthought to his being a queer.

It had always been assumed that he'd be a Razorback. And the great day came when the University sent someone to watch him play. Quentin scored three touchdowns that day and the man had come to the Dookes house afterwards and talked to him in his room. But only for about twenty minutes.

"I guess Quentin musta kissed him somethin' fierce."

It was her only possible explanation for why Quentin, breaker of every running and passing record in Arkansas high school history, never heard another word about a football scholarship.

"Then he just started goin' to the saloon with Daddy."

"And what makes you so sure he's gay?" I tried to think of a more believable reason for an athlete being rejected by a college.

"I'd have to know you lots better before I could tell you that."

I told her that I had every intention that she would and she said she wished I hadn't said that and I asked her why and she said because it made me sound just like that Hollywood talent scout.

It had been less than a week since he'd brought her to Los Angeles. During their long nonstop drive, he'd said it was a toss-up between their staying at the Beverly Hills Hotel or the Bel Air. And then he claimed she'd heard him wrong when they pulled up to this simply god-awful motel.

"Bel Air and Bolero don't sound that different," I said.

"Now how in the world did you guess it was the Bolero?"

I told her it was a favorite haunt of imitation talent scouts misleading star-struck young ladies.

"Lucky Quentin trailed us," she said.

That he had, across sixteen hundred miles and five states. Was there any devotion greater than a fag step-brother's? She still didn't know how he'd found out where she was heading. He'd even managed to get the room right next to theirs. I could have impressed her again by guessing the room number.

"Would you believe he wasn't a talent scout at all?"

"It's hard to," I said, "but I could try."

"I guess some men will do just about anything for a piece of ass."

It was precisely then that she snared me. Cheerleaders and baton twirlers didn't say things like that, not even in the heat of a bowl game. With one line she'd shattered my typecasting. But it wasn't the words themselves. Venables barnsides and Harlem public toilets probably spoke with a common tongue. It was her delivery, hovering between derision and wonder, tossing a crumb to an unfathomed value. She was pure RFD, reared in nature's fundamentals. She'd watched the deer and the antelope play and the pigs and the goats fornicate with equal detachment. Humans going at it were just a slight variation on a familiar theme, minor and over-rated. She was going to be an easy lay.

At my age, this wasn't a factor to be taken lightly. But more important or almost as important—I wasn't sure which—was that the pleasure of having her would include an extra dimension born of pain. I would take many Polaroid pictures via the bedroom mirror and mail the clearest of them to Quentin Dookes, General Delivery, Venables, Arkansas.

"I had this new bra that hooked in front." She pointed

in its general direction and I wanted to jump inside her blouse. "And he was still fidgetin' with it when Quentin broke down the door."

"And?"

"If we'd been downstairs it wouldn't a' been so bad."

Her throat went dry about then and I ordered her another Seven-Up.

"Seven-Up makes you piss more than Dr. Pepper," she said.

Another throwaway, more proof that what was still unmentionable to most was incidental to her. No suggestion during our sweating and heaving would shock her, no touch would be questioned.

"I didn't know that," I said.

Back to ringside. It wasn't much of a fight. Quentin only hit the guy two or three times before heaving him out the window. As she said, if they hadn't been on the second floor the police might not even have been called. It also would have helped if the window had been open and unscreened. With a second floor window and screen came an ambulance and two squad cars.

"All the cops here look like movie stars."

I said the same applied to the moving men and urged her to go on. There wasn't much more to tell. She hadn't liked the way Quentin kept looking at her in the police car on the way to the station. Plus, he'd kept calling her a "cheap, good-for-nothin' whore." So when the police finished questioning her and started in on him, she'd accepted their offer of a free drive back to the motel, grabbed her suitcase and lit out for a safer place.

She'd had her life's savings with her, which she figured would be enough for a week at the famous Beverly Hills Hotel, no matter how fancy it was. Little did she know. But the Beverly Hills was full-up and her cab driver suggested she try the Beverly Wilshire. That proved somebody was watching over her because if she'd managed to get into the Beverly Hills, she wouldn't have been at the Beverly Wilshire to see me hugging with Otto Preminger, whom she recognized because he was always being interviewed on TV.

Again, she didn't know how Quentin had managed to track her there, except he was always showing up like that. In any case, she went into the El Padrino room for something to eat, after Mr. Gomez brought back his card with my name and address written on the back, and she was helping herself at the salad bar when there he was. She'd managed to get him to sit down with her and order a beer and he seemed calm and friendly enough and it wasn't until she was off getting a second helping of mushrooms and chickpeas that he started looking through her handbag for money. Unfortunately, he'd found Mr. Gomez's card.

Then he'd become the same old Quentin she'd seen put so many people into the hospital. A waiter had noticed him slapping her around and sent for the house detectives. The first two who showed up had to call for reinforcements, but they'd finally managed to get him outside.

"They sure know some fancy holds."

During the application of which, Quentin kept yelling all kinds of unwholesome things at her and promising he'd be back.

"And he will." She looked at me resignedly and tried to shrug off her helplessness and fear. "Enough about me," she said. "Now let's talk about the movie you're writin' for Mr. Preminger."

The lies I invented aren't worth repeating. I did some assorted name-dropping. I managed to mention some of the pictures I'd rewritten and a few that I wished I had.

I was vague about Otto. I casually mentioned F. Scott Fitzgerald, hinting that his was the source material. She surprised me by saying she thought she'd heard of him. It also surprised me that she seemed to believe every word I said. What surprised me more—but that came much later—was that I'd believed all of hers.

Of course, by then my mind was mostly on the rescue operation. I had to get her out of the hotel and find someplace for her to stay where she'd be safe from Quentin. And the same applied to me and the North Sweetzer Arms. The network meeting the next day offered our only immediate chance of escape. But I'd walked away from survival hatches before. And I'd told women much more attractive than her that they'd have to find their own ways out of their dilemmas. There was no reason this time should be any different—but I already knew that it would be.

Chapter 12

THE BARRIERS at the network entrances are exactly like the ones that separate East and West Germany. The guards make full use of their authority; their faces radar screens for terrorists as they wait for each driver to name the executive he's come to see. But my car got the same look as the Rolls ahead of me. Snobbery isn't part of the new militarism.

I felt I could give any name. The executive turnover being what it was, the guard couldn't know everybody in the huge building, so no matter what I said the barrier pole would be raised. I considered Dolfuss and Masaryk. Were the names still remembered? Or Mr. Torquemada of the Situation Comedy Department. But smart-ass answers had landed me in the soup more than once.

"Mr. Averies," I said. "Mr. Burdick to see Mr. Averies."

"Just take any parking space that doesn't have a name."

Impeccable grammar. "Doesn't have" where I'd expected "ain't got." I was glad I hadn't tried to be clever.

The unassigned parking spaces, naturally enough, were the furthest from the main entrance. It was a long hike to the glass doors, and the lobby could have been cooler.

No one waited here. The receptionist sat alone at the far end, glancing up from her paperback as I crossed the halfway point. She was bored and listless. Either a discotheque regular or moonlighting as a hooker. I gave my name and destination again and she found my red tag in a drawer full of red tags. It had a clamp which left no permanent scars on the lapel.

Averies was on the third floor. The reception area here was more like it. A bouncy greeter, very dusky with miscegenated features, immediately asked me how I took my coffee. I said "Black" without getting a racial blink. I said "No" to her "Sugar?" and she played it rejected. Another hopeful.

Perry was one of the eight sitting on the deep-cushioned couches. He motioned to the one empty space as if I wouldn't be able to find it by myself. He looked gloomy. So did the other seven, most of them thumbing the trades. Then a secretary came out and asked Mr. Hutton and Mr. Dubrynsky to follow her. That gave me a chance to move next to Perry.

"Did you bring the money?" I whispered it and the five other guys pretended they weren't listening.

Perry nodded, still gloomy. Either he wasn't optimistic about the meeting or his wife had bought another ermine wrap.

"The ante's now got a codicil." I made this barely audible, a wasted effort.

"What codicil?" It was probably the loudest question ever asked in a network reception area.

The dusky girl bounced over with my black coffee in a plastic cup. During the interruption, Perry took out a gold pencil and lizard-skin appointment diary. It had a notepad attached and he scribbled his message.

If!!!

He underlined it twice. Then he added, *Think Fitzgerald!!!*

Enough crap has been written about F. Scott Fitzgerald. In Hollywood, he's been written off. None of the pictures he worked on made any money. Neither did *Tender Is the Night* nor the attempts at *Gatsby*. The verdict is unanimous: "Too literary."

I'd heard it from every producer I'd talked to about my idea. Not one of them knew the Pat Hobby stories Fitzgerald wrote and only a few bothered to look at them. "Too literary" ranks just below "Anti-Semitic."

I'd argued myself blue. I'd offered to do a first-draft screenplay for minimum. I'd even considered doing one on spec. But not too seriously. Out here, words on paper are harder to sell than words in midair. There've been a few exceptions, but generally speaking, a picture doesn't get made unless the producer's moronic "input" is present at the inception. Besides, there was no point in doing a screenplay without the rights to the original property. Fitzgerald wasn't public domain yet, so I needed a producer with front money. The option alone on the stories would come to a hell of a lot more than Fitzgerald ever got for writing them.

He wrote seventeen stories about Pat Hobby. This was during the last year and a half of his life. He was living in Encino then with Sheilah Graham. He wrote the stories on weekends, grinding out garbage at Universal Mondays through Fridays. He was on the wagon, but in hock. He wanted a hundred and fifty per story. He needed the money then as much as I needed it now. *Esquire* paid him a hundred. Nothing's changed.

The one producer who finally read all or most of the stories was on the couch at the time. So he was more interested in analyzing my affinity for Pat Hobby than in the stories' film potential. He had a couple of valid points. Hobby's car was as old and beaten-up as mine. And he only owned two books: the *Motion Picture Almanac of 1928* and *Barton's Track Guide, 1939*. I pointed out that our prose styles were different and that mine was slightly better. He jumped on that, accusing me of competing with a dead giant and saying it had all kinds of anal connotations. I didn't bother explaining that I'd been comparing my writing style with Pat Hobby's, not with Fitzgerald's.

Pat Hobby wouldn't have minded the comparison. He never took writing seriously, not that it would have helped. Even reading a script gave him a headache. His was the world of silent footage and mosaic swimming pools. Given somebody else's plot and a bright secretary, he came through. But the advent of sound ruined him. Dialogue came hard to Pat Hobby. "Let's get out of here!" or "You're going out feet first" were sweated onto the page. The line he was proudest of was "Boil some water—lots of it!" He quoted it often, never acknowledging his debt to Ibsen. Not that he'd ever heard of Ibsen.

All this is background in the stories. They take place when Hobby is forty-nine and hasn't worked in years. It's been a long time since he's managed to get onto studio grounds. But he's still in there trying. And his various attempts and the chaos they cause could make the definitive picture about this town. I'd been saying that for years and this appointment at the network was the first sign I'd had that my opinion wasn't alone.

Perry had told me to be ten minutes early and Averies kept us waiting a full half-hour. Then his secretary came out and led us into a small conference room. Averies and his staff of five greeted Perry like it was his surprise party and I received warm handshakes from all. One of Averies' assistants muttered that he was a fan of mine.

Four of the five were young men, maybe twenty-seven to thirty-two. The one girl still had pimples. Averies was the only one in shirtsleeves. No doubts about who did the hard work in his department. He was about ten years older than the others, but looked in better shape. His coal-black hair was thick and cropped and perfectly complemented by a small beard. Within the first minute, he threw in a remark about free-fall skydiving. Fitzgerald wrote on weekends; Averies jumped out of planes. It was going to be a weird marriage.

Introductions over, we sat around the table. Averies was at the head and I'd somehow been elbowed into a chair at the opposite end.

"We'll save time," he said, "if you're tuned into my thinking right away."

His assistants must have heard this opener every hour on the hour, but they gave him their rapt attention. The pimpled girl had her pencil poised over a yellow pad.

"Television is a reality," continued Averies. "What appears on television is also a reality. But that is not synonymous with portraying real life. If we did that, viewers would be bored stiff and the birthrate would increase accordingly."

The assistant who claimed to be my fan gave this an appreciative titter. Averies marched on.

"Our business is unreality. That's why the bleeding hearts who accuse us of fostering violence are full of shit. Unreality does not produce reality. At most, it places the recipient in a semi-comatose state in which to absorb advertising absurdities."

Averies paused to let the shock of his daring honesty sink in.

"But there's good unreality and bad unreality," chimed in the assistant on his immediate left.

"Agreed," snapped Averies. He opened the folder before him. "And that brings us to Mr. Fitzgerald's little stories."

"Has everybody here read them?" My question got me some strange looks.

"We've all read the synopsis," said Averies. "And it's been fed to the computer." He turned to my fan. "Mason?"

Mason leafed through the computer printouts. They would take longer to read than the stories.

"Well," he said, "family viewing time is out because of Hobby's drinking problem."

"It isn't a problem," I said. "He likes to drink."

That got me a warning look from Perry. He not so subtly touched his sports jacket in the vicinity of his wallet.

"Also, young people, who comprise fifty-three percent of this audience, are not very interested in a forty-nine-year-old man."

"A forty-nine-year-old drunken has-been," expanded Averies.

"Then why am I sitting here?" I asked.

"Carry on, Mason," said Averies.

"The computer has tossed up some possibilities," said Mason. He thumbed through a few sheets and found one of them. "The basic situation of a character on the outside, trying to penetrate an impersonal embodiment, has dramatic vitality."

"That's exactly what I've been telling you." Perry finally opened his mouth. "Like Don Quixote."

"I think you're oversimplifying Cervantes," said Averies.

"The computer also doesn't like the time period of the stories," said Mason. "They seem to take place in 1939 and 1940, which were watershed years."

"Name any year that wasn't," I said.

"You seem to be resisting us, Mr. Burdick." I had Averies' full attention now.

"I'm just wondering why the computer suggested that we get together."

"Are you open to suggestions?"

"Try me."

"Suppose our version took place in the present."

"We'd lose a lot of flavor."

"And suppose the impersonal embodiment wasn't a motion picture studio but a television network."

"I'm still with you."

"And suppose our hero was considerably younger than forty-nine."

"You're beginning to lose me."

"And suppose we had a heroine instead of a hero."

"Now wait a minute." I was hanging on by my teeth. "What would that have to do with Fitzgerald's stories?"

"Nothing," said Averies. "At least, nothing that was a violation of copyright."

"I love that computer," said Perry.

"Maybe you've found a soul mate," I said. One function of agents is to take remarks that you're afraid to make to the people who deserve them.

"The fact that you were attracted to these stories," said Averies, "is what makes us think you may be right for our approach."

"How old is the heroine?"

"Twenty to twenty-five."

"And why does she want to write for television?"

"She doesn't. We've decided she should be an aspiring actress."

"From some little jerkwater place," added the assistant on his left.

"Before we go any further, Mr. Burdick," said Averies, "are you interested?"

Perry gave me the money in the parking lot. He looked hurt when I counted it.

"Don't worry. I didn't take any commission."

"Either I can't count or there's seven hundred here."

"So I'm generous." He opened the door of his Bentley. "I'll call you with the figures later. I'll ask for fifty, they'll offer thirty and we'll settle for thirty-five thousand."

I'd received a lot less for rewriting epics. And the two-hour script I'd agreed to do was only an eighty-six-minute script after allowing for commercials, promos and news updates.

"What about my codicil?"

Perry had one foot in his Bentley, but got out again. "What's with the codicil?"

"I need a place to work." I pointed to my dark glasses. "The guy who did this will be coming back for more."

Perry smiled and I misinterpreted it.

"What's so funny? One more eye and we're out of business."

"This is our day," he said. "Let me enjoy it a little. You've got a codicil. I've got a director going on location this afternoon who needs a house sitter. No rent. All you've got to do is feed two cats."

"Where's the house?" Now that I was working again, I could be choosy.

"Laurel Canyon. With the beams and the log fireplace

and the whole bit. It'll make you write better than Fitzgerald."

"Are the cats tame?"

"My client's plane leaves at two. When do you want to move in?"

"Two-thirty."

"Some days, everything falls into place. Like once every twenty years." Perry got into his Bentley and electrically lowered the windows after closing the door. "Good meeting, Corey."

He backed out of his parking slot and gave me a victory tap on his horn before speeding towards the exit gate.

It took me awhile to find my TR-6. Then I sat in it for a few minutes, looking up at the tower of tinted windows. I had penetrated the impersonal embodiment. And I had agreed to do the one thing that I had so far refused to do. It might have been excusable if I'd done it strictly out of fear. But I wasn't kidding myself about my main reason.

I laid the money on Demetrious's desk with almost an hour to spare. He didn't bother counting it.

"You see what you can do if you try hard enough?"

"I got a big advance on a script," I said.

It was my way of telling him my credit was again good, but he looked at me as if I'd sprouted a new face.

"You write things?" Until then, I hadn't realized he didn't know what I did for a living. "Like stories and movies and things?"

"When I can." I braced myself for his idea which would make a great motion picture. Saved by the bell. Two bells. Both phones started ringing at the same time. But he made them wait.

"I might have something for you," he said.

"Another sure thing?"

"Not so sure. But the payoff could be beautiful."

"Count me in."

"Keep in touch."

He picked up one phone, told the caller to hang on and answered the other.

I went back to the North Sweetzer Arms to pack my two suitcases. Mrs. Fogarty always did her shopping after an early lunch and I planned to skip while she was at Alpha Beta. Perry's secretary had already called. He'd remembered that he'd forgotten to give me the address in Laurel Canyon and she'd left it on my answering machine tape.

Bambi wasn't in her room when I phoned the Beverly Wilshire, so I had her paged at the pool. I could hear the water splashing as I told her about the house and arranged what time I'd pick her up. I almost added that she was perfect for the leading role in the script I was writing. But I decided to save that for later. I also didn't mention the two cats we had to feed.

Chapter 13

THE HOUSE IN Laurel Canyon was laid out to thwart seduction. There were seven small rooms off as many narrow halls and four staircases. There was no soft lighting, the artificial log fireplace didn't work, the stereo was broken and both cats were schizoid.

Bambi immediately grabbed the only one of the three bedrooms that had a proper bed. It also had an adjoining bathroom and a door that locked from the inside. Of the other two, one had a sagging divan bed and the other a double bunk only usable by short, fat twins home for Christmas from military academy. In spite of my disk problem I had to go with the divan.

The director the house belonged to had "standards," which is the industry's accolade for not being willing to let your mother do a full frontal walk-on. The pictures he'd made about migrant workers and Hiroshima guilt had paid for a sauna, a microbe-sized pool and a Ben Shahn wash drawing. I have the habit of judging people by the fiction they buy, so I upgraded him when I spotted my collection of short stories amongst the other books on his shelves. Then I opened the flyleaf and saw that it was the copy I'd inscribed to Perry Lutz. The cats' names were Fellini and Kurosawa. Both were Persians. Fellini seemed to find me tolerable.

There followed the most frustrating four days of my life. According to French theory, there are three ways of taking a woman: by assault, trickery or starvation. On the first day, I tried assault. There is a magic moment when all resistance gives way to sustained aggression. Except with her. She squirmed out of my holds like a boneless mud wrestler. She left me far behind on the staircases. Once I managed to corner her in the double-bunked room and, outweighing her by at least sixty-five pounds, I sensed victory. I was pressing her back on the lower bunk when her eyes bulged at what she saw beyond my left shoulder.

"Quentin!"

I spun around to defend myself, staring at the empty doorway until she filled it on her way out. The oldest trick on the silver screen, perfected by Mary Pickford, and I'd fallen for it. Bambi had also managed to bang my knee while making her escape and it hurt when I hobbled after her. I sat on one of the staircases and reassessed myself. I'd been many things in my time, but never pathetic. I decided to change tactics. Trickery wasn't my strong suit and I couldn't starve someone who never seemed to eat. French techniques were best left to the French. It was time for American know-how, and the more knowing would triumph. It would be no contest. I had read between four and five thousand books to her seventy or eighty cheesy magazines. Knowledge and maturity were in my corner. But, even more important, I had the staple of my craft, a facility with words.

I chose the living room for the field of battle. I waited

there in its best chair, stroking Fellini and returning Kurosawa's glare. She finally strolled in, wearing a pink leotard.

"Hi," she said.

"I've got a problem," I said.

"Don't I know it."

"May I be allowed to state my own problem?" I said it scathingly, getting just the right edge into it. This was going to be enjoyable as well as easy.

"Sure," she said and started her waist exercises.

"My problem is that I don't know whether to call you Bambi or Fortunata." The false dilemma was chosen to disarm her.

"How about Bambi when we're alone and Fortunata if there's anybody else around?" She'd given it all of three seconds' thought.

"That makes sense."

"I always do," she said and switched to knee bends.

"Now could we talk about us?"

"Sure."

"Sure," "huh" and "so" were the syllables she most often took refuge behind. But they were useless ploys against well-chosen words.

"Do you regard me as old?"

"You ain't that old."

"Would you spell out the that?"

"T-h-a-t."

"I didn't mean literally. I was trying to establish the line of demarcation between old and *that* old."

"You know something, Mr. Burdick?"

"What?"

"I never know what you're talkin' about."

"All right," I said, "I'll try to put this into a capsule tiny enough for your mind to absorb. But meanwhile,

would you do me the favor of not calling me Mr. Burdick?" I felt my face heating. Calm, I warned myself,
stay calm. "Would you?" I repeated it because she was
mulling it over. What the hell was there to mull over?

"Okay." She made it a concession. "What should I
call you?"

"Try my first name."

"Corey," she said. "I ain't never known any Coreys."

"You've also never known anyone intelligent, articulate and sensitive."

"Boy, ain't we modest?"

"Would you prefer false humility?"

"Suit yourself." It was time for more contortions. Her
rib cage was actually sensual.

"I was merely suggesting that, despite the disparity
in our ages, you might find the attention of an intelligent, articulate and sensitive man more rewarding than
those of the lunchtime customers at Smitty's." I let that
sink in before applying the clincher. "Don't you even want
to know why that intelligent, et cetera man desires you?"

"Somethin' tells me that you're gonna tell me," she
said.

"I can't."

"Why not?"

"Because I don't know myself." I felt a twinge of dis-
taste for my dialogue. "But I do, very much."

"So?" she said.

"Just 'so'?"

"What do you want, a marchin' band?"

"Faulty image," I said.

"Huh?"

"A marching band is the wrong image. When I questioned the responsive sound you made, you should have
countered with another sound. Try something besides 'so'."

"Yuck!" she said.

"Better, but not ideal."

"I'm sure enjoyin' this intelligent, articulate and sensitive conversation." She wasn't a complete dope. She'd remembered all three adjectives and got them in the right order.

It was time for effective silence. No one knows the value of a pregnant pause better than a screenwriter. She continued exercising. I searched her contortions for the answer to my own question. Why the hell *did* I desire her?

One of my few blessings has been a nonanalytic mind. When the scenes are coming right or during a winning streak at the track, I never try to figure out why. I've found the good moments of life as fragile as they are rare. When not accepted whole, they tend to decompose.

Matters sexual are no exceptions. An unexamined orgasm is definitely worth having. I'll admit to some hours idled away on autopsies of why I've succeeded with one woman and failed with another. But generally I stick with the abstracts: emanations and charisma and unfathomable feminine moods.

That doesn't mean I regard all women as one. During my years in the Hollywood salt mines I've assembled my own private chorus line. Some of the members are in most men's my age: Garbo in her prime, Carole Lombard, the young Ava Gardner and what else is new? But I have some special honorees. I once saw Joanne Dru at Chasen's and she remains the most stunning woman I've ever seen. Then there was dear Jean Seberg with the haunted eyes, met many years after Preminger discovered her, and Lizabeth Scott of the husky voice and sultry splendor. I have about a dozen more and on sleepless nights I put them through some dazzling routines.

Bambi couldn't get into that chorus line as an under-

study. Sequined bras weren't made in her size. Feather
boas would be indistinguishable from her hair. Her baton-
twirling knee action was all wrong. Bambi was Kraft
cheese on Wonder bread and neither could take an am-
ber spot. Then there were her aberrations. She bit her
nails. She wiggled a double-jointed big toe in time to
whistled self-accompaniment. Her voice could lull the
demented. Raised, it could summon hogs. I ticked these
off daily, trying to dismantle my obsession. I imagined
imperfections that had worked before: pimples in un-
likely places, scars and birthmarks. I tried a Swiftean
attitude toward her entrails, a portrait of her in middle
age. Nothing worked. For four days and nights I beat my
head against a solid wall of Kraft cheese and Wonder
bread. And no matter what I did or said, her response
was the same.

"Only if I get a good part in your movie."

That was another problem. By movie, she meant a
movie movie. I hadn't yet told her that the script she
kept asking me about didn't quite qualify. From the moment we'd moved in, she'd shown an aversion to the television set. Even when I switched on the news she walked
out of the room.

"That barfy little box," she called it.

Her favorite word again. I should have realized she
had her reasons. But I just chalked it up to big-screen
monomania.

"Only if I get a good part in your movie."

She made it a water torture. That's my only excuse
for eventually breaking one of the cardinal rules of my
craft.

There are three such rules for screenwriters. First,
never write fast. (Illiterates refuse to believe that anything written quickly can be good.) Second, *never write*

intelligent dialogue. (When the audience has to think about what's been said, it can't follow the plot.) Third, *never show what you're working on to a broad you're trying to make.*

I'd never broken the third rule before.

Chapter 14

THE OAK TREE meeting at Santa Anita started on the twenty-third. I picked up a Racing Form the night before when I went out for some fast food junk and found a few entries I fancied. I called Demetrious in the morning to make twenty-buck bets.

"Five nine seven," I said.

"Hey! Where you been?"

"It's nice to be missed."

"You moved or what?" he said. "I tried to call you."

"What's the problem?" I couldn't think of one.

"I want you to sit in on something," he said. "How about tomorrow night?"

"Mornings are better for me." They were. I'm a slow starter. I never get much writing done before noon.

"This is gotta be with no interruptions," he said. "The Aqueduct action starts nine-thirty."

"How about eight o'clock?"

"You outta your fuckin' mind?"

We settled for the end of the afternoon. There wasn't any California betting to speak of after five o'clock.

"What's the meeting about?" I said.

"You think you could make up a story about a horse race?"

"Does it have to have a happy ending?"

"It better have," he said.

Gus let me in when I got there. Demetrious was at his desk, counting the day's take. Damon, his other goon, was pouring himself something that wasn't coffee into a coffee cup. The Kid waved to me like we were old friends. The surprise package was Pooch Padilla.

Pooch was getting fewer and fewer rides these days. He had some at the Pomona fairground, but at Hollywood Park or Santa Anita or Del Mar, he was lucky to get two a week. He never had a decent animal under him anymore, so when he did bring one in it was a testimonial to his skill. But I'd known the days when his name would be chanted from the stands every time he came back to the winner's enclosure and dismounted. He'd already done that eighty-seven times the year he was suspended. "Pooch! Pooch! That'sa way, Pooch baby!" And he'd grin up at them, showing most of his big, white, Panamanian teeth, in sharp contrast to the grim look he always wore when riding out of the tunnel for the post parade. Nobody ever commented on the difference—on the grimness before and the grin after—not until he was caught. A mouthful of straight pins doesn't make for smiling.

During his hearing, Pooch confessed to jabbing a horse with the pins as much as ten or twelve times during a race. The amazing thing was that he'd never swallowed any. More amazing was that none of the stewards was ever sober enough to notice the repetitive hand movement. Pooch might still be getting away with it if his dentist hadn't turned him in. Lacerations in Mr. Padilla's mouth had aroused his suspicion. Either the jockey was doing something illegal or eating hay. So Pooch had been caught cold at the starting gate and had to spit out the evidence.

The only remorse he showed at his hearing was that he hadn't let the dentist in on a certain thirty-to-one shot. Pooch was suspended for three years, and that had been eight years ago. What I never could figure out was why somebody with his teeth was going to a dentist.

"Here's the guy with the answers," said Demetrious. He motioned me to the only chair that wasn't occupied. "You know everybody?" His phone didn't give me a chance to say I didn't. "Sonofabitch!" he said. But he took the bet. After that he left both phones off their cradles.

"Okay. Everybody's here." Demetrious pocketed the stack of money from his desk. "The way I figure, we take one shot. So it's shit or bust." The others all nodded agreement.

"Wait a minute," I said. "I think I'm a lap behind."

"In due time," said Demetrious. "First we talk split." He let his forefinger drift as if sighting the five of us. "If we pull it off, you're each in for ten percent." He saw me smile and stopped. "I said something funny?"

"I feel like I'm at William Morris," I said.

"Who the fuck's William Morris?"

"Ten percent is agent territory," I explained. He never changed expression. I was glad when Pooch Padilla butted in.

"What about the other fifty percent?"

"There's expenses." Demetrious turned on him. "We got your boys to take care of, don't we?" No one seemed inclined to argue the point. "And I get what's left."

"Ten percent a what?" I'd never heard Damon speak before. It was strangled speech, polyps on the vocal cord. "How much is in it?"

Demetrious put his head back and stared at the ceiling as if it was a scratch pad.

"I figure a million."

It was a lot more than I was ready for. I had to do a quick rewrite on my next line.

"I would be grateful if someone would tell me why I'm to receive one hundred thousand dollars."

"I already told you," said Demetrious. "For making up a story."

"Nobody every got paid a hundred grand for a story."

"Okay." Demetrious sounded impatient. "I figured we need one more to make a bet. You go to the track a lot. The tellers know your face. Nothing suspicious if you put down some big ones."

"Wait a minute," Pooch had been smouldering ever since the percentages. "All he does is make a bet," he jerked a thumb in my direction, "and he gets the same cut as me."

"He also happens to be a writer," said Demetrious. "A very big, important writer." I had to resist correcting him.

"So what?"

"You ever read guys like Mickey Spillane?"

"What for?"

"I read lots." Demetrious rubbed his eyes as if to prove it. "Writers come up with gimmicks you and me couldn't."

"Yeah," said Pooch. "And every time the cops get wise." The meeting had become a typical script conference.

"That's right." Demetrious pointed at me. "But he's gonna come up with a story where they don't." He seemed to be waiting for me to corroborate this.

"It sometimes helps," I said, "to know what the story's about."

"We're fixin' a goddam race!" Demetrious yelled it at me. "Why the hell you think we're here?"

"Good enough." I used the level voice I'd honed on top producers. "Now tell me more."

And he finally did.

One thing that sets horse players apart is that we're able to rationalize our addiction. And we can do it with one word—excitement. Other addictions numb. Ours works the opposite. Where else but at a race track can you get nine thrills a day? It has noble animals charging around bends at forty miles an hour. It has the whole octave from groans to victory screams. It's got all the scheming and fakery made of coin. Only a Baptist or mossy idiot could ask for anything more.

Fixing a race is as old as racing itself, but this was to be my introduction to it. So far Demetrious only had the basics. The operation would be limited to one race. Pooch would take care of the arrangements on the track. He'd ride a long shot and he'd be trying. The other jockeys wouldn't be. It was as simple as that. There was nothing original in this. If it didn't happen twice a day, it happened at least three times a week. That's per track. The only thing different about this time was what the Kid was going to do.

The big fix, and with it the big score, has been killed off by the pari-mutuel system. For all the lighted numbers flashing on the infield tote board and scaring the uninitiated, the system is primitively simple. Everything wagered goes into the pot. The state government and the track and all the other so-called disinterested parties immediately take their cuts. That comes to roughly seventeen percent of the total. The other eighty-three percent is divided proportionally amongst all those lucky souls holding winning tickets.

Demetrious had stated a target of one million dollars. Twenty thousand dollars on a fifty-to-one shot would do it. But the more bet on a horse, of course, the lower its odds. If the twenty thousand goes on a fifty-to-one, its odds come down to about nine-to-two. Even making the bet in Vegas doesn't help. The bookies there pay out according to track odds and they have guys at the tracks laying off parts of any hefty bet to reduce those odds. So when a fix is on, a long-shot killing—of the kind Demetrious was talking about—is impossible.

That's where the Kid came in. He was chewing gum and looking bored until Demetrious came to his part of the operation. Horses obviously held no interest for him. I doubt if the money was that important to him, either. His incentive was strictly electronic.

From the time the betting starts on a race until the horses go into the starting gate, the infield tote board clicks over every thirty seconds. The amounts bet on each horse are up there for all to see. And every thirty seconds those numbers change. If the amount bet on a horse changes enough, so does the horse's odds. The Kid's part was to see to it that the odds on one horse didn't.

He'd found a way. He had a high-pitched voice and sometimes sniggered when there was no reason to and his explanation was laced with a lot of "you know"s. But I got the gist of it. There were hundreds of conduits from the betting counters at the track to a central control and another set of wires that fed the betting monitors and infield tote board. The Kid claimed he could get to the central control and choke off the lead wires affecting one of the entries and keep them cut off for three clicks. Three was the limit during which the betting figures on any horse didn't have to change. After that, a buzzer indicated a malfunction. If the Kid was right, anything bet during those three clicks on that one horse wouldn't show on the board or affect its odds. Three clicks meant one and a half minutes.

"That's what we got," said Demetrious when the Kid finished. "You think you can make up a story?"

"I've done it with a lot less."

"Nothing on paper," he said. "Just tell it to us—who does what and when and how we get away with it."

"I'll need a few days."

"Days?" He was genuinely surprised. Still, few people realize that working out a plot takes time.

"Meanwhile," I said, "I assume you're working on your own version."

"Sure," he admitted. "But yours might be better."

"And if it isn't?"

"Then you only get five percent instead of ten."

"Aren't you worried I'll blab if I feel cheated?"

"You won't blab." Demetrious looked toward Gus and Damon to be sure I got the message. "Anyway," he said, "we shouldn't think like that. You make a living from stories, so you must be pretty good at it. Why should this time be any different?"

There were many reasons why, but I didn't go into them. Every time I'd been assigned a script, talk had proved pointless. It had always come down to me alone in a room grappling with thousands of threads and shadows and imponderables. This time would be the same, only more so. This time was for real. This time I wouldn't have the luxury of loopholes. Even the best caper scripts had them, *The Thomas Crown Affair* and *Topkapi* and *Big Deal on Madonna Street*, holes that tanks could get through, and they didn't hurt the box office. But my scenario for this one had to be airtight and perfect. And, if I could come up with it, I'd have a hundred thousand dollars instead of thirty-five thousand and I wouldn't have to write a television script about the penetration of an impersonal embodiment.

Chapter 15

THE INVITATION was in gold lettering on imitation pool-table baize.

PERRY LUTZ
*invites you to help him celebrate
another milestone
in his fast-disappearing youth.
Flowers gratefully accepted.
(But items that increase in value preferred.)*

When he phoned to check on how the script was coming, Perry assumed I'd be at his party.

"And bring the bimbo."

"Which one?"

"She who answered yesterday when I called you. Maybe you should tell her *Gone With the Wind's* already been cast."

"I don't know if we can make it," I said.

"Why not?"

"Sociability is a disease." When cornered, I sometimes quote Freud.

"Be there."

"But if I show up, some people might think I wrote your invitation."

"Your script should be so well-written." After automatically taking the offensive, he had doubts. "What's wrong with it?"

"It lessens you."

"Five people I hate told me it's cute."

"You're right to hate them."

"And don't show up pissed."

"Who else is coming?"

"Streisand, De Niro and Brando."

"Seymour Brando?"

"Is there any other?"

"Her name is Fortunata."

"I thought we were talking about Seymour."

"Fortunata," I repeated. "Introduce her to a solvent producer in case one happens to show up by mistake."

"It's gonna be fun," he promised. "Strolling musicians, the whole bit. And Gillian found this pyschic who's for real."

"I can't wait," I said.

"Who was that?" She said it as soon as I hung up. My back had been to the doorway so I didn't know how long she'd been standing there. This was the morning after I'd let her in on my writing act and I was still brooding.

"Cat got Corey's tongue?"

Baby talk would get her nowhere.

"It sounded like somebody's havin' a party."

"Mmmmmm," I said.

"Who?"

"Sax Rohmer."

"Now don't be silly," she said. "Besides, he's probably dead."

"So what?" I said. "He's got you keeping his spirit alive."

"I only said he's a terrific writer."

"Exactly," I said. "Apropos of nothing and right in the middle of reading my treatment."

"I still don't see why you got so het up." She pouted it, trying to horn in on my wounded manner.

"Oh, don't you?" I snapped. "You with your massive, unfilled brain space can't figure out why a writer who takes his work seriously objects to being compared to the creator of Dr. Fu Manchu. Why didn't you go all the way? Why didn't you say you preferred Louisa May Alcott or that other dreary broad who wrote *Uncle Tom's Cabin*?"

"Harriet Beecher Stowe," she said.

"Thanks for nothing." I went back to my brooding act.

"I wasn't comparin' you." She sat on the arm of my chair and fingered a tic-tac-toe pattern on the back of my hand. It was unbearable. "I just think you should read *The Insidious Dr. Fu Manchu*."

"I don't want to read *The Insidious Dr. Fu Manchu*."

"In *The Insidious Dr. Fu Manchu*, Sax Rohmer has this Dr. Petrie helpin' Sir Dennis Nayland Smith who's a real good guy and maybe Mr. Preminger would like it if you did somethin' like that."

"I am not writing a mystery about a Chinese detective." I almost cracked a crown clenching my teeth. "I am writing a script about the penetration of an impersonal embodiment."

"It sounds pretty dirty to me." She slapped the back of my hand as she got up. "Anyway, I bet I know who that was." She pointed to the phone. "It was Mr. Lutz, wasn't it?"

"If you say so."

"What am I gonna wear?"

"We've been invited," I said, "but we're not going."

"Then I'll go without you." Her face assumed the stubbornness I'd come to know so well.

"Good enough. All you have to do is find out where he lives."

"You think I can't do that?"

"He's unlisted," I said. "And his secretary wouldn't give out his address to anyone who sounds remotely like an aspiring actress."

That changed her tune. She knelt before me.
"Why you bein' so ornery, Corey?" She began to giggle.
"Ornery Corey. Don't that sound funny?"

"This will get you nowhere, Bambi."

"Not even to silly old Perry Lutz's party?"

"The secret entrance, as Dr. Fu Manchu used to say, is at the junction of your thighs."

"Now there you go again."

"Let's fuck, Bambi."

"When I get a good part in your movie."

"How about let's fuck, Fortunata?"

"Now why would you want to do such a thing with someone who has so much unfilled brain space?" That was another device of hers, pretending not to notice an insult and throwing it in my face later.

"I withdraw the comment on your mental capacity."

"And if you're so much better than Sax Rohmer," she said, "how come you never won the Nobel Prize?"

"My similes are too good," I said.

"Your what?"

I spelled it for her and she went to the dictionary to look it up.

"A figure of speech . . ." She read with a head-bobbing

action. ". . . using as or like . . ."

"Keep going."

". . . in which two dissimilar things are compared."

"And now you know what a simile is."

"Maybe you'd better give me an example."

"Better still." I went to the bookcase and scanned the shelves. "Since you're partial to Nobel Prize winners." I tossed her a paperback Saul Bellow that proclaimed the award on the cover. "Just yell when you think you've found a simile."

She went out onto the small patio and settled down on the deck lounge to read. It was the first time she'd been on it without cotton balls on her eyelids. I'd never known her to be quiet for so long.

"Got one!" If there'd been hogs in Laurel Canyon they would have come running.

"Okay. Let's hear it."

She came back in, her finger marking the place. She squinted at the line as she read it.

" 'They looked *like* the fruit in an eccentric still life.' "

"What did?"

"Elvis's balls." She managed to keep a straight face.

"Bambi," I said, "either go to bed with me or stop talking like that."

"I like talkin' like that." She stopped and thought about it. "Hey, did I just say a simile?"

"No."

"I said 'like' twice."

"You didn't compare dissimilar things."

"Oh." She stared at the page of the novel by the Nobel Prize winning novelist.

"Read the whole thing," I said.

She did, with gestures. " 'Her eyes seemed to have been displaced by stress; they looked like the fruit in an ec-

centric still life.' " I'd heard worse readings from star ingenues, but only just.

"You think that's a good simile?" It was obviously
bothering her.

"I'm not a critic, Bambi."

"I don't think it's so good," she said.

She went out to the patio, her nose in the book, but
not for long.

" 'Those people are sweet and mostly air, like Nabisco
wafers.' " She read it out as she waltzed in.

"Good for you." I clapped my hands twice as a reward.
She looked troubled again.

"You ever see anybody who was like a Nabisco wafer?"

"Nabisco wafer, no. Kraft cheese and Wonder
bread, yes."

"That's what I call a lousy simile." She pointed to the
page to make it clear whose she meant, then tossed the
paperback on the couch.

"The Nobel committee didn't think so," I said.

"They don't know fuck-all about Nabisco wafers."

This time when she stretched out on the deck lounge
she used the cotton balls. I went to the typewriter and
started pecking away at my script treatment. I considered using a character who was some kind of assistant
and could serve as a foil. After all, Conan Doyle had Dr.
Watson and Sax Rohmer had Dr. Petrie. The assistant
could work for the president of the network. He could
keep the plush office scenes from being flat. He could
provide some comic relief.

I forced the notion away. Any similarity to anything
in *Fu Manchu* and she'd have me dredging the China
Sea for a hero and giving him a name like a Mr. Chow's
appetizer. Was that another simile? Can a name be lik-
ened to an object? What kind of shambles had she made

of my mind? For ballast, I read over the treatment I'd
shown her. The scene where the aspiring actress got a
job delivering sandwiches and Danish to the network's
cubicle dwellers had definite possibilities. Another part
was a dead steal from Scott Fitzgerald. He'd had his Pat
Hobby tend the stand of a man who sold maps to the
movie stars' homes. A tourist couple stopped to buy one.
They wanted to see where Shirley Temple lived and
Hobby pretended he knew her. He offered to take them
to her house for a price. They agreed and he drove them
to a big house in Beverly Hills, picking it at random,
and it turned out to belong to the studio executive he
was in trouble with. Fitzgerald's version was hilarious.
Mine was going to have to be more heavily disguised to
avoid a plagiarism suit. There weren't any tourist maps
to the homes of television celebrities, so I'd have to come
up with another device. And I could change the house to
a condominium.

There was also the party scene I'd roughed out. Every
script about the entertainment business had a party scene.
In mine, the aspiring actress, having crashed a star-
studded soiree, would have too much to drink and make
a fool of herself and . . .

Whenever a good idea comes, it's a wonder it took so
long. I stopped reading and looked toward the patio.
Bambi lay limp and delicious. Assault, trickery or fam-
ine? It was time for the second method. She must have
felt the outer winds of my brainstorm, for she removed
her left eye patch and turned her head toward me. I went
outside and stood over her.

"Besides," I said, "they don't serve Dr. Pepper at Hollywood parties."

"I only asked for that," she said, "to make you think I
was a hick."

"You are a hick."

"When Daddy takes me to the saloon, I drink everythin' except bock beer."

Everything except bock beer was good enough. All I'd have to see to was the quantity.

"You really want to go to this shindig?"

"Sure."

"Then we'll go."

"You darlin'!"

She jumped up and threw her arms around me and we pressed cheeks after she slipped my attempted kiss.

Chapter 16

"OUR HEROINE, bless her little heart," said Averies, "doesn't come off the page." He tossed my treatment onto the conference table. "I think she needs a disadvantage." All the members of his staff sank visibly into deep thought.

"How about a harelip?" I offered.

"The comedy department is down the hall," said Averies.

"Would a sociopolitical disadvantage do it," asked his right-hand man, "or should it be an infirmity?"

"If I'd meant infirmity," said Averies, "I would have said infirmity."

"Is a stammer an infirmity or a disadvantage?" I asked it deadpan, but the girl with the bad complexion giggled.

"It depends on what one had for lunch," said Averies.

"I was thinking of something akin to the Vietnamese boat people," said the sociopolitically oriented one.

"Don't," said Averies.

"Why can't she be white and Protestant?" asked Mason, the computer fiend. "Or isn't being a member of two minority groups enough?"

"We seem to be getting nowhere," said Averies. He turned both eye-barrels on me. "Doesn't our writer have any nonfacetious suggestions?"

"She could have absolutely no talent," I said. "That's a disadvantage for an aspiring actress."

"Not in television," he said and drew a round of laughter from his flunkies.

"There's always dyslexia," said the pimpled girl.

"It would take the first twenty minutes to explain it."

"Suppose she has an allergy," said his right-hand man. "And suppose it's to something vital to her success." He warmed to his idea. "E.g., the show she's trying to get into is built around a dog, a sort of Russian wolfhound-ish Lassie, and she's allergic to wolfhound hair."

Averies slowly rinsed his mouth with the notion. I began to feel light-headed.

"Not bad," he granted.

"I have a better idea." I said it out of desperation.

"Goody gumdrop." He turned to me and waited for it.

"Why doesn't she have the greatest disadvantage of all?"

"Which is?"

"She's a true innocent."

The faces around the table told me I'd struck gold.

"Enlarge upon, please," said Averies.

"She's a true innocent," I repeated. "She really believes all the crap she's fed. She thinks margarine's better than butter. She thinks the Kennedys cared about poor people."

"She even believes that ingenues can get good parts without putting out." Averies said it before I could.

"Exactly."

"Now we're getting somewhere."

He smiled and his staff smiled. I tried to but couldn't quite make it. If he'd gone with any of the half-assed ideas, with the boat people or the allergy, I could have tossed off the script without working up a sweat. But I'd had to go and open the floodgates and let the idiots come pouring in and now they were all busily improving on what I'd said. The pimpled girl excelled, using her inside knowledge of dermatology and the single woman to enlighten us.

Meanwhile, back at the conference table, our heroine, mutated from a fictional character and shaped by greed, lay truly innocent, waiting for the scalpel. Given a limp or a scar, the viewing public would have wept for her. But how did I make it empathize with innocence? How could I teach it to distinguish trust from naiveté? How would I convince anyone that to be unsuspecting was not the same as being dumb? And why should I even try? Listening to the voices around the table, I knew that the day would soon come when they would all agree that my conception of innocence was not the world's conception of innocence, and that mine was the more expendable. And I could already hear Averies' executive summation.

"It's just a matter of semantics."

But perhaps that day didn't have to come. The body on the conference table still had a slim chance. If my story for Demetrious made a thousand times more sense than this one, it might still be possible for Bambi and F. Scott Fitzgerald and me to walk off, hand in hand in hand, into the Pacific sunset.

Needless to say, I'd been giving much more thought to the fixed horse race scenario than to the television script. And with this conference slated to end by three o'clock and the track in Arcadia only twenty minutes away, I'd left my final research for that afternoon.

. . .

Arcadia has the highest smog level in the Los Angeles basin and the racing surface at Santa Anita is one of the most punishing to horses. The beauty of the place makes up for both. The fifth race had just finished when I got there. The mountains were purple against the October sky. The turf course had the special autumnal tint of California grass. It was great to be back. But I'd been smart enough to bring only enough money to get me past the turnstiles. There's nothing like empty pockets to keep me from betting.

I'd approached it as a story, just as Demetrious suggested. I'd started with the happy ending of my six characters getting away with one million dollars and worked backwards. With the bones in place, I was ready to flesh out the scenario.

I covered the betting halls in both the Club House and General Admission section and made notes that would be indecipherable to anyone else. CH:MH—3,10—7,5, for instance, meant that in the Club House's main hall the betting lines averaged three people at ten minutes before the off and seven people with only five minutes to go. There were fewer at the betting windows for large bets. I couldn't get into the Turf Club upstairs, but I'd been there many times in better days and knew it had a separate enclosure with two counters for the big spenders and not many big spenders.

There'd been a time when I prided myself on being a careful and thorough researcher. But rewriting screenplays had canceled that. In a film, it's assumed that the audience has no perspective beyond last week. Feasibility never has to be considered. Anachronisms go unnoticed. A hundred-piece orchestra is heard in the middle of the Congo. So what? George Washington has a Bronx accent. Who remembers? Arguing for a modicum of accuracy, the writer is reminded by his employer of all the pictures that made a fortune while shafting the truth. *Casablanca* usually heads the list.

But this time was going to be different. My old compulsiveness, long thought dead, came back in full bloom. I had never been so exact. I included everything that could have the slightest bearing on the outcome. I recorded every tote-board change after each click. I found variations and refinements I'd never noticed before.

I finished my research before the eighth race and stayed to watch it as a sporting event. Shoemaker won on a Charlie Whittingham horse. I would have bet something else and had the empty pleasure of not losing.

All the track phone booths are locked during the racing, so I called Demetrious from a gas station on my way back and told him I was ready for another meeting.

"We've got problems," I said.

"Big problems or little problems?"

"Some little," I said, "and one insurmountable."

Chapter 17

BEVERLY HILLS department stores don't cancel charge accounts until six months after you're dead. So I took her to Robinson's and she picked out a white lace dress that was tight enough to be a new layer of skin.

"You don't think it makes me look too virginal?" She waited until we were driving to the party to start worrying.

"No woman can look *too* virginal."

"You're doin' it again," she said.

"Doing what?"

"You know, pickin' up what I say and turnin' it into somethin' out of the Bible."

"Which isn't easy," I said.

"You know what I think?"

"What or if?"

"I think you have a low opinion of women."

"And you're not raising it."

"I guess your wife musta been truly awful."

"Only when she wanted to be."

"Do you fret about her bein' married again?"

"Nope."

"Liar," she said. "I bet you lie awake nights thinkin' about what she's doin' with another man that very second."

"Sometimes," I admitted. "But actuality never lives up to my imagination."

"You're doin' it again," she said.

Perry lived on a winding street with no parking except by permit. So he'd had to hire a student valet service and borrow all his neighbors' driveways. The uniformed attendants took my car in stride. Sociology majors. One of them opened the door on Bambi's side and handed her a long-stemmed rose. I could feel her apprehension as we went toward the open front door.

"Relax," I said. "You look sensational."

Perry and Gillian Lutz were greeting the couple ahead of us in the front hall. Perry had the habit of talking to one person while looking at another. All the time he was telling Sidney somebody how glad he was to see him, his eyes were roaming over Bambi. Then it was our turn. I did the Many Happy Returns and let Bambi hand him the Beethoven's Ninth she'd spent an hour gift wrapping.

"She who belongs to the voice," said Perry. "Boy, am I glad it isn't disembodied."

"This is Fortunata." I had to shout to be heard. The strolling musicians were close.

"No surname?" Gillian shouted back as she shook Bambi's hand. She seemed traumatized by Bambi's hair.

"What's this surname crap?" Perry's voice was the loudest. As with most second-class citizens, marrying someone from abroad had made him a superpatriot. He not only wanted Gillian to embrace everything American but to give up the frame of reference she'd brought with her from England. "We got first names and middle names and last names," he said. "That's enough."

Either he'd already had too many or he figured that his birthday was the one time she wouldn't wipe the floor with him.

"She does have a surname." I played peacemaker. "But why spoil the effect?"

"Eat, drink and join the luminaries." Perry was already looking at the people behind us. He motioned us toward the mob inside, then leaned closer for a parting confidence.

"Dustin's gonna try to stop by later."

"Terrific," I said.

"Did he mean Dustin Hoffman?" Bambi waited until we were out of earshot before asking.

"None other."

"You think he'll be here?"

"I know a bookie who'll give you a thousand to one he won't."

We reached the perimeter of the crowd and she did a quick scan.

"I don't recognize anybody," she said.

"That's a good sign," I said. "The real muscle in the industry is anonymous."

"I like that." Her giggle was forced.

"What?"

"Anonymous muscles."

"Marilyn Monroe did it better," I said.

The B-Team was out in strength. There were a few familiar faces: a weather girl from a local channel, an afternoon game show host and a character actor from "Knots Landing." Most of the rest were bit-players and writers who got pieces of multiple credits and directors who had to go to Guild arbitration to collect their fees.

The business-end representatives were ass-kissers and hangers-on who spent the first hour of every day reading the trades. Gossip was their fodder and firings their joy. There were two I'd had encounters with: an assistant V.P. at Fox and a story-department mole from Columbia. I considered introducing Bambi to them, but they'd be just the type to have heard about my taking on a television assignment.

"Is that Jack Nicholson?"

I followed the movement of her shoulder.

"Granpa Dookes looks more like Jack Nicholson."

"Well," she said, "are we just gonna stand here gawpin'?"

I steered her to the bar and ordered my usual Scotch and water. The Korean bartender waited for her request.

"Try a margarita," I said. "They're harmless."

The bartender made mine just right and hers extra strong. A sly wink came with them. I slipped him a dollar.

We threaded our way through the crowd, drinks aloft. The clusters of partygoers were giving off their usual sounds. There was the dirty joke cluster and the recent surgery cluster and the party game cluster. That one had room for two more.

The game was "Guess the Hoary Chestnut" and the pipe-smoking butterball conducting it was a bottomless pit of the inane.

" 'If you don't think I want your arms around me,' " he quoted, " 'you're crazy.' "

No volunteers.

"Errol Flynn. And he said it to, believe it or not, Ruth Roman."

Proper admiration, halfhearted.

"Your turn, Judy."

Judy, pasty-faced with a hooked nose and golf-ball earrings, dredged the cinema of her childhood for a memorable line of dialogue.

" 'You wanna call me that . . . smile.' "

"Gary Cooper!" Three guesses rang out in unison and Judy looked squelched.

" 'You have to get this message to Lotus Blossom in Macao,' " quoted the butterball.

"Somebody or other to Anna May Wong," said the wit of the group.

"What the hell they talkin' about?" whispered Bambi.

Her glass was empty, so I went for a refill. A plump little redhead was asking the bartender for an Iced Tea. I expected to see a Lipton bag appear, but the Korean mixed five liquors in a tall glass. The redhead sampled it and staggered off.

"Potent?" I said.

"More kick than a Cajun gin martini," said the bartender.

"Make it a double."

The game had changed slightly by the time I got back to it. But the butterball was still in charge.

"Who was the first cowboy to say, 'Let's head them off at the pass' . . . Tom Mix, Hoot Gibson or Johnny Mack Brown?"

"Hoot who?" said Bambi.

On the derisive chord this got, I headed her toward the garden and handed her the Iced Tea.

"What a stupid game," she said.

"No argument."

"What's this?" She'd tasted the drink and pulled a face.

"I thought you drank anything."

She gave it another try.

"It's kinda sweet, but I like it."

I saw the woman single us out. She looked like a re-
tired porno queen, her dress stitched together from a
magician's scarves.

"Want to hear all about tomorrow?" She planted herself in our path and handed each of us her card: *Alysia
Zembo, Psychic and Futurist.*

"If you mean my tomorrow," I said, "we'd both be
bored."

"I don't believe that." She fluttered spider-leg lashes
and started pitching hard. Leave it to Perry to have her
working solely for tips. I almost gave in. I've always had
trouble saying no to fortune-tellers and shills and elixir
salesmen.

"You can tell me about mine," said Bambi. The booze
was beginning to show.

"Alysia," I said, "meet Fortunata."

The both smiled as they said their howdy-dos, but I
didn't like the curve of Alysia's. There were too many
years and too much poundage between them. Maybe
Bambi reminded her of how she'd once looked. Maybe
futurists didn't like being reminded of the past.

"I have a table set up near the pool," she said. She
fastened a claw on Bambi's arm and led her away.

Typical. As soon as Bambi was gone I started bump-
ing into people I knew. I made small talk with a production manager from Lorimar and a writer I'd rewritten
with on a Gene Hackman picture. I could see Bambi at
the far end of the pool with Alysia Zembo. A waiter
stopped at their table and proffered his tray of champagne glasses. The psychic waved him off but Bambi took
one.

I went to get a refill. The house was getting even more
packed and the strolling guitarists had to push their way
through. I followed in their wake, then had to stand in

line at the bar. By the time I got back outside, Alysia Zembo had a new customer. I couldn't spot Bambi anywhere.

At first, I took my time. It was just a matter of moving around until we connected. Then there was the possibility that she was upstairs in the john. The mix of champagne, liquors and tequila could have made her sick. I went up to make sure, but the bathroom was empty. I resumed my search downstairs. I began to step on shoes and got some dirty looks. I wished I'd looked in the bedrooms to see if she'd passed out. I was beginning to sweat.

"Corey!"

It was a theatrical lawyer I'd once used, standing with his drab little wife and desperate for company. I waved a hello and made it back to the garden. Then I saw the white lace in the darkest part of it. As I moved toward it, I could hear her laughing. There was an arm around her waist, an arm in a checkered sleeve. Someone at the pool took a flash picture and the light carried. I saw that she was with Averies.

I should have guessed that he'd be at the party. No agent neglected to invite a new contact. I kicked myself for not remembering that. I called myself names for being there. Now the question was whether I was part of the glue between them. It wasn't much of a brain teaser. He was bound to ask who she'd come with and sure to tell her I was writing a script for him. So, she'd have dishonesty to throw in my face. But not necessarily. Not unless he told her what my television assignment was about. If he hadn't, I could pretend I was doing it on the side, in addition to the script for Preminger. It all depended on how much I'd been discussed.

I lingered behind a potted palm, watching them and trying to think of what to say if she knew everything.

Then she laughed again. Either I'd never noticed how melodious her laugh was or the drinks had relaxed her larynx. Averies moved in on the sound, encircling her more with his arm and giving her a good squeeze. She held her champagne glass to one side but she didn't pull away. He kissed her and she didn't try to dodge that either. I came out of hiding.

"Everybody know everybody?"

"Oh, hello." Averies slowly released her.

"This is Mr. Averies," she said.

"I know," I said. "I'm a big admirer of his free-falls."

Averies gave me a quizzical look as if trying to place me. I'd had a meeting with him less than eight hours before and the bastard didn't remember my face. That was how much they'd discussed me.

"Mr. Burdick is a writer," said Bambi.

That did it. He knew me now.

"A great writer," she added. She said it through taffy. He'd help set her up for me with more champagne.

"Not as great as Sax Rohmer," I said, trying to take the edge off the compliment.

"Rohmer?" He was better at placing the dead. "You mean the Fu Manchu guy?"

"It's an inside joke," I said.

He was quick. A glance at our faces and he put it all together.

"If only the writers nowadays could write like him." He said it more to Bambi.

"You like him too?" It was a shriek of delight.

"He's the best," said Averies. He snapped his fingers at a passing waiter and exchanged her empty glass for a full one. Her first sip of it was an audition.

"How many you had?" I tried not to sound fatherly.

"She can handle it," said Averies.

Her hiccup said otherwise. His hand was snaking around her waist again.

"Corey's writin' a script for me," she said.

"Small world," he said. "He's also writing one for me." He smiled in my general direction. "Could they be one and the same?"

"She's with me," I said.

Averies gave me the look he probably gave a cumulus cloud before jumping into it.

"I was going to suggest a game of musical beds," he said.

"She lives with me," I said, "and we only play games with each other."

It came out louder than I'd intended and managed to get through her fog.

"Are you two sillies fightin' over me?"

"No, my dear," said Averies. "You're not quite scintillating enough."

"That stinks," I said.

"What stinks?" She was having trouble focusing.

Averies slowly finished his drink, then handed me the empty glass.

"We have many battles ahead," he said. "Let's not waste punches on this one." He gave Bambi a courtly bow. "No offense intended, dear."

We stood watching him walk away. I half-expected her to run after him. Then the best looker in the garden intercepted him and hugged him like she'd never let go. Watching him, I felt old and unimposing. I envied him his build and thick hair and the unflinching eyes that went with his avocation. I even half-envied him his job. At his age and with his looks and career, most of this town and a lot of the women in it were his for the taking.

"What'd he mean?"

"Who knows?" I shrugged it off, thinking she meant his crack at her.

"You should know if you're writin' the script."

"What script?"

"He said you're writing a script for him." She enunciated it carefully. I fought back my aversion to the speech patterns of drunks.

"It's just another script," I said.

"He told me he's in television."

I could have invented a complicated explanation. But Averies had admitted to being in television and hadn't attracted her the less for it. In fact, it might have worked in his favor. In places like Venables, the local picture palace had long shut down and the TV sets got bigger and bigger. Her walking out of the room when our set was on didn't mean she'd turn up her nose at television stardom. Maybe she just couldn't stand the commercials.

"For Preminger, read Averies," I said. "For *movie* movie, read movie of the week."

"Huh?" said Bambi.

"I'm not writing a motion picture for Otto Preminger," I said.

"Then how can you get me a part in it?"

"I can't," I said. "But I was hoping to get you one in the television film I'm writing."

"An' you thought I was gonna sleep with you for a part in a lousy television show?"

"Who says it will be lousy?"

"If it's on television, it's lousy."

"There've been some good things on television." I couldn't believe what I heard myself saying. "And if it wasn't for television, you wouldn't have recognized Otto

Preminger and be standing here right now."

"Our deal is off." She tried to stand straight to announce it.

"That's fine with me," I said. "But just out of curiosity, who the hell are you to be so particular? Let's see your rave reviews. Or how about a little sample of your great acting ability."

"I got a special quality," she said. Her voice carried across the pool and garden. Faces were turning toward us. "I got somethin' that turns men on, little men, big men, hard-up men." I wasn't sure if she was talking to me or giving me the sample of her talent. Then Alysia Dembo came out of the darkness and descended on us. Working under the pool lights had made her eye shadow run.

"We had a fascinating session," she said, tilting her head toward Bambi.

"Like hell," said Bambi.

"Ignore her," I said to the psychic. I gave her five bucks.

"Oh, goodie," she said. "Now I can buy a new crystal ball."

"An' you'll still be full of it," said Bambi.

"Words you shall someday eat." Alysia blew her a kiss before flouncing away.

"What's all that about?"

"I need a drink."

"You've had too many," I said. "Let's go home."

"No." She backed away. "Not until I meet Dustin Hoffman."

"I told you. Dustin isn't coming tonight."

"And neither are you."

On that note we made our way back to the bar.

Chapter 18

IT STARTED pouring when we were halfway along Sunset.
I pulled off into a side street and managed to get the top
up while she went on sulking. Watching me get soaked
mellowed her a little and when I got back in the car she
started to sing. I though it was a rock number until the
punch line.

"March on, Venables High!"

"Doesn't it always?" I said.

"A lot you know, Ornery Corey." She let her head loll
against the back of the seat. "You don't even know what
that fortune-teller told me."

"I could guess."

"G'wan, try."

"All about a tall, dark stranger and an ocean voyage
and suddenly coming into a lot of money."

"An' you call *me* dumb?"

"All right, what did she tell you?"

"She don't know nuthin'."

"Drop the other shoe, Bambi."

"What shoe?" She peered dazedly toward her feet.

"What did the fortune-teller tell you?"

"First she spread out her lousy cards. Then she turned over the lousy queen of hearts."

"The suspense is killing me."

"An' then she said that proved I like women better than I like men."

"Why not? Women are superior creatures."

"She didn't mean it like that, dopey."

"Oh."

"That's what I call a faulty fuckin' sound," she said.

"I'm glad I only gave her five bucks," I said.

"How could anybody say that about me?" She was starting to sulk again.

"Well," I said, "at least it would explain why you've turned me down."

"Prick," she said.

"Spoken like a true lesbian."

There are times my dialogue is too sharp and this was one of them. She wouldn't speak again all the way back to the house. She pushed me away when I tried to help her out of the car. It took her a full minute to manage it by herself. Then she walked into the garbage cans.

I made strong coffee. While it was brewing she started going on about the psychic again.

"Why didn't she turn over the jack of clubs or somethin'? Why'd she have to turn over that lousy queen?"

"Because she wanted to."

"Why'd she want to do that?"

"Because she was jealous of your youth and beauty." I never sound convincing when I'm drunk. "Because you've got something that turns men on." I managed to get my arms around her. "Especially me."

I'd said the wrong thing again. She struggled to get away. She said "that phony bitch" at least six times. She wanted me to drive her back to the party so she could belt Alysia Zembo right in the mouth. She got one arm free and demonstrated the punch that would do it.

"Calm down," I said. I kissed the back of her neck, but she went on with her imaginary fight. I planted one on her lips and she kept talking, proclaiming her femininity right into my mouth. Then she suddenly went limp and I let her sink onto the wooden stool near the pantry.

"What if she's right?" She looked thoroughly crushed.

"She isn't right."

"She was right about a lot of other things."

"Like what?"

"Like my comin' from a small town an' bein' a cheerleader."

"Educated guesses," I said.

"An' how about that fuckin' queen of hearts."

"Forget the queen of hearts."

"I can't," she moaned. "I ain't ever goin' to be able to forget it until I find out for sure." She tried to draw herself up. "An' there's only one way to do that."

"Two ways," I said. "There's a positive way and a negative way." I lifted her chin with my finger and leaned down to kiss her again. "Let's try the negative one first."

Her lips didn't respond. I tried to force my tongue and hit a roadblock of tooth enamel. I got the fist she'd rehearsed for Alysia Zembo right where it hurt most.

" 'Course women are lots prettier than men."

"No argument," I gasped.

"I might as well try it while I'm drunk."

"Try what?" I had trouble straightening up.

"Go get me a woman," she said.

"Now, don't be silly."

"I'm gonna find out tonight," she said. "With you or without you."

She made it to her feet and almost to the kitchen door. I tackled her from behind and we both went down. I carefully separated our legs before trying to get up.

"And exactly where," I said, "do you expect me to find a dyke this time of night?"

"I dunno." She thought about it. "Try the Yellow Pages. Everything's in the fuckin' Yellow Pages."

"Good enough." I decided to humor her and crawled toward the living room to get the phone book. She was pouring out coffee when I came back with it and a bottle of cognac that the house-owner had forgotten to hide.

"It might be more fun with this." I plunked down the cognac.

"Right." She emptied both the coffee cups into the sink, then smashed the Silex on the side of it. She did it all thumbs, the same way I was riffling through the classified pages.

"Nothing under 'Lesbians,' " I said.

"Gotta be." She found two relatively clean glasses for the cognac. "Look under 'Escort Services.' "

I did. There were three pages of display ads.

"How did you know?" I withered her with besotted suspicion."

"I read things besides Sax Rohmer, don't I?"

"Do you?"

"Or maybe it was in one of your shitty television shows." She motioned in the general direction of the phone book. "What does it say?"

The ads all said pretty much the same thing. The *Geisha Escort Service* and the *Hello Dolly Escort Service* and *A Touch of Class* all offered companionship that knew no bounds in the privacy of home or office or hotel suite, and most of them accepted Visa or MasterCard. But they were all downtown or in the valley. The only one anywhere near us was *Mrs. Murphy's Girls*. The small print said, "Beautiful, young, sophisticated ladies for your pleasure," and there was nothing about credit cards.

"You'd better call this off," I warned, "before we get in too deep." I tried to sound firm but my tongue was too floppy. I wished she hadn't thrown out the coffee and broken the Silex. I drank some cognac.

"I ain't callin' off nuthin'."

"In that case . . ." I made it to the kitchen phone and took it off its hook and stood there giving her one last chance to change her mind before I dialed.

"Mrs. Murphy's Girls." It was answered on the first ring. The woman sounded sultry but had a distinct German accent. I had a quick flash of Dietrich in *The Blue Angel.*

"Am I speaking to Mrs. Murphy?"

"Yah. This is her."

"This is she," I said. I only correct people's grammar when I'm sloshed.

"So?" She was waiting.

"How do you do," I said. I covered the mouthpiece and whispered to Bambi, "We're both gonna regret this."

"Do it," she hissed. She'd finished her cognac and was pouring another.

"Mrs. Murphy," I said.

"Yah. I'm still here."

"Mrs. Murphy, would you by any chance happen to have a beautiful, young, sophisticated lady available?" Her assumed or married name had given me a slight brogue. The same thing happened when I rewrote a picture that featured Barry Fitzgerald.

"How young?" she said.

"Oh . . ." I looked at Bambi and realized I didn't know her exact age. ". . . say early twenties."

"When would you like to meet her?" said Mrs. Murphy.

"Soon as possible." Either excitement or heartburn was rising in my chest.

"You're in luck," said Mrs. Murphy. "Consuela just walked in."

"Just a minute," I said. I mouthed the name to Bambi and she shook her head vehemently.

"I should have told you," I said, "that, though we have nothing against Hispanics, we're in sort of an Aryan mood tonight."

"And no coons," yelled Bambi. I couldn't cover the mouthpiece in time.

"And vott did you mean by vee?" said Mrs. Murphy.

"I'm with a friend," I said.

"Male or female?" She made gender sound like Volkswagen parts.

"A young ladyfriend," I said.

"Is there anything else you'd better tell me?" said Mrs. Murphy.

"Well, uh . . ." It was probably the first time in my life I was at a loss for words.

"What's wrong?" Bambi was lurching over to find out. I waved her off.

"I think it might help," I said to Mrs. Murphy, "if your young lady likes other young ladies."

"Vy didn't you say so in the first place?" said Mrs. Murphy.

"Does it make a difference?"

"You mean you don't know?" She had a guttural laugh, but at least she laughed. "How about Valerie?" she said. "Thirty-six, twenty-five, thirty-six."

"She sounds perfect," I said.

"Seventy-five dollars to the agency for the introduction," said Mrs. Murphy.

"And how much to Valerie?"

"She usually gets a hundred. But in this case, she'll want another twenty-five."

"Okay," I said. "Two hundred even." I couldn't remember if I had that much in my wallet.

"Maybe you should tell me more about your lady-friend," she said.

Bambi was fuzzy to look at, so I sized her up from memory.

"Thirty-two, twenty-two, thirty-two," I said.

"Maybe she should take B-complex," said Mrs. Murphy.

"What the hell's goin' on?" said Bambi.

"These are very delicate arrangements," I said. I asked Mrs. Murphy if there was anything else she wanted to know and she said it would help if I gave her my address. She assured me that Valerie would be with us in about twenty minutes.

I relayed this to Bambi after I hung up and suggested she use the time to run a comb through her hair. Then I went to check my wallet. There were two hundred and forty-five dollars in it. I hid it behind my collection of short stories on the bookshelf. By the time I got back to the kitchen, Bambi had wandered off. She answered the third time I yelled her name and I found her in the bedroom, flat on her back and ready to be crucified.

"Now what?" I said.

"Tie me up," she said.

"What for?"

"I want to be helpless."

"What for?"

"Will you stop sayin' 'what for' and get some rope?"

"Where'm I gonna get rope?"

"How do I know?"

I started looking. There was no rope in the closet. I

got down on my knees and peered under the bed.

"What you doin' down there?"

"Lookin' for fuckin' rope."

"Look in the cellar," she said.

I'd never been in the cellar and fell down the last three steps. It reeked of fuel oil and homemade strawberry jam. I found a rake and a coal shovel and a basket of moldy onions. A coil of telephone wire was in with the onions.

"Success!" I waved the wire triumphantly as I stumbled back into the bedroom. The stumble was partly because she'd turned off two of the three lamps. Also because she'd taken off her lace dress and everything else except bra and panties.

"What's that?" She fluttered one hand toward the telephone wire.

"You are about to be rendered helpless."

Easier said than done. I'd seen repairmen bend the stuff like overcooked spaghetti, but they were sober and stronger. I began with her left wrist. The bed didn't have posts or a headboard, so I had to fasten the loose end of the coil to the metal frame underneath. For the first time in my life I regretted never joining the Boy Scouts or Sea Scouts. I gave the wire the same knot I gave my shoelaces. There looked like plenty to spare, so I wound it around her wrist and halfway to her elbow before realizing I had nothing to cut it with. Her nail scissors got through most of the plastic coating before breaking.

"Be right back," I said.

I went to the kitchen and scooped up all the carving knives. The one with the serrated edge worked out best, but it took a lot of pressure. When the wire finally snapped, I almost lost a finger.

"Now my left ankle," she said.

"You mind if I stop bleeding first?"

"Why you bleedin'?"

"You and your goddam hang-ups."

"What hang-ups?"

I soaked a washcloth in her bathroom and wound it around my hand. It immediately started turning pink. I ignored this and went to concentrate on her left ankle. I did a better job this time. Nothing like experience.

"'S too tight," she said.

"Good," I said.

By the time I finished her right wrist, I felt like I'd played three sets of tennis. I sat on the edge of the bed and waited for my arms to stop quivering.

"Incidentally," I said, "her name's Valerie."

"Who?"

"The broad who's on her way."

"What if she doesn't like me?"

"For two hundred bucks, Valerie would go down on the bride of Frankenstein."

"Is that what lesbians do?"

"You're the one who reads filthy magazines."

"I thought they just went in for tit munchin'."

"You could still call it off."

I couldn't tell if she was thinking about it or falling asleep.

"Tie my other ankle," she said.

There was just enough wire left. I was too weak to cut it off and left the spool attached.

"See if you can squirm loose," I said.

She couldn't. I stood there, admiring my handiwork and watching her writhe. It began to get to me. How often do you get a girl you want tied up and at your mercy, especially one who's recently punched you in the balls? She was looking up at me and not liking what she saw. I moved to the side of the bed and touched the tip of her nose with my forefinger. She turned her head away and I ran the finger down her neck. She shuddered, but it seemed more sensual than scared. My finger had reached a collarbone. I followed it to her shoulder. Her skin was even more soft to the touch than I'd imagined.

"Don't," she said.

"Don't what?" I said.

I put the traveling finger in my mouth and wet it. Then I let it descend slowly to the dip between her breasts. I traced the edge of her bra and lifted one cup by its strap. And the doorbell rang.

It had never rung since we'd been there and the volume must have been set to reach the house next door, and it was more buzzer than bell. No wonder Pavlov chose an ear-splitting buzzer for his dirty work.

"You better let her in," said Bambi.

"I fully intend to let her in," I said. My head was still ringing.

I went through the living room to the small entrance hall. My feet felt heavy and my throat felt dry. I stared at the front door. A sudden knocking on it make me jump.

"Just a minute!" I made a big deal of sliding off the chain.

That left only the bolt. Only one bolt between me and a brand new experience. I always stop to savor such moments, gearing myself the way I've seen good actors do before making an entrance. I tried not to visualize Valerie or anticipate her first words or prepare mine. Everything was to be fresh and natural and unrehearsed.

I turned the bolt and opened the door. Valerie stood waiting. She stood under a big umbrella and wore a belted trenchcoat and a floppy rain hat. All I could see of her face was a lot of lipstick and a chin. I could see more of the green station wagon she'd parked in the driveway.

"I'm Valerie," she said.

"Come in," I said, all natural and unrehearsed.

My first impression was of brisk efficiency: the way she introduced herself to be sure she was at the right place, the way she collapsed her umbrella, shook off the water and stood it in a corner of the front hall so it wouldn't drip onto the scatter rug. Mrs. Murphy had trained her well.

"Miserable night," I said.

"Yes," she said. Her 'yes' sounded a little bit like a 'yah.'

"This way," I said.

She followed me like I'd once followed a weary bleached whore up a flight of stairs in a Chicago cathouse. I'd been almost as drunk then as I was now.

"In here."

I motioned her to precede me into the bedroom, so I didn't see her face when she first saw Bambi on the bed. Not that I could have seen much of it, wherever I stood, with her rain hat still on.

"Good evening, darlink," said Valerie. Her accent was definitely German or Belgian or Dutch.

"Hi," said Bambi.

"All ready for some B and D, I see."

"What's B and D?" I said.

"Bondage and discipline," said Bambi. "And I don't want any."

"First vee do the lights," said Valerie.

She went to the lamp on the dresser that was the only one still on and turned it off. We were reduced to what came from the small bulb in the bathroom.

"That's better," said Valerie. She efficiently took off her rain hat and shook loose her long hair. In the semi-darkness it looked brassy. She unbelted and unbuttoned her trenchcoat and tossed it over the back of a chair. Then she stretched as if limbering up. "So what did you haff in mind?" she said.

I suddenly felt in the way. I hadn't thought through what my part in the proceedings would be. I felt I should leave, but I didn't want to miss anything. I couldn't think of anything better to say than the truth. I pointed to Bambi.

"She wants to find out if she's more attracted to women than to men."

"Some do and some don't," said Valerie. She kicked off her shoes expertly. "So . . . ?" She waited for instructions. Bambi could have helped, but she just stared at her.

"Mrs. Murphy gave me to understand that you were experienced in these matters."

"Did Mrs. Murphy also tell you how much?"

"She said two hundred dollars."

"Two twenty-five," said Valerie.

"Mrs. Murphy definitely said two hundred."

"You didn't tell her it was B and D."

"It isn't and how do you know what I told her?" A suspicious thought was squeezing through my stupor.

"I happened to be in the office."

"And maybe you're who I was talking to."

"Sometimes vee sound the same." Valerie resumed her limbering-up exercises. "Ve're both from the same part of Switzerland."

Every Nazi I've ever met has pretended to be Swiss. My suspicion was hardening.

"And maybe Mrs. Murphy is all her beautiful, young and sophisticated ladies rolled into one."

"All right," she said. "I von't argue over twenty-five bucks."

"Then you *are* Mrs. Murphy."

"Valerie said she's got flu and I didn't vant to disappoint you." Her shrug dismissed the whole charade. "So two hundred even . . . in advance."

"Half in advance." I'd been taken by hookers before.

"Whateffer makes you happy," she said. "But nothing kinky."

"Put the lights on," said Bambi.

"Later, darling," cooed Mrs. Murphy.

"Right now! Put them on!" Bambi was tugging against her telephone wires.

"Take it easy." I headed for the nearest lamp, but Mrs. Murphy blocked my way.

"Go put on some music," she said. "Vot's her favorite song?"

" 'March on, Venables High,' " I said.

My joke didn't go unrewarded. There was a flash of lightning and the curtain was slightly open and Mrs. Murphy didn't cover up in time.

"Jesus!" said Bambi.

She took the name right out of my mouth. Even allowing for the harshness of lightning, Mrs. Murphy was anything but young and beautiful. Fifty and all fucked-out would be closer.

"Don't let that old bag near me!" screamed Bambi.

"Who you calling a bag?" yelled Mrs. Murphy. Anger thickened her accent. "You rotten little whore!"

"No," I said. "You've got it backwards. You're the whore."

"Okay, you vant it mitt hostility, vee do it your way."

"Get her outta here!" Bambi was tugging so hard she was rocking the mattress.

"I think we'd better forget the whole thing," I said.

"Gut enough." Mrs. Murphy picked up her hat and

trenchcoat. "Pay me and I'll leave."

"Pay you for what?" I said.

"For the abuse!" said Mrs. Murphy. "For coming out in this piss to get pissed on!"

"Fifty bucks for your trouble," I said.

"A hundred." She sat down in the chair and gripped the arms. "Or I'll giff you my order for breakfast now."

"My wallet's in the other room," I said.

When she went with me to the door, I knew she'd turn back to Bambi and get the last word. She took her time, as if committing the shadowy figure on the bed to memory.

"Don't worry, darlink," she said. "You vould haff enjoyed it more than me."

I looked under the sofa cushions for my wallet. That's where I usually hide it. Mrs. Murphy stood tapping one foot until I remembered putting it behind my book of short stories. When I handed her the two fifties, I pointed to my name on the jacket.

"That's me," I said.

"You're sick," she said.

I let her out and went back to the kitchen for some more brandy. I heard her station wagon start up and expected to hear a crash as she rammed one of my fenders as a farewell gesture. But it didn't come. I downed the brandy and poured another. I wasn't in any hurry to get back to the bedroom. I didn't want to hear Bambi's comments or voice my own. A messy orgy would have left me depressed, but at least I'd have had images to revive when the shame wore off. This encounter had the emptiness of farce. The only feeling I could summon was a strange sympathy for Valerie or Mrs. Murphy or whatever her name really was. Of the three of us, she had emerged with the most dignity.

I don't know how long I sat there or how many brandies I had. But when I finally got back to the bedroom, Bambi was sound asleep. I couldn't decide whether to untie her or leave her like she was until morning. I switched on one lamp and her eyes opened.

"I'm sorry," she said.

"For what?"

"Costin' you all that money, and the bother."

"Forget it," I said.

"I knew before she got here that fortune-teller was full of it."

"Maybe the drinks wore off."

"No," she said. "I knew when you touched me."

That was my cue to touch her again. But whatever had been unique about it was due to the mood we'd been in. I had to resurrect that first. I let my gaze drift down the length of her body. The sensation was pleasing, but not exciting.

"You can untie me now," she said.

"Maybe I prefer you helpless."

"It'll be better if I ain't tied up." There was no mistaking what she meant.

"Our deal's off, remember?"

"You sure don't know fuck-all about women," she said.

That did it. My mania returned full strength. I started the forefinger routine again, the tip of her nose, the point of her chin, her throat. She purred and that made it unbearable. I knelt on the bed and kissed everywhere my finger had been.

"Please untie me," she whispered. "I want the first time to be special."

Either I would have made the world's worst Boy Scout

or her pulling and tugging had tightened the knots. The one on her right wrist wouldn't give. The ones on her ankles were just as bad.

"You're hurtin' me," she said.

Shades of Janet when she wasn't in the mood. But the great lust-killing line didn't work this time. Back to the knife. All glory to the genius who invented the serrated edge.

"Someone's at the door," she said.

Loud as the buzzer was, I hadn't heard it. Then it rang again. It set off one of those lucid moments forged by drink and exhaustion. I immediately knew who was ringing and why.

"She left her goddamned umbrella."

I remembered it in the corner of the front hall, still dripping as she'd slammed the front door behind her. I wished I'd grabbed it and run after her.

"The hell with it," I said.

The buzzer went a few more times before the pounding on the door began.

"Maybe you better let her in," said Bambi.

"She'll give up."

The pounding got louder.

"She's gonna break it down," said Bambi.

"Hold still," I said. The knife was almost through the wire on her left wrist. Nothing could stop me now, not even the tinkle of breaking window glass which sounded close. If some semiretired call girl wanted to risk a severed artery for a five-dollar umbrella, let her. If she wanted to come in and watch, she could do that, too. Maybe she'd learn something. "Success!" I cut the final strands and the left wrist was free. Bambi flexed it, then looked past me toward the doorway.

"Quentin!" she gasped. It was the same wide-eyed bit,

the same Mary Pickford trick she'd pulled before. That
was how special she wanted our first lovemaking to be.

"Not this time," I said.

But I instinctively glanced around and there he was.

Chapter 19

THERE'S BEEN A lot of unnecessary mourning over what "Hollywood" does to a writer's sensibilities. Those sensibilities, like everybody else's, are hardened young, and no environment short of a maximum-security prison can dent them. What happens here to a writer's memory is something else.

Maybe it's the standard screenplay format. Maybe it's the FADE IN at the beginning and the FADE OUT at the end and every scene having to be labelled EXT. or INT. and DAY or NIGHT and every gesture and nuance having to be spelled out in detail. The main reason the motion picture will never be an art form is that it leaves nothing to the imagination. And that starts with the script. Maybe that's why, after I'd rewritten my first dozen or so, everything that ever happened to me before I typed that first FADE IN got out of focus. And there went all those juicy real-life experiences that a writer is supposed to draw on.

I remember my first FADE IN like it was yesterday. It began a screenplay about a Hoosier poet. Having spent almost two years at Purdue and having once written a profile article on e.e. cummings, I was eminently qualified for the assignment, which may have had a little to do with my getting it.

The picture was made by a producer who regularly worked out during our meetings with a rubber chest expander and by a director who was heavily into health foods and meditation. The studio putting up the cash was Warner Brothers.

Came the great day in Burbank when, morning script conference over, my producer and director announced that they were taking me to lunch in the Executive Dining Room. The slight hitch was that Jack Warner was still running the studio then and Jack Warner did not allow writers in the Executive Dining Room. So I went anyway and was introduced as a production assistant. The three of us sat midway down the long mahogany table, not too far from Mr. Warner to go unnoticed, but not close enough to get much of his attention.

The talk was mostly business—grosses and profits and percentages. I was surprised to find that while Warner had total recall of box office receipts, he had little or none for the faces on the screen.

"You know who I mean," he said at one point. "The broad who looks like a wolf."

"Sophia Loren," muttered one of his vice-presidents. The prompt didn't seem to bother Warner. He got three more when he couldn't think of the names of Lee Marvin, Kim Novak and Rod Steiger. In fact, the only stars he managed to name were Bette Davis and Edward G. Robinson.

Then, during the break between the beef stew and the cherries jubilee, Warner pointed an imperious forefinger toward us.

"This thing you're doing with James Bond," he said.

"Sean Connery," muttered one of his other vice-presidents. Connery had been signed to play the Hoosier poet. This was over twenty years ago and his Scottish accent then was thick enough to stuff haggis with. We knew this was going to be a problem and had kicked around some possible explanations for why, when he said Fort Wayne, it sounded like Dundee. But all got lost along the way and when, in the finished version, Connery said he was going home to Indiana, all the cartographers at Rand McNally must have gone back to their drawing boards.

"We talking about the same picture?" said Warner. When assured by still another vice-president that they were, he turned to us again.

"It going to have lots of action?"

"Lots," said my producer.

"Plenty of shooting and fighting and tits?"

"Plenty," said my director.

I saw the picture when it came out. Even for its time there was a notable absence of cleavage. And the only person the Hoosier poet took a swing at was Joanne Woodward. I later heard that when Jack Warner saw it in the studio screening room it took all three vice-presidents to hold him down.

Other absurdities were to follow, all with heroes and villains and budget problems as more and more of the outside world wound up on the cutting room floor. The bulk of my life was spent taking ridiculous positions in asinine conversations and I wrote accordingly. I wrote descriptions like "the slug leaves a hole in his forehead the size of a walnut," and dialogue like "You know what I mean, man. I mean, you better know." I wrote a scene where a wife stood on her head to help her husband's spermatozoa travel her Fallopian tubes and a scene where an army bomber dropped a bale of confetti on a World Series game. I wrote about an outbreak of rabies on a cruise ship and ditto for syphilis in the Continental Congress. I wrote about a fuck-up Mexican general who recaptures the Alamo and a constipated chimp who swallows the plans for the definitive nuclear device. I wrote about a geography teacher who turns out to be a psychotic killer and an evangelist who turns out to be a psychotic killer and I wrote about a psychotic killer who rehabilitates his fellow inmates by muscling them into a production of *Porgy and Bess*. And there was many a time, between my DAY and NIGHT and EXT. and INT., that I came close to writing, "You have to get this message to Lotus Blossom in Macao."

Grousing went with the territory, and when I complained too much, Janet was always "supportive"—another word that has screwed up family life.

"Why don't you try something less pointless?" she once said.

"Law, medicine and professional golf are just as pointless."

"But less parasitical."

"If film writing is parasitical, what's film criticism?"

"I'm not suggesting you become a film critic."

"But you read their crap."

"Do I detect a note of defensiveness?"

"You sure as hell do."

"All right. Then defend what you do for a living."

"It's a form of autoeroticism. The people I work with make me feel more intelligent than I am. And I get a few laughs. The only laughter ever heard from a critic is maniacal."

"Why do you keep going on about critics?"

"Because I hate critics."

"Just because they panned your last picture."

"It wasn't my picture. I rewrote it."

Then she got around to the routine about being willing to follow me anywhere.

"I'm perfectly willing to live on less," she said.

That was right after the birthday when I'd given her a necklace that set me back almost eight grand. I've already mentioned who got the house.

"There are always literary pursuits," she said.

"You know how I feel about literary pursuits."

"I know how you *say* you feel."

"Same thing."

"If you say so."

"Literary pursuits make screenwriting look honest."

"Really?"

You know who the world's two leading authorities on Shakespeare are right now?"

"Who?" She'd heard it all before but tried to look fascinated.

"A Jewish professor from the Midwest and a Jewish professor from Brooklyn, both determined to prove that Shylock was really a swell guy."

"Yes, Mr. Eichmann."

"I am merely suggesting that an American professor of Jewish persuasion couldn't appreciate an Elizabethan sonnet unless it was printed in Braille and shoved up his ass."

"Which has nothing to do with what we're talking about."

"All you need to be 'literary' is a library card and an obscurantist title. *Virginia Woolf at Ringside; or, The Secret Secretions of Violence.* How's that?"

"And you prefer rewriting *The Clone from the Deep Lagoon*."

"You know what every Professor of Fucking Comparative Literature has in his bottom desk drawer?"

"The *Penthouse* calendar."

"Plus an unfinished screenplay. Don't forget all their unfinished screenplays in blank verse. And you know what every true-blue literary pursuer really wants to pursue?"

"I can't wait to find out."

"All the Hollywood prizes," I said. "They go home every night to their fat, hairy, Ph.D. wives and dream about Bo Derek's snatch."

"Or Clint Eastwood's cock."

"Touché," I said.

"Cliché," she said.

"Next question," I said.

"I only have one more," she said. "Where does it end?"

I'd already given some thought to that. Anybody my age does. Where would it end? People usually die pretty much the way they've lived. The lucky go out lucky, and so on down the ladder. So it figured that my last fade-out would find me doing something pretty boneheaded. But I never thought I'd be bending over a semi-naked girl, trying to liberate her from telephone wires, as a nutcase who'd broken every running and passing record in Arkansas high school history came charging in. And never in a million rewrites could I have come up with his opening line.

"What the hell you doin' to my wife?"

Chapter 20

So MUCH FOR screen credits. He'd been in a fleabag downtown with nothing to do but guzzle beer and watch TV when a Rock Hudson movie I rewrote came on. He didn't know until then that I was a writer and he asked everybody who would listen how a famous movie writer could be located until somebody knew. The Writers' Guild referred him to Perry Lutz's office. Perry's secretary was out having an appendectomy and the temp apparently hadn't been told not to give out clients' addresses. Dookes would have arrived much sooner, but he'd gone through all the money he'd lifted off me and had to wait until it was dark enough to steal a car. Then it had taken him a few hours to find the place.

He thought I might know where Bambi was. It had even crossed his mind that she could be with me. But he sure hadn't expected to find her the way she was. The few seconds it took him to come out of shock probably saved my life. That and Bambi.

"Don't hit him, Quentin. It was all my doin'."

It wasn't what she said as much as the way she said

it. Meryl Streep couldn't have done better with twenty takes. And Bambi did it twice, identical readings of the exact same words, hitting just the right note somewhere between a command and a whimper, stalling whatever was about to explode inside his thick skull. Then she slipped in the clincher.

"If you don't hurt him, we can stay here."

And so it was that twenty minutes later the three of us were sitting in the living room, drinking tea because the last of the coffee had gone down the sink. Bambi was rubbing her chafed wrists and ankles (Dookes hadn't been very gentle when he tore off the telephone wires); Kurosawa, who'd taken an immediate liking to him, was trying to lick the pattern off one of his hand-tooled boots; and I was getting a hell of a draft from the window he'd broken and climbed through.

She'd been right, of course. Anything short of killing me and I'd have eventually brought in the police to get rid of both of them. This way, I had no legitimate complaint. It wasn't my house, they weren't disturbing the peace, and they were married.

That was the toughest part to accept. I'd never fully swallowed her intimations of virginity. The good citizens of places like Venables lose it young. But even in Arkansas, most baton twirlers don't marry their stepbrothers.

The first item on the agenda was the Subaru he'd filched. It was almost new and he was reluctant to give it up, but Bambi again displayed a knack for nudging him into practicality. So she stayed put and I followed behind him in my car and we dumped the Subaru behind the Chateau Marmont where the cops would be sure to find it. It was during our drive back to the house that I got his side of the story.

Her married name was Dookes and her own was

Fruehoffer. If her paternal grandfather was in World War One he'd probably been on the German side. Her father only drank on New Year's Eve and her mother had been a breeder. Bambi was the youngest of seven.

"She told me you were her adopted brother," I said.

"That's Bambi for ya," he said.

As for his running and passing records, he'd been a defensive guard and he'd been dropped from the squad after two games because he drew so many unnecessary roughness penalties. That left her allegations of homosexuality, but I'd had enough of that subject for one night.

There hadn't been any fake talent scout. Bambi had just up and left. But she'd been going on about changing her name to Fortunata and being a movie star for so long that even he could guess where she'd lit out for. She'd taken a Greyhound bus and he'd hitchhiked and caught up with her at a rest stop near San Bernardino. Being so close to her dream, she'd carried on like crazy and he'd never been able to deny her anything she really hankered for. So he'd given in and they'd traveled the last fifty miles together. But after two nights at the Bolero Motel, she'd sneaked off again, this time with all the money he had except twenty dollars.

"Then I found her in that fancy Beverly Wilshire place and was just goin' through her purse for what she took and I found that card with your name."

"I know the rest," I said.

I could have added that, though his version made a lot more sense, hers was much more interesting.

"Is there anything else I should know?" I said.

"Sure," he said, "but we got us loads a' time."

That made me die a little. More chest pains followed in my lumpy divan bed. High Santa Ana winds had followed the rain and I tried to blame them for every creaking sound. But, though she'd gone to bed before we got back, she'd left her door unlocked and he'd walked right in as if there was no question of where he was to sleep.

I tend to be offhand about my agonies, but not this time. All through what was left of the night, I suffered fantasies as never before. My writer's voyeuristic eyes wanted to watch the two of them make love. My brain didn't want to know. If it hadn't been a standoff, I'd have slithered through the backyard mud to their window, praying that his prick would be a panatella and she'd be responding like a felled tree. I settled on creeping down the hall and listening at their door. I thought I heard her gasp. It may have been the Santa Ana wind.

Morning was even worse. I heard a war whoop and a splash and went to look. The pool fit him like a bathtub. He'd belly flopped into it and displaced half the water.

"How ya doin', Old Fucker?" He waved and dove for pearls. I hoped the nickname wouldn't stick.

Dookes had left Venables with only the clothes on his back. The boots and ten-gallon hat had held up, but the white suit was looking grubby. Not that he needed it. He just paraded around in jockey shorts and the hat. Even the shorts were a concession. He was in love with his own flesh, all the pink pulp of it, every one of its faded freckles. The hat was something else. He kept it on most of the time to hide what wasn't underneath. What there was of his hair was cropped close and shaved high at the back and sides to minimize its thinning.

I noticed that Bambi avoided looking directly at him as much as possible. He must have been aware of it too, for he started deliberately standing in front of her so she had to look at him, just standing there, rubbing his big stomach and scratching his crotch. And the noon performance ended with his going off to the bedroom and calling out to her to join him.

"Come on in, little whore. Quentin's got somethin' for ya." I couldn't stand it, not so much his cooing, but the way she looked as it went on.

"Don't go," I said. But she shook me off.

"I can talk him out of it."

"Bambi!" His voice got louder. "I ain't tellin' ya again!" And she went to him, as to the gallows, and I died some more. When they came out, he did some chortling for my benefit.

" 'Course we ain't done it tied to the bed yet."

He still hadn't asked me to explain what she was doing in that position. It was as if he could hold it over me more if I didn't, that the moment of reckoning was still to come. But what had or hadn't happened in the bedroom had fouled his mood. It got worse as he consumed the six-packs of beer he sent me out to buy.

His threats got more obvious and all were directed at me through her. She was the hostage. Any displeasure I caused would be vented on the parts of her he obscenely labeled. With his glasses off, his pale eyes would measure her for a coffin and there'd usually be a show of power. He picked up an apple and turned it into sauce with one crunching squeeze—things like that.

I knew I couldn't take much more of him. His high nasal twang grated on my eardrums. He droned idiocies nonstop with the total smugness born of brute strength. He took delight in his own belches. If I'd only been concerned for myself and not for her, I'd have gone off for more beer and never come back. If I'd had a gun, like almost everyone else in Los Angeles, I would have gladly emptied it into him.

I considered substitutes: the knife with the serrated

edge, the moldy onions in the cellar in a poison stew, anything heavy while his hat was off. I honestly believe I would have made the try if we hadn't got into our first three-way conversation. The subject was Now What?

"If you want me to go home with you," said Bambi, "I will." I knew she was doing it for my benefit.

"No way," he said. "I ain't crawlin' back to Venables. If I go back, I'm goin' in style."

Bambi couldn't argue. There wasn't much to go back to. Their home emerged as two rooms above somebody's garage. The reason he'd hitchhiked to California was that his beaten-up old Dodge had been repossessed. She'd often worked double shifts in the diner because he'd never been able to hold a job.

"Like in one of them Porsche 944s," he said. "Whooeee! That'd make 'em sit up and take notice." Once he'd said it, no other make or model would do. "If Old Fucker here had one, I might just swap my little whore in for it."

It was a glimpse of daylight. He kept drooling about the car, his offer of a swap repeated enough to make me later check the used-car ads in the paper. Even a three-year-old Porsche 944 went for about twelve thousand. Of course, there was every chance that he wouldn't stick to his bargain, that if he drove off in a Porsche or anything else, she'd be sitting next to him. But I had to risk that.

Twelve thousand dollars became my immediate goal. A week before, it would have been laughable. Now I had two shots at it. If the fixed race worked, I could buy the car with plenty to spare, even a brand new one, if necessary. But I couldn't count on that. As I'd warned Demetrious, we had a problem that looked insurmountable. The television script was a better bet. I'd done round-the-clock rewrites of seventy to eighty pages. This script could be ground out the same way. And concentrating

on it would keep my mind off him. I went to my typewriter and started pounding the keys.

"What you doin', Old Fucker?"

He'd taken another dip in the pool with his jockey
shorts on and loomed over me, dripping wet. I kept my
sightline above his waistband to preserve the panatella
image.

"Just knockin' out a few notes," I said.

"What for?"

"I have a story conference at five o'clock," I said. That
was the time Demetrious had set for our meeting.

"For one of them movies you write?"

"It's for a television script," I corrected him gently.

"That's right," he said. "Bambi told me."

I hoped she'd told him all the time they were in bed,
that she'd verbalized him into impotence.

"She says she's gonna be actin' in it."

"It's a possibility," I said.

"She'll be right unhappy if she ain't." He let the new
threat sink in. "Let's see what you've writ."

"It's just a treatment so far."

"What's a treatment?"

"Sort of a florid prose version of an outline." His face
showed I wasn't getting through. "I'm only just beginning the script."

"Then let's see that there treatment," he said.

"You don't want to see it," I said. "It's just to give
idiots something to fight about at story conferences."

"I like a good fight," he said. He was getting his coffin-
measuring look again.

Luckily, a copy of the treatment was within reach. I
think I handed it to him just in time. Then he plopped
down on the sofa without drying himself off and stared
at the title page.

"It's only a working title," I said. I automatically tried it for size. " 'New Star In Town.' "

"I can read."

He turned to the first page to prove his point. He read like a producer, mouthing every syllable and shifting his weight to ease the pain.

Watching him, hating him, I still wanted him to be impressed. I'd had the feeling before, the longing for the approval of some illiterate. It had something to do with my esteem for words and my faith in their being able to penetrate any brain. But mostly it was because approval, whatever its source, would make my chore easier. So this time wasn't all that different. I wanted Dookes to be impressed because I wanted the leverage. What I had put on the page, however hyped-up and platitudinous, was the equivalent of his lifting up a freight car. The script treatment was my show of strength. If he acknowledged my superior mind, there'd be more daylight ahead.

He read through all of two pages before commenting.

"What they payin' you for this here?"

"The first draft fee," I said, "less agent's commission and withholding, will just about pay for a three-year-old Porsche 944."

"Well, what d'ya know?"

He turned to the next page, then suddenly slapped it with the back of his hand.

"Goddam!" he said.

"What's the matter?"

"You keep callin' her Loretta."

"That's the character's name."

"Isn't that the one Bambi's gonna play?"

"As I said, it's a possibility." I almost inserted "remote." "It's up to the network brass."

"Then why don't you call her Bambi so they'll know."

"I think that would be too on the nose," I said.

He rolled over to look at me and I didn't like the look.

"I think you should call her Bambi," he said.

"Okay." I decided to humor him. "I'll change it to Bambi in the first draft."

"And I got some other ideas, too," he said.

Bambi came in from the patio then, wiping the suntan oil from her arms.

"What you up to now?" she said.

"Just gassin'," he said. "I'm gonna help Old Fucker here write his TV script."

So much for screen credits. So much for glimpses of daylight.

Chapter 21

THE INSURMOUNTABLE problem with fixing the race was how to get away with a million dollars when there wouldn't be a million dollars to be got away with. Since giving Demetrious the bad news on the phone, I'd managed to improve the figures. But they still fell far short of his target.

I reached his place twenty minutes early and wasn't anxious to be first. The saloon next door looked reasonably safe, so I decided to kill the time there. Pooch Padilla was sitting alone at the bar with a Heineken. I took the next stool and ordered my usual.

"Could I ask you a personal question?" I said. He shrugged and waited for it. "Why was a guy with your teeth going to a dentist?"

"A broad hit me with a bottle." He pointed to his front uppers. "Caps."

"I often miss the obvious," I said.

"Yeah," he said. He wasn't agreeing with me. Some people just say "yeah" when they can't think of anything else to say.

"Now let me ask you one," he said.

"Sure."

"Demetrious said you write movies."

"I've been known to."

"So how come you never use jockeys?"

"For what?" My first thought was that he meant to type my scripts.

"For your movies. How come you only use football players?"

"You mean *in* the movies."

"What you think I mean?"

"We don't *only* use football players." I tried to think of how many of them had made the jump from gridiron to screen. Jim Brown and O. J. Simpson had and maybe one or two others.

"So how come you never use us?"

It wasn't an idle question. There was indignation behind it, as much as he'd shown at his suspension.

"Just one of those things," I said.

"Yeah." He concentrated on his beer.

I thought about his gripe. There was some validity to it. A jockey weighs about as much as a wet canary. His saddle gives his nuts the same protection they'd get from a tea room doily. The jarring he takes from the dirt track would disassemble a normal spine. And every time he goes into the starting gate he's risking his life. Pound for pound, jockeys are the strongest and bravest of all athletes. And the motion picture, the medium that made the most noise about muscles and guts, had yet to recognize jockeys' existence. Pooch deserved an explanation.

I could have argued height, but it wouldn't stand up. Charles Bronson doesn't actually tower over Willie the Shoe. Chris McCarron can face Kirk Douglas, eye to eye, without heel lifts. Robert Redford and Angel Cordero, Jr. probably have the same inside-leg seam measurements.

Or I could have put the onus on diction. Pooch's vocabulary was obviously limited and I'd had trouble making out the little there was of it. But Sylvester Stallone never had to say more than twenty-five different words in any one picture and he pronounced most of them wrong.

"I can give you my opinion, for what it's worth," I said. "I think that when your colleagues deliberately lose a race, it's too apparent."

"Talk English," he said.

"I'm saying that most jockeys are lousy actors."

"So are most actors," he said.

"Yeah," I said.

We finished our drinks and went to see Demetrious. The Kid and the two goons were already there. Demetrious didn't like Pooch and me arriving together.

"You two been talking?"

"Only about actors and acting," I said.

He gave me a long fishy look before deciding to drop it.

"So let's hear the big problem."

"I'm going to have to play devil's advocate," I said. I found myself facing five puzzled faces and decided to stick to the kind of dialogue I was paid to write. "No matter how you slice it," I said, "there ain't a million bucks in the pie."

I went on to spell out the numbers, most of which they knew as well as I did. The betting handle at Santa Anita averages out at around four hundred and fifty thousand dollars per race. That's for straight win, place and show bets. Then there are the exotics, the daily double and the exactas and the Pick-Six which had just been intro-

duced. These fattened the pot and we had to fix a race
when it was at its fattest. There would be times during
any racing day when the money in the cashiers' tills
might go over the million-dollar mark. But as soon as
the result of a race became official there'd be everybody
with a winning ticket lining up for his payoff. The only
leftovers would be the seventeen percent that went to
the track and the government and what was there from
the exotic bets. And at no time would that come anywhere near a million dollars.

"How much is there in the daily double pool?" said
Demetrious. I was sure he knew and was just testing my
research. The daily double money, of course, is in the
tills before the first race and not paid out until after the
second. So, by fixing the first we'd be long gone before
the shortage of cash was noticed.

"It depends on which day," I said. "Wednesdays average about two hundred and fifty thousand. Weekends are
more."

"The first race is tougher to fix," said Pooch.

"How come?" Demetrious seemed surprised.

"The jocks like to have something on the double," said
Pooch. All jockeys bet through their agents or cousins
and they invariably bet on the same horse.

"Then the first race is out," said Demetrious. He gave
me a signal to continue.

"The Pick-Six gives us a couple hundred thousand
cushion," I said.

The Pick-Six jackpot was starting to catch on but hadn't
reached anywhere near the proportions it would later.
At that time the "Six" ran from the second race through
the seventh. So the one thing I knew for sure was that
our race had to be one of those. The seventh was a possibility because the jackpot results weren't announced

until about ten minutes after the race finished. But it would give us more time to get away if we chose one of the earlier races. I said as much. I also said it should be an exacta race because that would fatten the tills and make the coup less obvious.

"It's gotta be the fifth," said Gus.

"Genius." Demetrious flattened him with the word. It was obvious to all of us, except maybe the Kid, that we were stuck with the fifth race. It was the only exacta race between the second and the sixth.

"Shit," said Pooch. "Small field."

This was generally true. The fifth race usually had fewer horses than the others and you don't get odds of more than fifteen or twenty-to-one in a small field. We needed longer odds than that.

"Then we gotta see it ain't small," said Demetrious.

"We're still skirting the real problem," I said.

I spelled it out again. The problem was all those winning tickets in other people's hands. When the Kid managed to freeze the odds at higher than they should be, those tickets would also be worth proportionately more. So there still wouldn't be enough left in the tills for us.

"You're forgetting a couple of things," said Demetrious.

"Like what?"

"My bets," he said. "I can get maybe five grand down in Vegas and lay off another couple with books here." Seven thousand at forty-to-one. The pot was growing. "Also, a lotta mugs don't pick up their winnings until they make their bets for the next race."

"I thought of that," I said. "But it's more true of small payoffs. With a long shot, we can't count on it."

"Maybe," he said. From his lips, this was a concession.

A long and glum silence followed. Demetrious finally

broke it by putting some figures down on his yellow pad and talking them.

"So there's let's say four hundred grand in from straight bets and another two hundred from the exacta. And figure half the winners don't pick up their dough right away."

"Make it a third to be safe," I said.

"Okay, a third. So that's a third of six hundred thousand."

"Two hundred Gs," said Pooch.

"No shit," said Demetrious. He wrote down more numbers. "Plus a couple hundred from the Pick-Six and I pick up maybe two-fifty more from Vegas and books."

"Six-fifty," said Pooch. He ignored the look he got. "I settle for that."

"I won't," said Demetrious.

His pencil kept scratching on the pad, but whatever was written down was soon crossed out. Nobody spoke. I found myself watching the Kid. During all my talking, he hadn't looked very concerned. I'd had the impression again that he was only interested in the cables and conduits underneath the track and not in what was happening on it. But now he seemed to realize that he might not get the chance to do his thing.

"What if I drop the odds first?" he said.

"Yeah," said Demetrious.

He'd caught on immediately and I still hadn't. I was again reminded of how stupid it was to think I could beat a bookie.

The Kid's idea was simple. All good ideas are. If he could freeze the odds on our horse for three clicks it would be duck soup for him to set those odds first at any number he wanted. Suppose, for example, that the few bucks bet on the nag by the miracle believers would make it a ninety-nine-to-one shot. Ninety-nine was as high as the tote board went, though the real odds could be much higher. Demetrious used round figures so that even his goons could understand. If the real odds were a hundred-to-one and the Kid dropped them to forty-to-one, the pipe-dreamers would only be picking up forty percent of what they were entitled to. That left the other sixty percent or about another two hundred and fifty thousand dollars in the tills. The total had now passed the nine hundred thousand mark. I expected Demetrious to settle for that.

"Maybe I can get down another few grand in Vegas," he said.

I'd been so involved with the insurmountable problem that I hadn't finalized all the details of who would do what when. So I had to wing some of it. I made the mistake of thinking Demetrious would be one of us at the track on the big day. But he set that straight. For one thing, he was too recognizable and there'd be a line of big mouths eavesdropping on his bet. For another, he had to be on the phone making his last-minute bets in Vegas and with the other illegal bookies in town.

Pooch and the Kid would be otherwise occupied, so that left Damon and Gus and me to hit the big play windows at just the right time. We were sticking to the magic odds of forty-to-one and there'd be a total of six hundred thousand in the tills that we could take out. That meant each of the three of us had to plunk down five thousand dollars.

"You did a good job." Demetrious's compliment came out of nowhere. "You're in for the whole ten percent."

"And where do I get my stake money?" I said.

"From me," said Demetrious.

Then he summarized the essentials. The fix would be on the fifth race the following Wednesday. We'd have one more meeting the day before. This one was ready to be adjourned.

"All we need now," I said, "is the right horse."

"Leave that to me," said Pooch.

"It's gotta be one that a lot of idiots won't play." The worrywart in me was showing.

"You ever see Invidious run?"

"Shut up," snapped Demetrious, but the name was out.

"They gotta know sometime," muttered Pooch.

I had seen Invidious run. But that had been in the bullring track at Pomona at least three years ago. And he'd been coming apart at the seams *then*.

"Don't tell me he's still around," I said.

"Even the glue factory wouldn't take him," said Pooch.

Not that this would increase suspicion until too late. More than one glue factory reject had come in at long odds at a major track.

"So that's it," said Demetrious. "And anybody who says Invidious before three o'clock Wednesday will wish he didn't."

He looked straight at me when he said this. But I don't think he trusted my discretion less than the others. He was operating on instinct and he was right. I was the one most likely to say Invidious. I was the only one in the room who knew what it meant.

Chapter 22

BLOOD ON THE TUBE

Original Teleplay
by
COREY BURDICK and QUENTIN DOOKES

First Draft

I HAD GOOD reasons for letting him in on the act. By keeping the few brain cells he had occupied, I reduced the risk of violence. And by working on the script with him around the clock I kept him out of Bambi's bed.

The title was his. So were the descriptions of the characters and just about everything they said and did. I made a suggestion here and there to keep it looking like a collaboration and did all the typing.

FADE IN:

EXT. TELEVISION STUDIO   DAY

A Bus stops at the corner and BAMBI gets off. She's carrying a suitcase. She's terrific-

looking. She starts across the street toward
the studio.

CLOSE SHOT—POLICE CAR
It's black and white and squeals to a stop in
front of her. BIGGS gets out, all slow and
thinking he's something, the way cops do. He
walks with this thumbs in his belt toward
BAMBI.

It soon became obvious that he knew a hell of a lot
more about television than I did. I'd watched it rarely
since its golden days in the fifties. He seemed to have
seen every show that ever was.

"Ain't nuthin' to do in Venables but drink and fuck
and watch the tube."

What better source for her dubbing it a barfy box. He'd
not only watched it, he'd memorized everything on it. If
I questioned any of his dumb ideas, he'd quote chapter
and verse, program and star.

"That ain't the way Jack Lord did it in 'Hawaii Five-
O.'" And he'd tell and usually act out exactly the way
Jack Lord did it in "Hawaii Five-O" and the way Tom
Selleck did it in "Magnum, P.I." and somebody in "Mis-
sion Impossible" and somebody else in "Fantasy Island"
and on and on it went.

CLOSE SHOT—BAMBI AND BIGGS

He looks her over, the way cops do.

BIGGS
You're jaywalking, Miss.

BAMBI
I'm sorry, officer. I didn't know. I just got
here.

>   BIGGS
> Ignorance of the law is no excuse. That's
> going to cost you a twenty-eight dollar fine.

>   BAMBI
>   (aghast)
> Twenty-eight dollars!

I told him along about here that opening scenes were
best kept brief and short on dialogue.
"Not in 'Hill Street Blues' they ain't."

>   BAMBI
> All right, officer. I'll pay you soon as I
> get a job.

>   BIGGS
> And when and where will that be?

>   BAMBI
> Today and right here, I hope.

Then she points toward the TELEVISION
STUDIO.

>   BIGGS
> You know anything about television?

>   BAMBI
> Well, back home there ain't nothing to do
> but make love and watch the tube.

Getting him to agree to leave out drinking as the other
local activity took some doing. I finally persuaded him
that most viewers didn't like heroines who drank.
"It's frustratin' not bein' able to write things the way
they are," he said.
I heartily agreed.

DISSOLVE TO:

INT. CORRIDOR—TELEVISION STUDIO

DAY

> BAMBI comes along, pushing a refreshment
> cart. She wears a thing like a waitress. She
> opens one of the doors and yells in.

BAMBI
Doughnuts! Crullers! Coffee!

This was the only scene resembling anything in my treatment.

INT. CONTROL ROOM   DAY

> THREE MEN with stocking masks over their
> faces are doing something to one of the
> complicated machines that sends the pictures
> out to millions of American homes. The door
> suddenly opens and BAMBI leans in.

BAMBI
Doughnuts! Crullers! Coff . . . . !

> Her jaw drops open when she sees the men.
> She turns and runs. They run after her.

I tried to talk him out of the stocking masks. I tried to convince him that it would be better if the men were in the shadows but thought she'd seen their faces.

"They always wore stocking masks in 'Starsky and Hutch'."

I dropped my case.

INT. STAIRWAY   DAY

> BAMBI is running as fast as she can. The
> stairway's only there in case of fire, so there's
> nobody else using it.

CLOSE SHOT—BAMBI

She stops on a landing and listens. Three lots
of footsteps are coming at her from above. She
starts running again.

INT. BOILER ROOM   DAY

BAMBI comes running in. She can't go any
lower. It's dark. She makes her way between
the boilers and is grabbed.

                CLOSE SHOT—BAMBI

She looks up in stark naked fear at the man
who grabbed her.

                     BAMBI
     Officer Biggs!

                     BIGGS
     Well, hello again.

"What's Biggs doing in the boiler room?"
"Lookin' for a bomb," he said.
"Shouldn't we explain that?"
"What for?"

                     BAMBI
     Help! There's three men chasing me.

                     BIGGS
     Only three? There must be more fairies in
     L.A. than I thought.

Dookes laughed so much when he came up with that
gem that he had to take off his glasses and wipe his eyes.
I didn't think it the time to tell him that no network
continuity-acceptance department would approve it.
    In all honesty, I was beginning to enjoy what we were

doing. My suggestions became more frequent and closer to his way of thinking. I began to feel all sense and reason and logic slipping away. It was a pleasant feeling.

"I think that we should be very clear in our own minds what those three men were up to."

"They're Commies," he said.

"But we have to give them a specific plan."

He came up with it all by himself. Of course, I don't know how much it owed to "Magnum, P.I." and "Hawaii Five-O" and all the "Starsky and Hutch"es.

The Russians had found an ingenious way to make the first strike. They'd infiltrated television-set assembly lines and had little valves, that were invisible to the naked eye, planted behind the picture tubes. Dookes and I spent a good ten minutes debating whether the sets should be imported or domestic. He leaned toward Sonys, Sanyos and Toshibas. I favored Sylvanias, Magnavoxes and Emersons. We finally decided on both.

The gimmick was that when a certain image was projected by this particular network, all the sets tuned in to that channel would explode. Dookes had drawn on his own personal experience here. When twelve years old, he'd taken off the back of a television set and had been blown across the room. It was as good an explanation as any for the end of his mental development.

"And the set only was on for about ten minutes."

Since most TV sets in America were rarely turned off, the implanted, invisible valve would approximate a hundred times that voltage buildup.

"Shouldn't we explain that?"

"What for?"

He was right. What for? This was television. This was entertainment. This was to keep people from thinking about sickness and death and what their lives were all about. This was to keep them from wondering what anything was about.

The plot thickened and I warmed even more to my task. Bambi waltzed in a few times to listen and pull faces. The third time, she had put on a nightgown. I'd never seen her in one and he looked like he hadn't either. The steel-rimmed octagonal glasses came off and were blown on and wiped and replaced so he could see her better.

"Maybe we better take a break, Old Fucker."

"We're going good," I said. "And the network's screaming for the script."

That was Sunday night about eleven. I convinced him that, if we kept going, we could deliver the first draft the next day. Bambi gave me a grateful smile before going off to bed alone.

Dookes and I agreed that Officer Biggs should be married to a woman who didn't appreciate him. Also that he be devoted to his seven-year-old son, so that going off with our fictional Bambi shouldn't be too easy. Also that Bambi and Biggs be ensnarled in endless police and network red tape while trying to unravel the Communist plot. I don't remember which one of us came up with the scene where a rookie cop accidentally stumbles across it and is shot through the heart and just manages to tell Biggs what he's found out before he dies. But I came up with the sequence that followed. Biggs's first thought is to save his little boy from the explosion that could go off any second. He drives home wildly, with Bambi in the car trying to calm him down. He runs into his nice little house in Sherman Oaks to find his son watching some moronic puppet show on television. Biggs grabs the set, races into the bathroom and dumps it into the tub. And his wife, who's taking a foam bath, gets an instant home permanent. I was proud of coming up with that.

"Maybe we'd better talk about the image," I said.

"What image?"

"The one that comes on the screen and blows up a third of the country."

"I already figured that out."

"Want to let me in on it?"

"I should think a smart old fucker like you could guess."

"It'll save time if you just tell me."

"It's gotta be somethin' special, right?"

"Right."

"If it ain't somethin' unusual, it could come on TV by mistake and ruin everything."

"Absolutely."

"So what's so special it can't come on by mistake?"

I tried to think of something clever to say, but couldn't. I also didn't like the way he was licking his lips.

"Come on, Old Fucker. What's never been on TV?"

"Your molars and mine," I said.

"An' how about a big close-up of a nice, juicy pussy?"

He sat waiting for my reaction. He was actually serious.

"Quentin, we can't put that in our script."

"Why not?" His wet mouth went tight.

"This is network television," I said. "It reaches a national audience. The show will be on prime time for family viewing. During prime time, except for tampon and hemorrhoid-ointment commercials, there is no life below the waist."

"It's goin' inta the script," he said.

And so it went in, in his exact words. The first-time-ever image would be projected from Maine to California, followed by eight hundred and seventy-four thousand

explosions for every point the network got in the Nielsen
ratings.

My predicted work schedule turned out to be right. By
the time the sun came up, we were on the last page.

INT. MOTEL ROOM   NIGHT

    BIGGS and BAMBI are in bed together, looking
    at what's left of the TV set. There ain't much
    left, just part of the box and some broken
    glass. There ain't much left of the room either.
    Or the motel, either.

                 BIGGS
    Now there ain't nothing to watch.

                 BAMBI
    What we going to do?

The real Bambi came in, rubbing the sleep from her
eyes, and I typed on.

    BIGGS looks her over.

                 BIGGS
    Can't you think of something?

                 BAMBI
    Nope.

                 BIGGS
    I can.

    He kisses her like he means business and
    turns out the light.

    FADE OUT
               THE END

Dookes insisted that Bambi sit down and read the whole script right away. She started it while I scrambled some eggs. He must have forgotten or had never known what a slow reader she was. He wolfed down his eggs and went out to the patio and I could see him pacing. I didn't like her infrequent page-turning any more than he did and joined him.

"Relax," I said. "It's only a first draft."

"What the hell she know about writin', anyway?"

"Exactly."

I knew from experience that a writer in this state had to be agreed with, even a writer who wasn't psychotic.

"You think those network guys'll like it?"

"Well . . ." I had to hedge this one. "It does depart a lot from the treatment."

"But it's better, ain't it?"

"I like it better," I said.

We waited together for Bambi's verdict. We saw her turn over the last page of the script and we gave her about ten seconds of what he called "mullin' time" before going back in.

"What d'ya think?" he said.

"Is this what you two been doin' all night?" She tapped the neat stack of typewritten pages.

"Ya know fuckin' well," he said. "Ya like it?"

" 'Bout as much as I like moose-turd pie," she said.

He went for her throat with both hands but I grabbed him from behind and slowed him down enough for her to get away. By the time he shook me off she was in the bedroom with the door locked. It was an easier door to break down than the front one. Two kicks and it began to give.

"Don't," I said. "You've got to learn to take criticism."

"Not from her!" He kicked the door again and the bottom panel splintered.

"It's the dumbest script I ever read!" yelled Bambi. It sounded like her voice was coming from the en suite bathroom.

I thought it the worst thing she could have said. But she knew her man better than I did.

"You never read a script before!" he yelled back.

"An' you never wrote one before!"

"The trouble with you is you're ignorant."

"Look who's talkin'."

"If it's so dumb, you ain't gonna want to be in it."

"There ain't gonna be nuthin' to be in."

She gave me a clue with that one. I pretended to share his indignation.

"If she feels like that, we'll get someone else to play Bambi."

"You're damn right," he said. The idea began to calm him down.

Which brings me back to the third reason I went through with the whole charade. Somewhere near the beginning, I'd decided to deliver whatever we came up with to Averies.

Perry had mailed me the contract with the network and I'd signed and returned it. By now, it would have been countersigned and binding. It was a standard Guild contract and it called for payment of two-thirds of the total fee upon delivery of the first draft teleplay. It didn't say the teleplay had to be acceptable or even literate. As long as the script was in proper format, I was entitled to two-thirds of thirty-five thousand dollars when I turned it in. I'd decided to have six copies made at Barbara's Place, the best script service in town, and was on the patio reading over the pages for typos when he came out.

"Maybe we should change her name back to Loretta," he said.

"Good idea," I said. "The typing service will do it."

I would also have to make a change in the title page. The copies I delivered to the network would give me a solo writing credit. I wasn't hogging it. The contract didn't allow for my having a collaborator.

Chapter 23

THE FINAL meeting at Demetrious's place was on Tuesday morning. My cover story to Dookes was that I was going to drop in at the network. I told him that Averies probably hadn't read the script yet, but some of his assistants might have and I wanted to sound out their reactions.

All the racing arrangements had been made. Invidious was entered in the fifth and, barring scratches, there'd be nine horses in the field. Pooch was down for the ride and had also managed to get one in the first race. It would have looked more suspicious if the long shot he brought in was his only mount of the day. Nothing was said about the arrangements with the other jockeys, and I didn't ask.

I went through the itinerary I'd laid out. I left the Kid's schedule up to him and all Pooch had to do was steer Invidious to the finish line without falling off. Demetrious would be at his desk, making his phone bets in the last two minutes before the off. That left Damon and Gus and me.

The approximate starting time of the fifth race was 3:05, so the betting on it would begin about twenty minutes to three. The Kid would start dropping the odds on Invidious at a quarter to. He'd do it gradually, so as not to start a stampede from the tote-board believers, and freeze them at forty-to-one. There are always some nuts in the stands with slide rules and calculators and it was possible that a few of them would divide the proportionate amounts on each horse and discover that the odds on Invidious should be more like a hundred-to-one. But we had to take that chance. Besides, slide-rule boys are always two-dollar bettors.

With the odds frozen, the Kid would shift to pinching off the cables that recorded our bets. He said he'd need five minutes to do it. That brought us close to three o'clock. I thought that was drawing it too fine. No matter how carefully we timed it we had to allow for the unexpected—a cashier's machine jamming or a spread player betting every horse in the race and slowing down the line. But there weren't any minutes left to shave off, so we agreed on three o'clock sharp as the kickoff time. Damon and Gus and I would then have ninety seconds maximum to make our bets.

I'd assigned myself the window in the Club House that was reserved for big bettors. Damon would make his in the hall of the general admission section, also at the large transaction window. Gus got the smaller hall near the quarter pole. He was going to have to bet at a regular window and I told him to use window number twelve because it seemed to get the heaviest action.

We discussed transportation, whether the three of us should go to the track separately or together. I favored different cars and Demetrious wanted to know why.

"Cars break down," I said. "Cars are run into by other cars."

"What about afterwards?"

"We all meet back here and divide up our just deserts."

"Never mind the fancy talk." He gave it another few seconds' thought. "Okay. You go in your own car." He turned to Damon. "You go with Gus."

"I also think we should be there before the first race," I said.

"What for?"

"The more normal everything appears the better. There are too many sharp eyes and noses at the track and too many big mouths. We don't want to walk in like we're robbing a bank. In fact, I think we should make some token bets on the earlier races."

"He's right," said Pooch Padilla.

"With your own money," said Demetrious. "I know you guys. You'll start with your hunches and go through a few hundred before the fifth."

"Good point," I said. "No matter what, we don't bite into our stake."

Demetrious took out the biggest wad of money I'd ever seen and divided it into three neat piles. He told me to count mine in front of him. There were fifty fifties and twenty-five hundred-dollar bills.

"Five thousand exactly," I said.

"And you bring back two hundred and five thousand."

"Maybe a little more." The actual payoff usually comes to more than the official odds. Most two-to-ones return $6.20 or $6.40. In this case, that little bit extra could come to four or five grand.

"Don't lose any part of it," he said. There was a double

edge to the advice. He wasn't just talking about getting rolled.

In my better days, I often went to the track with two thousand or more on me. Luckily, the one time I had my pocket picked was late in the day and I'd already lost most of my stake. But it taught me not to keep all my cash in one pocket. Demetrious stood waiting for me to put away the five thousand, but I deliberately made a ritual of it. Twenty of the hundreds went into my wallet. The other five and ten fifties went into my other breast pocket with my glasses. Then twenty fifties in my left pants pocket and the other twenty in my right.

"Good idea," said Demetrious. He turned to his goons who'd been watching the whole routine. "You guys do the same thing."

That left the synchronization of watches. The Kid's looked like the dashboard of a 747. There was no way it couldn't be accurate, but Demetrious got the exact time on the phone to make sure. Then we all set our minute hands.

"Just like in a movie," said the Kid.

It was the first time he'd ever spoken to me directly. He was grinning as usual. I didn't have the heart to tell him that in a movie all the things that go wrong can be reshot.

"Okay," said Demetrious. "The race should be official by a quarter after three." He motioned to the two goons and me. "You guys be at the windows waiting to collect. By twenty after, you're outta there."

"Should we use valet parking?" asked Damon.

"You don't use anything you can do yourself." Demetrious said it wearily. "How many times I gotta tell you?"

"That's another reason for getting there early," I said. "We'll be able to park closer to the stands."

"By half past at the latest you're outta the parking lot." Demetrious went on with his timetable. "Take the Harbor Freeway down and the Santa Monica across." He pointed to the floor between us. "By four-thirty, you'd better be standing there."

"What about us?" Pooch included the Kid in his hand movement.

"We'll wait right here for ya," said Demetrious. He stopped to think something through. "Tell you what. I'll give you your cuts off the top. It'll take me a couple days to get mine from the bookies."

"If you can't trust your bookie," I said, "who *can* you trust?"

"Yeah," said Demetrious.

Chapter 24

DOOKES COULDN'T wait. He came out of the house as I got out of my car. But he'd made a concession to passing motorists and put his pants on.

"What'd they say?"

"Nothing yet." I sounded like an obstetrician comforting a first-time father—a movie obstetrician, that is. The one who'd brought Zachary into the world kept puffing cigar smoke in my face and talking about marlin fishing.

Dookes followed me into the house. "When they gonna read it?"

"They scheduled a script meeting for tomorrow noon," I said, "so they'll all have to read it by then."

"Mr. Averies too?"

"He'll probably just get a synopsis from one of his flunkies."

"An' you gotta be there noon tomorrow?"

"That's right." I'd decided to say this on the drive back. It would get me out of the house and to Santa Anita in plenty of time. I hadn't yet figured out the lie I'd tell him when I got back. I had bigger things on my mind.

"Ain't that a funny time for a script meetin'?"

"Not at a network," I said. "They'll give me their general thoughts for an hour, then we'll break for lunch, then go back to the conference table for their nit-picking."

I was just complimenting myself on how well it all fit together when he swung. This time he caught me flush on the temple. I spun almost a full circle while staggering backwards and, if I hadn't landed on the couch, I might have kept going through the French doors and into the pool. He was immediately on top of me, one knee on my chest and an elbow crushing my Adam's apple.

"There was a phone call for ya right after ya left." He waited until I managed to make a croaking sound. "From his secretary. Mr. Averies wants ya there for a meetin' at two o'clock today." He pressed harder and I could feel my eyeballs coming out on stalks. "So what's this horseshit about tomorrow?"

I couldn't have come up with a ready answer even if I'd been able to speak. But the fact that he'd spared my face so far gave me hope. He wanted me at that meeting today and looking presentable. He was going to let me live, at least for a little while. But, if he didn't let some air through my windpipe soon, I wasn't going to make it. I tried to tell him that and another croaking sound came out. I was only dimly aware that I was fighting back.

There are times when standard movie dialogue is just right. This was one of them. If I'd been able to, I would have grunted some: "You've gone too far this time, you bastard!" or "You ain't the only one who played high school football, Dookes."

Of course, I'd played it long before he was born. I'd

played it when there were ends instead of wide receivers and the quarterbacks, not the coaches, called the plays. I also wasn't that good. It was a subject better left alone. I groped for a carotid artery. I arched my back to shift his weight and did contortions with my legs to try to get one of my shoes over his head and under his chin. Nothing worked.

A numbness was expanding in my brain. All thought was disappearing, all concern, and I didn't care. There was nothing to be missed by leaving the planet now, no words still to be written, no great statements to be made. I'd been right about death coming in ludicrous disguise. I should have guessed that it wore a ten-gallon hat and octagonal glasses. There was only one last strand of remorse left, that I wouldn't live to see the fixed race the next day. But I'd never really believed we'd get away with it. The only thing I'd never know was where I'd miscalculated, which hole in my scenario led to disaster. But it was all unimportant now, thoroughbred speed and literary grace and money, all were the same and fading fast. All that was left was the core of me. No tunnel, no fading of the light—they were Hollywood hokum, too. Just the core, hard and rough and colorless and incredibly small. This was death, being reduced to this infinitesimal speck of dust. And this was what would soon rise to join all the others. Smog was a trillion spirits farting, nothing more. End of dialogue forever. FADE OUT.

And I would have died then and there if Bambi hadn't come in.

"What you fightin' about this time?" Her voice echoed from far away. "Somethin' to do with that dumb script?"

"You stop callin' it dumb!" He turned toward her as he yelled and that eased the weight on my throat.

"What'm I s'posed to call it—brilliant?"

I was managing to sip some air, but they both looked fuzzy. So did the heavy ceramic ashtray on the coffee table, but it came into focus first. Then the back of his thick neck as he stood up, still facing her.

"You oughta be ashamed, hittin' an old man."

"He's been lyin' to me."

"About what?"

"I dunno yet."

"Ya never will if he's dead."

They went on this way, back and forth, getting nowhere. And all I had to do was combine the ashtray with the back of his neck. I lurched to my feet and was just about to try it when she got between us.

"You shouldn't lie to Quentin," she said.

I thought her move was intentional, that she'd guessed what I was about to do and didn't think it would work. I took her line as a cover-up, too, until she followed it with a roundhouse slap to my face. It stung. And while I was rubbing my cheek, she went and patted his. The patting hurt more than the slap.

"Never you mind." She was cooing to him now. "I'll make you a nice Smitty's Special for lunch." Then she seemed to remember me. "You can have one, too, but you don't deserve it."

We adjourned to the kitchen. She kept fluttering around Dookes as she probably had around the long-haul drivers in the diner. Through her coquetry seemed to calm him down, I could have lived without it. I'd never been able to understand the attraction of opposites. Not that it was hard to guess what a slobbering pig like him saw in a slender nymph like her. It was the reverse angle that was unfathomable. Still, I'd seen it at premieres dozens of times, lily-white creatures with aristocratic bone structure hanging on the arms of lemurs who'd had lucky hits.

A Smitty's Special turned out to be a ground beef patty layered with green pepper strips and onion rings and simmered in a sauce made from beef bouillon cubes. I finally knew why she'd included beef bouillon cubes on her shopping list.

"It ain't all your fault that the script's so awful." She tried to console him as she served him first. "He musta done a lot of it." My plate was shoved unceremoniously toward me. "And he's so dumb, he don't even know great actin' when he sees it."

She'd stopped to stroke his cropped, thinning hair when she delivered that. She was behind him, so he couldn't see the broad wink she gave me. Only then did I catch on. But I had an excuse for not doing so sooner. My head was still numb from his punches.

So it had all been an act and I owed my existence to her talent. I gave no sign of acknowledgment, but as she went on, playing him the way the truly great ones played the balcony, I tried to make my silence more appreciative. A good actress would be sensitive to that and, if the last ten or fifteen minutes were any sample, she was more than good. I looked forward to the time I'd be able to tell her that. I'd expand on it. I'd tell her that she had Hepburn's panther grace and Harlow's sexiness, plus the rare ability to improvise her own dialogue. Meanwhile, I could only sneak her a quick, grateful smile.

"What you grinnin' at?" Dookes had caught it.

"Why not?" I said. "I like the food. I like the company."

"You won't like it for long if you don't tell me where you was this mornin'."

"I went to a meeting."

"What kind of meeting?"

"It's called a pitch session," I said. "I pitched an idea for a movie."

"So why'd ya tell me different?" His boar eyes were narrowing in a way I was learning to fear.

"Because, if this one happens, I want to write it alone." I said it defiantly and it rang with conviction. The danger light dimmed and he gobbled some more Smitty's Special. "And I have another important meeting tomorrow," I said.

He was holding his fork in his right hand and his knife in the other. He stared at me between tines and blade as if considering using them on me.

"You gotta be at that network at two o'clock today," he said.

"I know. I'll leave in a few minutes."

"An' after that you don't go nowhere without me."

"Don't be ridiculous," I said. "My meeting tomorrow could go on for hours."

"An' I'm gonna' be right there with ya," he said.

I watched him break off a piece of bread and sop up the last of his beef bouillon gravy. I think it was then that the germ of the plot twist first reared its gorgeous head.

Chapter 25

A LARGER NETWORK conference room had been commandeered for the occasion. Its table was more polished and its leather armchairs were deeper, so it took Averies' kind of posture to avoid insignificance.

Nobody got up to greet me when I arrived. There were none of the firm handshakes and offhand quips that had accompanied my other two appearances. The pimply girl smiled faintly and the computer expert nodded. Otherwise, I was ignored. I started to take the nearest empty seat.

"I think Mr. Averies would like you to sit there." The staff assistant pointed to the chair that would have me directly facing the head of the table. I took it and we waited for Averies. There was no mistaking the courtroom atmosphere.

Averies wore a suit and tie. He'd probably just returned from a Le Serre lunch with one or more of his higher-ups. He had a copy of "Blood on the Tube" in his hand. He placed it on the table in front of his chair before sitting down. Then he interlaced his fingers, using them to prop his chin, and stared at the script as if his first words were hidden somewhere inside.

"I take it we have all read Mr. Burdick's master-piece." He didn't wait for sounds of assent. "Would any-one like to venture an opinion before I give mine?" It was the typical lip service to democracy that precedes an execution. There were no volunteers. "Was anyone amused?" This time Averies looked down the rows of faces. All were pointed somewhere else. His eyes arrived at me. "It appears," he said, "that we are not amused."

I was enjoying his act. It was one of the very few can't-lose encounters I'd ever been in. He could insult the script as much as he wanted. It wasn't mine. And no matter what he called it, it had to be paid for and part of the money would buy a Porsche 944 and good-bye Quentin.

"It's obvious to me," he said, "that Mr. Burdick is one of those people who prefers his fictions real and unspar-ing and true." His steady gaze shifted to me again. "Would that be an accurate assessment, Mr. B.?"

"Sometimes," I said.

"Only sometimes? Not even most of the time?"

"No," I said. "Only sometimes."

"And so we come to the oldest struggle of mankind: one version of truth against another."

"It had a few predecessors," I said. But he wasn't being detoured.

"Your version of the truth as opposed to ours." His use of the plural was deliberate. "Ours, of course, is out in the open. It's on public display between commercials." He smiled as he savored his candor. "So let's hear more about yours."

"My version is sort of personal," I said.

"But detectable to the intelligent eye."

"You having a good time, Averies?"

"Why not?" he said. "You've had yours." He motioned disdainfully toward the script.

"Then enjoy yourself." I made my postscript unmistakable. "Your company's paying for it."

"Perhaps truth is too abstract for you," he said. "Maybe you prefer facts—hard, honest facts."

"Sometimes."

"Your favorite word again. So what do we compare? Worthy causes contributed to? Ballots cast? How about the substance of our daily lives?"

"You call it."

"Of course, I have you at a disadvantage," he said. "Your mature years are evident. And I've met your young lady. And Mason, there, happened to notice your car in the parking lot."

"All of which proves?"

"A great deal," he said. "And it brings us back to your version of truth and how often we encounter it ad nauseam in this medium we're all so devoted to."

"I have one question," I said.

"Ask it."

"Why do you have to have an audience?" I spread my hands to include all his attentive underlings.

"I'll answer that gladly." He made a production of getting up and walking halfway along the table toward me as he spoke. "My staff is here because you've mocked them as well as me. I hope you don't think you're the first half-assed intellectual pretender who's done so. And every one of them has been middle-aged or older and shacked up with a young woman—and stooping to our level only out of financial necessity." He made it back to his starting point before delivering the dagger. "I'm afraid, Mr. B., that the very stuff of your life makes a more sudsy soap opera than anything emanating from this building."

When you've been added up to zero, there's only one thing left to say and I said it.

"I don't know what you're talking about."

"I'm talking about this garbage!" Averies came as close to screaming as he ever would and his fist came down on the script like a hammer.

"Nothing I write is garbage!" I yelled it right back. You don't live through as many script rewrites as I have without learning the tricks of the trade. I'd once had a reputation for recalcitrance and it had been deserved. When I'd been solvent I was nobody's punching bag. I'd seen plenty of Averies come and go and I was still on my feet. Practically.

He knew all the tricks, too. After the shouting came the sweet reason. He was the good cop and bad cop combined.

"What I'm trying to ascertain," he said quietly, "is the frame of mind that prompted this effort." No fist this time, but his nod toward the script was almost as bad.

"Money," I said.

"Money is not a frame of mind. Try again. How exactly would you describe this?"

"I'd call it the revenge of F. Scott Fitzgerald."

"I'm talking about the genre?"

"Satire, of course."

"Satire? I don't recall asking for a satire." He turned to his staff members. "Did anyone hear me mention the word?"

"I assumed it," I said. "It never occurred to me that you were being serious in our other meetings."

"So you decided to satirize what we discussed. All by

your lonesome self, you came to this momentous decision." He was using the same tone I'd so often used on
Bambi.

"Satire," I said, "is the last flicker of originality in a
boring time."

"And in what fortune cookie did you find that?" Every
member of his staff laughed at that one, a few of them
too much. I contributed the smile I gave a tennis oppo-
nent when he served an ace. "I haven't the time to enter
into a quoting bee," he said. "I offer you only one. 'Ninety-
nine hundredths of all the work done in the world is either
foolish and unnecessary or harmful and wicked.' "

"I'll buy that," I said.

"And this falls into the foolish category." He punched
the script again.

"I think it fairly reflects your contempt for your audience."

"Don't give me that!" It was the bad cop's turn. "You
start telling me about the innate intelligence and taste
of the American public and I'm going to throw up all
over this nice typing job."

"In that case, why don't you like the script?"

"Because it's contemptuous of me," he said. "Because
it's *deliberately* foolish, because the so-called satire falls
flat, because it's monosyllabic and idiotic and crude and
because you know goddam well that we can't show a close-
up of a cunt during prime time."

I thought he'd aimed for a laugh, but no one was
laughing. Averies picked up the script and hefted it.

"So if we remove the banalities and the terrible grammar and semiliterate dialogue, what do we have?"

"A lot of blank paper," said the pimpled girl.

"Not true!" Averies said it sharply enough to make

her recoil. "We then have something with definite possibilities." He turned back the mauve cover I'd picked
out at the typing bureau. "So let's go through it scene by
scene."

Chapter 26

HE WAS SPLASHING in the pool and hadn't heard me drive
up. I was in no hurry to make him happy with the news.
I hadn't yet figured out how to do the revisions Averies
wanted without his knowing about it. I didn't want to
envision the night when he told the whole population of
Venables that his show was on television and his name
didn't appear on the screen. I didn't want to think about
what would happen after that. What I did want and need
was Bambi's advice on how to handle the situation. It
was time I let her in on why I'd got myself into it.

I found her in the bedroom on the floor. She was naked
and bleeding from the mouth, but she was conscious.

"What happened?" As if I didn't know.

"I couldn't talk him out of it this time." The words
were spaced. It hurt her to talk.

I wet a washcloth and wiped the blood from her mouth
and chin. Her lips were swollen, her face distorted by its
bruises.

"Should I get a doctor?" Another cliché. Another score
for Averies. She shook her head.

"Lift me onto the bed."

I did it as gently as I could, the way Laurence Olivier carried Merle Oberon to the window in *Wuthering Heights,* the way countless actors held countless actresses in countless pictures. Was there any act of man that hadn't already appeared on the motion picture screen?

"He just kept hittin' me," she said. She pointed weakly toward the raised red welts on her body. I could see his hamhock fists thudding into her. I could see him enjoying it.

"Don't talk," I said. I spread a blanket over her and sat on the edge of the bed and took her hand. "There's something I have to know. Just shake your head for yes or no." She nodded and waited. "Would you care if something bad happened to him?" It got a vehement no, but I had to make sure. "Are you absolutely certain? After all, you did marry him."

"Only because he said he'd kill me if I didn't." She looked like she was resurrecting the moment he'd said it. "And he would have."

That was all I wanted to know. I went out to the patio and waited for him to come up for air. When he did and saw me, I made sure my face gave nothing away. He treaded water and waited, but I was determined not to speak first.

"Well?" One breaststroke took him to the edge of the pool nearest me. He hung onto it. "Well, how do they like it?"

"Their exact words," I said, "were that it's the worst piece of shit that any retarded six-year-old ever wrote."

"You're joshin' me," he said.

"That was one of the nicer things they said."

He got out of the pool and picked up a towel and started

slowly drying himself off. I watched his hands and kept thinking of them hitting Bambi.

"But they still got to pay us," he said.

"They don't intend to," I said.

"Then I better go talk to them."

"It wouldn't do any good."

"Maybe I could teach 'em to sit on this and spin." He held up a middle finger to emulate the spindle.

"Networks are tougher to get into than Fort Knox," I said. "And the guards have real bullets."

My countering him was making him suspicious. All the time the towel made its way down his big, beefy body, he was studying me, trying to figure out what I might be up to.

"Of course, we can sue them for the money," I said, "but that could take years."

"Then I guess I'll just have to stick around," he said.

It was intended to be menacing, but I didn't care. I'd reached the same conclusion that John Wayne had come to so many times. The world wasn't big enough for both of us. It had to be either him or me.

"But something else has come up," I said. "Something that could cushion the blow."

"And what's that?"

"A way to make some easy money," I said. "Do you know anything about horse racing?"

Chapter 27

DURING THE OAK Tree meeting the races start at one o'clock. We left the house about noon which gave us plenty of time. I'd spent most of the morning briefing him, but went over it again in the car.

"Now play it back to me," I said.

"I don't do nuthin' until the fifth race," he said. "Then I wait until it shows five minutes to go and I get inta line at the bettin' winda'."

"Which window?"

"Number twelve."

"Keep going," I said.

"I get inta line and if it moves too quick, I keep lettin' the people behind me go first until the announcer says they're gettin' to the gate."

"The horses are now approaching the starting gate." I told him the exact words for the twentieth time.

"Then I plunk down the hundred smackers on the horse."

"On what horse?"

"In-vid-u-ous." He still couldn't say it right.

"You don't use the name. It'll be number seven. So what do you say when you make the bet?"

"One hundred dollars to win on number seven."

"That's it."

"And as soon as it wins, I get back inta line for my money."

"And?"

"And I meet you back where you park the car."

"The easiest four grand you'll ever make," I said.

I took the Baldwin Avenue off-ramp from the freeway. The traffic to the track was heavy, so I used the back streets. In Arcadia, they all look like sets from a Doris Day movie.

"An' you're sure In-vid-u-ous is gonna win today?"

"Is the Pope gonna pray today?"

"What's he got to do with it?"

"Nothing," I said. I fished out the two dollars for the general parking as we approached the entrance. "Invidious will win unless he has a heart attack or swallows his tongue."

"A lot of animals swallow their tongues when they run too hard."

Now I had something else to worry about. This on top of his not yet doing what I'd counted on him to do.

"Now you're to go into the General Admission section," I said. "That's where window number twelve is."

"Why's it have to be winda' twelve?"

"We ain't the only ones in on this coup. Everybody's been given a different window."

"Where you gonna be?"

"Never mind. I've got to stay by myself. I wasn't supposed to let anybody in on this. If we do happen to meet up, you don't know me. Got it?"

"Got it," he said.

I pulled into the nearest parking space I could find to the turnstiles, turned off the ignition, and fussed around getting my Racing Form and Digest and binoculars, and he still didn't make his move. If he didn't make it here and now, I'd figured him wrong and it was back to square one.

I'd gone over the numbers a dozen times the night before. B-minus was the best I ever got at math, so I'd needed paper and pencil to calculate the different payouts and how much I'd have to deliver to Demetrious in order to figure out how much to leave in my wallet.

I was supposed to bet five thousand at forty-to-one. Easy enough. I'd pick up two hundred grand plus what I'd bet. Demetrious had said we could all keep our share of the take up front, so all I'd have to give him was a hundred thousand and the five thousand he'd staked me to. No matter what the payoff was, the split was the same: half plus the five thousand stake money to him, the other half to me. It was my half that made my plan possible.

Dookes had to bet enough on Invidious to insure his own funeral. A five-hundred-dollar bet would bring its odds down to about thirty-five-to-one. A thousand-dollar bet would drop them to around thirty. I wanted them down to twenty-to-one. It would take a two-thousand-dollar bet at a time when the Kid didn't have the cables pinched off to do it.

Then, as far as Demetrious would know, I'd have put down his five grand and picked up a hundred thousand. He'd only have his half of it coming, so I only needed to bet twenty-five hundred dollars at twenty-to-one to wind up with the fifty thousand for him. About the seventh time I went over my figures, I caught my one small mistake. In order to give Demetrious fifty thousand plus his five thousand stake back, I'd have to bet exactly twenty-six hundred and fifty bucks.

After that, the arithmetic held up. I was going to have to give up most of my ten percent of whatever the take turned out to be, but not all of it. Letting Dookes have two thousand still left me three thousand less twenty-six fifty. I'd wind up with three hundred and fifty bucks times Invidious's odds. This would only amount to about seven thousand, so it would have cost me over ninety grand to get Quentin Dookes out of my life and out of Bambi's life and, unless I greatly underestimated Demetrious and his goons, out of everybody else's. But it was worth it.

I'd played Dookes like some of the best con artists had played me, warming him up to the joy of a killing at the track, telling him I'd told a double lie about where I'd been that morning, that I'd really spent it scrounging around for a stake. I said I'd come up with a total of four hundred dollars and that he could have one hundred of it to bet.

"Now why you bein' so generous, Old Fucker?"

"Because you found me in a compromising position with your wife and I'm still around."

I was able to say it with total honesty and that's what made it work. But the suspicious glint was there behind his glasses. Later, I managed to drop my wallet so he'd be sure to see how full it was. I didn't think Dookes would settle for a hundred or even four hundred after that. I guessed that he wouldn't settle for less than everything that was in it. And I'd figured out exactly how much that had to be. Then why wasn't he making his move? What was he waiting for?

"You got the hundred I gave you?" I said.

"Right here." He tapped the brocaded breast pocket of his white suit.

"Let's see it." I was stalling. I couldn't think of anything else to do.

"What for?"

"Because with this much at stake, it's smart to double-check everything."

He chewed that over before taking out the two fifties.

"Satisfied?"

"Good enough."

"Now let's see yours," he said.

"I've got mine," I said.

"Let's just make sure," he said.

"I'm sure." I turned to open the car door, hoping he wouldn't knock me cold from behind. It was a relief to be grabbed in a choke hold.

"You wanna hand over your wallet or you want me to take it?"

Anywhere else but a racetrack, somebody being strangled in a TR-6 with the top down wouldn't go unnoticed. Even allowing for my end of the struggle being faked, we could have gotten more than a passing glance from the zombies going by.

"Okay," I said. "Here." I managed to pull my wallet out and gave it to him.

"Looks pretty fat, Old Fucker."

He counted the money out on one knee, wetting his thumb when the bills didn't separate easily.

"I make it nineteen hundred," he said.

"So do I."

"You said we were goin' partners."

"I didn't say fifty-fifty."

"You didn't say you were hoggin' it, either."

"All right," I said. "So I'm greedy."

"Me too." His grin emphasized the space between his front teeth. He dropped my now-skinny wallet back into my lap.

"Wait a minute." I made my protest desperate. "You've got to leave me some of it."

"Empty out your pockets," he said.

There it was, the one thing I hadn't counted on.

I'd worn my baggiest pants. I'd scrutinized myself in the full-length mirror on the back of my bedroom door, turning every way to be sure the ten hundred-dollar bills in each pocket didn't make a revealing bulge.

"Or you want me to take your pants off?" he said.

The specter of a ludicrous death again. Found in a racetrack parking lot in shorts and shoes. I considered it. The end now or after the fifth race. Two and a half hours more of life. The same amount of hope. Something else I hadn't counted on could happen. Invidious *could* lose. I would have died pantless for nothing. I emptied my pockets.

"Well, whaddya know?" He finally finished counting it out. "It looks like I've got myself four thousand smackeroos."

"You're not keeping all of it."

"Nope," he said. "I'm betting it." He did his calculations out loud for my benefit. "Let's see, four thousand times forty is one hundred and sixty thousand."

"And what if the horse loses?"

"You said it couldn't."

"I've been wrong before."

I was stalling again, trying to think of how to get fifteen hundred of the money back, but afraid to push him too hard. It wasn't only my neck I was worried about. It was the thousand dollars in my left coat pocket that he hadn't yet cottoned on to. As long as I kept that, I had an outside chance.

"Tell you what," he said. "You meet me right here after the race. And if Inviduous wins it, I'm gonna give you a piece of my winnin's." He gave me a broad wink as he opened the car door on his side. "A nice *little* piece." He looked at the nearest post marking our parking row. "Forty-three B," he said. "I'll meet ya right here."

I sat watching him walk away. His white suit and hat made him a standout all the way to the turnstiles. He'd be an easy target for Damon and Gus. I had the consolation that they'd take care of him before getting around to me. And there was still the possibility that they wouldn't have to get around to me at all.

I didn't panic. The ambiance helped. I've lost my shirt at the track but never my head. One of the buses from downtown was unloading senior citizens and I watched them negotiating the three-step drop. Their racing forms were well marked-up. What else did they have to do all morning? But there was no hope in their faces, no glint of anticipation. Better to conk out now than wind up like that.

But first things first. I went back to my original plan. Dookes had disappeared in the crowd going into the General Admission section. I pulled out of my parking space and drove to the opposite end of the lot. During the long walk to the grandstand entrance, I went over the numbers again.

Now, if Inviduous came in at twenty-to-one, I'd have to give Demetrious fifty thousand and I'd only have twenty. If the odds dropped to ten-to-one, I'd owe him twenty-five grand and I'd only have ten. The proportions were inviolate. No matter how I juggled the figures, I came out dead.

But words had saved my neck more than once. Maybe I could talk my way out of it. "I'm an addict. I admit it. I blew it on the first four races. You can't give an addict five thousand bucks and expect him to sit out four races. Go ahead. Kill me. It's the only cure for this goddam addiction!" And that's exactly what they would do. Or how about almost the whole truth? "I was rolled. By who? By the guy who ruined the sting by betting that four grand on Invidious." And *why* did he bet it all on Invidious?

There was no way around it. My only chance of survival was in running the thousand I still had on me up to enough to give Demetrious his share of the take. Turning the thousand into twenty-six hundred and fifty would do it. All I needed was a nice two-to-one shot that couldn't lose, and I had four races in which to find it.

Chapter 28

HORSE PLAYERS have an inverted sense of security. We're all firm pessimists where the state of the economy is concerned. A lot of us have been around long enough to remember what the Depression of the thirties was like. We know that the safe investment doesn't exist and that all symbols of wealth are transitory stuff. When the stock market collapses again (as it definitely will) and property values nose-dive and the banks fail, the only solvent survivors will be those who can go to a racetrack and make their food bills and luxuries. Horse players know something else. We know it isn't hard to do.

At most tracks there are nine races a day, five days a week. And every week, at least two or three of those forty-five races are gilt-edged. I'm not talking about the one-third of the races that are won by the favorites. I mean the times when the winners romp in by six or seven lengths.

The racing secretaries who make up the day's card are out to arrange balanced fields where no single horse is a standout. The trainers have to please the owners

who keep them in business by delivering winners. So they
try to get their horses into races where they're faster
than the other entries. That's the name of the battle.
Most of the time the racing secretaries come out on top.
But two or three times every week they don't. A trainer
manages to sneak in a superior animal. And any experienced handicapper can spot it when they do.

So all we have to do is stick to the gilt-edged nags.
They rarely pay big, but that isn't the reason we don't.
We don't because there's no kick to it. Of course, we play
them and that gives us something to cover our losses.
But the real juice is in coming up with the horse that's
been overlooked, the long shot, the overlay, the one the
tipsters didn't give a chance. And all the time we have
this sense of security. When things get really rough, when
it's do-or-die time, we'll only bet on the animals that are
standouts. We won't even make token bets on hunches
to pass the time. We'll make sizable bets two or three
times a week and that's all. And though we may drop
an occasional one to a fix or accident, we'll leave the track
every day the way professionals do, with the parking
captain announcing our names over the loudspeaker and
our Rolls Royces brought up right away.

I've said as much many times, mostly to myself. The
theory is right. I've never doubted that. The only question was if I had the discipline to put it into practice.
And now I was going to find out.

The four tipsters in their booths near the entrance
touted their sheets. I bought Baedecker's. He covered the
morning workouts and sometimes came up with a sleeper.
I had to break one of my remaining fifties to pay my ten-
buck admission. That meant ten dollars more times the
odds that I'd have to win back. I suddenly felt hungry,
something I rarely feel at the track. I got in line at a

sandwich counter and ordered a corned beef on rye. Santa Anita is supposed to have the best corned beef west of Caesar's Palace. The potato salad looked like it was today's, so I bought a tub and remembered to take one of the plastic spoons.

I found an empty table in the corner and spread out my Racing Form to discourage joiners. The plastic spoon broke on the second mouthful and the corned beef was stringy. The monitor showed eleven minutes to go before the first race. There wasn't enough time to handicap it. I concentrated on the second.

It was a six-furlong Maiden Claimer for two-year-old fillies. I try to keep away from Maiden Claimers and especially from fillies. It has nothing to do with chauvinism. It has to do with menstrual cycles. Besides, there were three first-time starters in the field of eleven. One of them showed some fast workouts, but I'd been burned by morning glories too many times. I decided to leave the race alone.

The horses were going in the gate for the first race. Pooch was on the two horse and it already looked tired. I watched the race on a monitor. The track bias favored those near the rail until the far turn, then an eight-to-one called Battlin' Barney moved up on the outside and ran away with it. I wouldn't have bet it with other people's money. Pooch's horse trailed in last.

I handicapped the third race. There are as many handicapping methods as there are explanations of the origin of life, and most of them are just as bad. I use a point system: ten points if the horse has run within the last two weeks, five points if within thirty days, any number from one to nine for the jockey according to his current win record, three points if blinkers are going on or off, three more if it's the first time on lasix, and so on to include finishing position last time, lengths made up in the stretch, weight changes and workouts. I put more emphasis on speed than class. A horse doesn't know what purse it's running for. It doesn't know what number it's wearing either, but I've seen old ladies from Pasadena who rely strictly on numerology hit some big ones.

The third race was a straight claimer for three-year-olds. My figures turned up the number-four horse. By the time I arrived at that, the second race was ready to start. I went outside to watch it. The first-time outer with the good workouts won by daylight and paid better than three-to-one. If I'd put my thousand on her my troubles would have been over.

The number-four horse my figures turned up in the third race was a bay colt named The Wheezies. I've got a thing against horses with cute names. But they don't know what they're called any more than what numbers they're wearing. Horses are only like people when it comes to temperament. They can be docile and eat sugar out of your hand or they can kick you into the next county. And all the stuff about counting with their hooves or tails is vaudeville. The least-admitted equine fact is that horses are as dumb as they are beautiful.

So The Wheezies it would be. My life would be riding on his not living up to his name. The morning line odds in the program were seven-to-two but the infield tote board didn't show much early wagering. I went back into the betting hall and tried to walk off the lump in my chest.

My handicapping system had given The Wheezies a total of forty-three points. The nearest to it was the number-one horse with thirty-five. An eight-point margin was more than my handicapping system usually turned up. The Wheezies showed improved speed ratings

for his last three races. He'd been bumped at the start
in his last one and still only lost it by a neck. He had a
hot bug-boy apprentice up and that took five pounds off
his back. I couldn't see the one horse beating him. Nor
any of the others, either. The only horse I couldn't handicap was the number nine, a shipper from Caliente. But
he looked cheap and his workouts were nothing special.

The monitor showed the horses parading in the paddock. I went out on the veranda to watch them come up
the path toward the track. The one horse was already
washy. The Wheezies was on his toes with his ears
pricked, two good signs. The Caliente horse was a gray
and looked seedy.

I followed the mob to see the horses come down the
track with their outriders. The Wheezies still looked good.
I wanted to go make my bet and get it over with. But
the odds on the tote board showed eight-to-one. If they
stayed there, I could hedge my bet. Two hundred at eight-
to-one would give me what I needed. And if The Wheezies
lost, I'd still have eight hundred dollars left to play in
the fourth race. As the numbers on the board rotated
every thirty seconds, I willed the odds to hold. They
steadily came down, all the way to nine-to-five. What I'd
spotted in the Racing Form had been seen by all. I was
going to have to risk my whole bundle.

I got into the shortest betting line and immediately
wished I hadn't.

"What you goin' with?" The guy in front of me was a
loser. He hadn't shaved in days, his eyes twitched in
counterpoint and his askew baseball cap read "Padres."
In scripts, I always dub my losers Manny or Morrie or
Moe. He was definitely a Moe.

"I'm not sure yet," I said. I never say what I'm betting. It's a jinx.

"They're sure pouring it on the four horse."

"They sure are." I buried my nose in the Baedecker poop sheet to discourage him.

"It broke down last time."

"It doesn't say so in the form."

"I was here!" Moe was ready to make a federal case of it. "After the race, he came back limping. Looked to me like his left rear fetlock."

A self-appointed expert who couldn't afford a razor blade. A twitcher who rooted for the Padres. He wouldn't know a rear fetlock from an armpit. I tried to ignore his existence. But it was his turn at the window and I couldn't help overhearing his bet.

"Two across on the nine."

The shipper from Caliente was eighteen-to-one. Longshot players always bad-mouth the favorite to justify their dreams. He picked up his ticket and patted my arm.

"Good luck, buddy."

The teller waited for my bet. The big black guy behind me was nudging my heels with his toes.

"Move, man."

But what if there *was* something wrong with the fetlock? I kept my hand on the money in my pocket and walked away.

The Wheezies broke in front. He took a two-length lead down the backstretch. I promised myself that if he wasn't caught I'd find Moe or whatever his name was and strangle him. Then the apprentice jockey went to his whip and I remembered how to breathe. The Caliente horse won going away and The Wheezies finished fifth.

"What'd I tell ya?" Moe had tracked me down to wave his winning ticket in my face.

"Thanks for talking me off the four," I said. "You saved my ass."

"Any time, buddy."

In spite of my vows, I almost told him out of gratitude to put everything he'd won on Invidious in the fifth. His small bet wouldn't change anything. But his kind wouldn't listen to a tip if all the horses in the race sang it to him in harmony.

"You know what I like in the next one?" he said.

Otto Preminger once told me how to field suggestions from actors. During the shooting of *Exodus,* one of its stars had come to him and said he had an idea for the scene they were to shoot that day.

"I don't want to hear," Otto had said.

"Why not?" said the star.

"Because your idea may be very good," said Otto. "And if I use it, tomorrow you'll have two ideas."

"I don't want to hear," I said to Moe.

"So next time," he said, "save your own ass."

I took an end seat with nobody close and went to work on the fourth race. I had almost twenty-five minutes, more than enough since there were only eight horses in the field. It was an allowance race at a mile and a sixteenth. My handicapping system has always been better at routes, and with a twenty-three-thousand-dollar purse the race was likely to be honest.

My numbers gave a three-point spread to the eight horse. I could have wished for more. The eight horse was a four-year-old gelding called Sheba's Uncle Sam. I liked the name. I've never known a Sheba and I took the rest of it to mean the national image and not some rich relative. When in doubt, wave the flag. It had worked with the minstrel shows and "Oh, Say Can You See" still evoked more tears than "Over the Rainbow." The solemn visage between top hat and white beard would symbolize my last hope. Never mind that his namesake had no testicles. Geldings ran more consistently to form.

The trumpeter strode out onto the track, did his ex-
aggerated about-face and blew his fanfare. I didn't wait
to see the horses come out. I'd made my decision and
didn't want anything to change it. I went into the betting hall and watched the odds on the big board. Sheba's
Uncle Sam was holding to its morning line of six-to-one.
The two horse, as expected, had gone favorite. The one
horse was seven-to-two and the six horse was four-to-
one. The bettors liked three horses more than mine and
that was fine with me. Success in America, more often
than not, relied on a negative stance.

There were only two ahead of me at the special window for large bets. I realized I should have got into this
line for the third race and the fact that I hadn't had saved
me. There still was a thing called luck. The thought made
me feel better. But there was good luck and bad luck.
With the horses at the starting gate, the guy ahead of
me started a consultation with the teller. The race could
start before I got my bet down.

"Let's go, fella."

Those in line behind me offered choicer remarks until
the guy finally moved away. The teller, hunched over
his keys, waited impassively for my bet. I'd decided not
to say it aloud. The nine hundred and eighty dollars was
in my program. I opened it and pointed to the number
eight horse in the fourth race. The teller counted my
money and didn't look impressed. Then he pushed the
magic button and the betting ticket came out of the slot.

I thought about not watching the race. If Davy Crock-
ett could hide under a mattress at the Alamo, I could
spend the most important race of my life in the john. But
how often does anyone get to witness his own fate? Besides, I needed air.

The horses were being loaded. I squeezed through to a spot where I could see the whole track. My bet had dropped the odds on the eight horse and the board showed it at five-to-one. Half of the nine hundred and eighty would have been enough, but the rest wouldn't have done me any good if I'd lost. I'd been right to go all the way.

The starter raised his flag. Children swung and teeter-tottered in the infield area. The unexplainable inland gulls hovered over them and the mountains looked more foreboding than picturesque. The usual hush came over the stands. I focused my binoculars on the eighth stall of the starting gate and silently begged Sheba's Uncle Sam not to stumble when it opened. The race began.

I was the only one who wasn't screaming or groaning or shouting advice and encouragement. I'd watched the same counter-clockwise run thousands of times, but never in a state of such total detachment. I would live or die according to what happened in the next minute and forty-four seconds. There was nothing I could do about it now.

Sheba's Uncle Sam was forced wide going into the first turn. But he was under a tight hold. I didn't panic. I'd long ago learned to watch only my own horse, not the race. He was fifth going into the backstretch, but running easily.

"That's the way. Move him up gradually."

Either the jockey could hear me mumbling or the trainer had given him the same instructions. Sheba's Uncle Sam passed one horse, then another. He was third heading into the far turn and in the catbird seat coming out of it. The front-runner, the two horse, was tiring, and mine just cruised past him. He was clear now. The track announcer said by a length and a half before the crowd drowned him out.

By then, I was screaming, too. No words, just a gut-

tural cry from way down deep, deeper than ever, a sound
of praise and gratitude, thanking the horse, blessing the
day I first saw a racetrack, congratulating myself on my
genius in having picked this beautiful creature with the
long stride and flowing mane. I lowered my binoculars
to take in the whole stretch during the last half furlong.
Sheba's Uncle Sam, its number eight flapping in the wind,
was the most glorious sight I'd ever seen. Then I saw the
number-six horse begin its run.

It was as if my gelding had slowed to a trot. The six
horse was gaining with every stride, digging new holes
in the surface, throwing up dirt. I didn't remember its
name, so I cursed its number. Six had always been my
nemesis. The jockey was wearing green. I'd never hated
the color before but I did now. I wanted a world without
shamrocks and half-dozens.

It was only a question now of how soon the finish line
would come. Sheba's Uncle Sam looked rubber-legged.
What else from a horse named after a toothless, urine-
bagged relative? The six horse looked twice as big, twice
as strong. The jockeys on both were out to win, both riding with hands and heels, both in perfect rhythm with
their animals. The horses were side by side now, nostril
to nostril and tail to tail as they crossed the line.

The photo sign lit up. I stood staring at it, vaguely
aware of being drenched with sweat, increasingly aware
of the voices around me.

"What do ya think?"

"It looked like the six to me."

"Naw. The eight held on."

"The line favors the outside horse."

"The angle's deceptive from here."

I heard sixes. I heard eights. I was the only one without an opinion. It could have been either, whichever one

stuck out his tongue at the line. The only thing I had to go on was that winning meant everything to me and I wasn't a winner. The horses were coming back. I tried to tell something from the reception they got. But both the six and the eight seemed to be getting equal cheers. The jockeys didn't seem sure, either. Usually, during a photo, one heads for the winner's enclosure and is almost always right. But both were hanging back, not willing to dismount until the result came up on the board.

It was a long photo. I heard talk of a dead heat. I was willing to settle for that. Half of five to one would give me more than what I needed for the fifth race. I started wishing for the track announcer to say the stewards couldn't separate the first two horses. Then the photo sign went off. The track was in total silence. I don't know how many seconds it was before the win and place numbers came up. All I know is that I never suffered so much for so long.

Sheba's Uncle Sam had won. The roar that went up was deafening. I gloried in it, but I still didn't move. I watched my horse being led into the winning enclosure. I saw its picture being taken with its owners. I saw them shake hands with the jockey and the trainer. I saw the horse unsaddled and the steam rising from his hide. But there were fiendish devices known as inquiries and objections and I didn't move until the result was official.

The eight horse paid $12.80 for two dollars. The beautiful ticket in my pocket was worth six thousand, two hundred and seventy-two dollars.

Now everything was up to the Kid and Pooch Padilla and Invidious. I wasn't going to have to handicap the fifth race.

Chapter 29

THERE ARE ALL kinds of ploys in the rewriting game. No matter how bad the script I'm given, I say I can fix it. No matter how good it is, I say it needs work. There are some staple remarks that always work: that the beginning drags and the ending is a little ambiguous and that some of the characters need fleshing out.

By this time, if producers or executives aren't hanging on the ropes, I hit them with the two big questions: "What's this picture about?" and "Who are we rooting for?"

Waiting for the fifth race, I asked myself both. I had approached the sting as a scenario. I had worked out the beginning, the middle and the happy ending. But I'd deliberately avoided the big questions. What was it about? The standard theme for a caper is Crime Doesn't Pay. That was out. But it still had to have a point. It didn't until I found Bambi lying on the floor, beaten-up. That was what it was all about. All the scheming and timing and the big payoff were based on that, on how a supposedly criminal act could have a noble purpose, for if we got away with it and my personal vendetta worked, Bambi would be free. And freedom was still the best theme of all.

Who was to be rooted for was something else. I could mentally cast all the parts. I knew a good character actor with a weight problem who could play Demetrious. He was Italian, not Greek, but so what? There were plenty of goopy-looking juveniles for the Kid and enough undersized Latins to pick a Pooch from. The two heavies were no problem and James Garner would be great as me. Put us all up there in Vista Vision and who would the audience be pulling for: a fat bookie, his toothless goons, an unethical jockey or an electronics freak? No way. That left the jaded Hollywood hack, and even with Garner playing the part, the character wasn't going to get any cheering section.

The subject matter got part of the blame. Except for *National Velvet,* horse-racing pictures have never made money. And that one had a steeplechase and a teenaged Elizabeth Taylor. That was what was missing in this scenario: the beautiful young girl who rides to victory. Ideally, she'd have leg braces from muscular dystrophy and there'd be some kind of homestead at stake. And Invidious would refuse to be curried by any hands but hers. Then he'd throw his jockey just before the big race and wouldn't let anyone else on his back except the girl. She'd strip off her clothes right in the paddock (a modern touch) and change into the jockey's silks, and the rest would be up to the second-unit director who shot the racing scene.

Back to reality. There were twenty minutes to go before the fifth race and still nobody to root for. Even I couldn't root wholeheartedly for me because, motivated or not, good guys didn't do what I was doing. Heroes took on villains twice their size. A hero kept throwing punches even after he was out on his feet. He didn't set his enemy up and have two hit men do his dirty work for him. Good guys wore white hats and bad guys dark ones. And the white hat this time was on the head of Quentin Dookes.

I wallowed in my villainy. Dookes would soon be dead and the indirect blood on my hands wouldn't lose me any sleep and I'd have a nice bankroll to show for my efforts. If nothing else, it proved that Averies had been wrong about me. None of this was in the soap opera manual. All the other platitudes that fit my life would soon be more than canceled out. And as I wallowed some more, I knew I couldn't go through with it. I couldn't decide who would live or die. If ever I was capable of murder, it wouldn't be premeditated or through middlemen. I wasn't going to be able to hide behind motivation and morality and all the other standard alibis. Sudsy or not, I alone was responsible for my actions.

I went through the gate which separated the Club House from the General Admission section to find Dookes. Easier said than done. After a few races, the General Admission area smells worse than the stables. It's deep in discarded losing tickets and there's hardly room to move. Today was worse than usual. Dookes could have been anywhere in the mob or outside in the stands. There wasn't a white suit or Stetson in sight.

I spotted Gus hanging around near window twelve. He was facing the other way and hadn't seen me. The monitors showed the team of Clydesdale horses dragging the starting gate into position. The board showed the early betting.

The morning line given in the program at Santa Anita rarely quotes a horse at more than thirty-to-one. Invidious's odds were listed as fifty. So far, only two hundred and seventy dollars had been bet on him to win and yet the tote-board showed him at forty. The Kid was doing his job. I suddenly felt sure that all of us would, that everything would work out according to plan. I had to find Dookes before it was too late.

I found him sitting at one of the crowded bars. His cowboy hat was on his lap and he was starting a fresh beer and looked like he didn't have a care in the world. I squeezed in next to him and kept my voice down.

"Everything's changed," I said.

He slowly turned his head my way.

"You talkin' to me?"

"Don't do it," I whispered. "For your own sake." He looked at me as if I hadn't spoken.

"You got me mixed up with somebody else," he said.

"Dookes, listen to me. Don't make the bet. If it wins, I'll give you ten thousand dollars."

"And where would you get ten thousand dollars?" He lowered his volume to match mine.

"Never mind where. I'll give you half of what you would have won."

"Half of a hundred and sixty thousand?" He couldn't keep from guffawing.

"It won't come to that if you make the bet," I said. "And there are some people who won't like it if you do, people who play for keeps."

He took out a dirty handkerchief and wiped his brow as if the beer was seeping out of it.

"I never seen you before, Old Fucker," he said. "And if you don't go 'way, I'm gonna hit ya. An' if I hit ya, you won't get up."

An opening in the crowd gave me another glimpse of Gus. He was still near window twelve but moving in our direction. If he saw me with Dookes, the plot would thicken beyond repair. Living with a bad conscience suddenly didn't seem so impossible.

"Will you listen for once?" I said.

He got up from the bar stool and loomed over me.

"Don't make me tell ya again," he said.

I didn't. Back in the Club House section, I checked my synchronized watch against the posted time. The track clock was a minute behind. I stuck with my watch. The odds on Invidious were holding at forty-to-one. I heard the trumpet call and went outside to watch the horses come onto the track.

The Program and Racing Form said that Invidious was eleven years old, but he looked older. He was swaybacked with knobby knees and a moth-eaten mane. His piebald coat had been worn too long. The quarter horse that was taking him to the post looked in better shape.

I got into the betting line at two minutes to three. It moved quickly and I was at the window too soon. So I did what I'd told Dookes to do, letting those behind me go ahead, one at a time. At exactly three o'clock, it was my turn again. The teller remembered me.

"You hit a good one," he said.

I had figured out how to make my bet so that no one could overhear. I opened my program to the instructions I'd written in it and slid him my winning ticket. $6,240 came up on the machine when he put it into the slot.

"Pretty, ain't it?" he said.

The tote board clicked over. Sixty seconds to go and he wanted to admire the view. I pointed to what I'd written in my program. *Five thousand to win on number seven. I'll take the rest.*

He leaned forward so he could see the tote board.

"What you trying to do, take home the track?"

"Everything or nothing," I said.

"It's none of my business," he said, "but I'd go for half."

"Like you said," I said, "it's none of your business."

I immediately regretted it. He started counting out what I had coming like he'd never counted before. Then he pretended to lose track and had to start again. The tote board clicked again. Thirty seconds to go. Telling him to hurry up would just slow him down more.

"Do my bet first." I tried not to sound hysterical and added "please."

"Any particular reason?" He looked like he wanted to discuss that, too.

"I'm superstitious," I said.

"Okay. Don't want you blaming me when you lose."

He hit the win key and my betting ticket came up with all of seven or eight seconds to spare. I pocketed my cash and took off. On the next click, the board and monitors showed Invidious at forty-five-to-one. On the click after that it was back to forty. The Kid's work was finished. I spotted Damon near the betting window assigned to him. He saw me and gave a slight nod. Our work was done, too. Now it was Pooch's turn.

"The horses are approaching the starting gate." The track announcer's voice was almost drowned out by the racket in the betting hall.

I didn't go out to watch the race. I'd come close enough to cardiac arrest for one afternoon. Besides, what was going to happen inside was just as crucial as what would take place on the track.

I concentrated on the big board. On the next click the odds on the seven horse went from forty to nineteen. Dookes had made his bet. A buzz immediately went up. I knew the words without hearing them.

"There's a big move on the seven."

"Maybe it's a fake."

"Not for that kinda dough."

"I'm goin' with it."

And go with it they did. The betting lines lengthened and became noisier.

"Hurry it up, will ya?"

"Get the finger out!"

"Somebody see if he's still breathing."

I stood watching the odds go down to sixteen, to fourteen, to twelve.

"What the fuck's happened?"

It was Damon, grabbing my arm and hissing in my ear. Before I could answer him, he saw Gus motioning from the entrance to the General Admission section. He ran to join him. There was a lot of pointing and gesturing as they went off.

Invidious won by three lengths and paid eight-to-one and change. I went back to the same window and picked up forty-five thousand, two hundred and eighty dollars. The teller counted it out without comment.

I stood on the steps outside to take in most of the parking lot. Dookes was already making his way between the cars toward the space where we were supposed to meet. Damon and Gus were about twenty yards behind. They'd obviously been tailing him since he picked up his money. I tracked them with my binoculars. Gus peeled off and Damon started closing the gap between himself and Dookes. The place where I'd originally parked was taken by a van. Dookes stopped in front of it and took off his hat and scratched his head. He checked the markers on the nearest pole to see if he had the right row. Gus's car and Damon got to him at the same time.

I'd expected it to end there, that they'd use a silencer or a knife or the car itself and take off leaving Dookes in a pool of his own blood. But there wasn't even a scuffle. Damon just opened the car door and Dookes just got in. Gus must have had a gun on him from inside, but I couldn't see it. Then Damon jumped in the back and the car joined the traffic toward the exit gate.

I'd overlooked the obvious again. In rewriting the scenario, I'd left a great hole in it. They weren't going to dispose of him until they found out what was behind his bet. I could guess where they were taking him and the first two questions Demetrious would ask.

"Where'd you get the stake? Who told you to put it on the seven horse?"

The answers to both were the same.

Chapter 30

I COULD HAVE driven east into the desert or south toward Mexico. But I didn't even consider running away. There is a point in a scenario when the turning and twisting has to stop, when the characters take over and, if the pieces have been assembled right, the end is inevitable.

I was glad I'd reached it and tried not to anticipate what I was heading into. Whatever, I wouldn't beg and I wouldn't lie. The commitment to truth provided a jab of irresponsibility and I drove relaxed. But I didn't break any speed records on the freeway.

I expected to see Gus's shiny black car parked near the pizza parlor. It wasn't. Nor was my knock on Demetrious's door answered. I tried it and it opened. Demetrious was alone, sitting behind his table and staring at the pad he'd scribbled the numbers on as if it was his mother's grave.

"I'm sorry," I said. It was the least I could say.

He looked up and there were real tears in both eyes. "Eight hundred grand down the toilet," he said.

"It could have been worse," I said. One of my pet

hatreds is Pollyannaism. Still, it wasn't a lie. "Invidious could have lost."

"But he didn't," he said. His tears had vanished. "Give me the twenty-five grand."

"Twenty-five thousand, one hundred and forty," I said. I put the exact amount in front of him.

"I coulda bought a yacht," he said. "I always wanted a fuckin' yacht."

Then the two goons came in. But Dookes wasn't with them. I searched their faces for any clue. Gus looked at me with killer eyes. Not lying was going to be a hell of a lot easier than not begging. But Gus always looked that way. Damon closed the door and said something in Greek that made Demetrious jump up. His jump made me jump. He came around his table on thick, stumpy legs. It was the first time I'd ever seen him on his feet and he was shorter than I'd imagined. I stood waiting for the three of them to spread out and come at me. Then the yelling began.

It had the fury of a street fight, but they never touched. They stuck to gestures, raised fists and accusing fingers and at one point Demetrious grabbed a chair and threw it across the room. The rest was verbal and all in Greek. This was it, my climactic scene, my denouement, my last page, and I didn't understand one word. The only Greek word I knew was emphysema.

"Wait a minute," I said. "How about letting me in on it?"

Mine was a rational voice in a Greek argument. It went unheard. But none of the fists and fingers were pointing my way. Hope started coming back fast. But it wasn't alone. It was riding a hell of a lot of bottled-up steam.

"You're in America!" I was as loud as they were. "Try talking the language."

Old Glory fell on its ass. My caustic tone landed on deaf ears. I don't know what set off the rest. Maybe it was relief or perverted paranoia or the masochism my wife so often accused me of. Maybe all three. But when they went on yelling and leaving me out, I blew like I'd never blown before.

"You fuckin' greaseballs!" I shoved Damon aside and grabbed Demetrious by the knot of his loud tie. "You wanted me to work out the story! I broke my balls on it! And I've got a right to know the goddam ending!"

Demetrious looked at my fist holding his tie. A signal from him and his two goons would use me for a wishbone.

"What's with you?" he said.

"I want to know what you guys know," I said.

"We don't know nuthin'." He pointed to the others. "The dumb sons-of-bitches went crazy."

"He made us mad," said Gus.

"So what?" Demetrious was yelling again. "You coulda found out first who he was! You coulda found out who sent him!" He looked down at his tie again and I quickly removed my hand.

"The bum tried to get tough," said Gus.

"Now he can bet on fish races," added Damon. His grin displayed both of his teeth.

Demetrious came up with a special Greek expletive that silenced them. Then he went to the closet and took out a cardboard laundry box.

"Somebody leaked it," he said. "Maybe one of the jockeys." He stopped to take us in. "Or maybe somebody closer." The Kid's arrival interrupted him.

"Getting to those conduits was tougher than I thought." The Kid immediately started angling for praise. From his point of view we'd succeeded.

Demetrious took one look at him and eliminated him as a suspect. He turned to his goons again.

"So fork up my share."

While they emptied their pockets, he unplugged both his phones from the wall and dumped them into the laundry box. The hundred-dollar bills that Damon and Gus laid on the table came to a lot more than twenty-five thousand dollars each. My casual count made it about thirty-five thousand more. The return on Dookes's bet would have come to about that. Demetrious gave the Kid his ten percent of the take and the Kid didn't even check it. Then Pooch came in mad.

"I told 'em it was my birthday!" he said. It was standard track gossip that jockeys let one of their own win a race on his birthday. "Now I gotta wait a whole year."

The money Demetrious shoved toward him calmed him down a little. Demetrious watched him as he checked it.

"Who screwed up on the odds?" said Pooch.

"Vegas had a guy lay off four grand to bring them down," said Demetrious.

"How'd they find out?" said Pooch.

"Somebody musta told them."

"Who?"

"Maybe somebody who was tryin' to square some markers." Demetrious's suspicion was openly aimed at him.

"I don't gamble," said Pooch.

And then there was one. Demetrious turned to me and waited. I could sense his gorillas ready to pounce.

"I haven't been to Vegas in three years." I could say it honestly.

"Just hope I never find out different," he said.

"I won't lose any sleep," I said. "Vegas isn't my scene."

"I'll bet it was one of the other jockeys," said the Kid.

The wide-eyed way he said it cleared the air a little.

"Anyway," said Demetrious, "whoever sent their boy won't like what happened to him." He dumped some yellow pads and all the remaining money into the box. "Everybody better disappear for awhile." His last line was an afterthought and only for me.

"You'll have to make your bets someplace else."

Chapter 31

PERRY LUTZ AND Associates was only a couple blocks out of my way. The door to Perry's inner office was ajar and I could hear him on the phone. The temporary secretary didn't know me and started the song and dance about his being in a conference, but I walked on in. The producer on the other end of the line was giving Perry a rough time, but Perry got the last word after he hung up.

"One of his thalidomide offspring winds up in the black, so suddenly he's an expert." He proffered the jar of hard candy he always kept on his desk. "So why aren't you home typing?"

"I want out," I said. "I want you to settle for the first draft payment."

"Twenty thousand?" He pulled a face. "With a little potchkying, you get thirty-five."

"Tell Averies I've lost perspective on the script," I said. "Recommend somebody else for the rewrite."

"You're throwing away fifteen big ones."

"I can afford to." I gave him a peek at what was in

my wallet. He looked suitably impressed. Then he leaned back in his swivel chair and tapped his lower teeth with a pencil.

"You know anything about Catherine the Great?" he said.

"Only that she had a thing for white stallions."

"I knew you were perfect for it." He buzzed the temporary secretary and told her to get Averies on the phone. We both knew that Averies wouldn't take the call or return it until the next day.

"You mind telling me what I'm perfect for?"

It was an epic to be shot in Yugoslavia and financed by an international cartel of gonifs. But Perry assured me he could get half my fee put into escrow.

"And first class, round trip, to Dubrovnik?"

"You didn't have to ask," he said.

"For two," I said.

There was a bookshop on La Cienega which specialized in pornography and out-of-print paperbacks. The paperbacks were arranged alphabetically by author. Somebody goofed. The one copy they had was in the middle of a shelf of Harold Robbins. The corner of the cover was torn off and the paper was yellowing.

"*The Drums of Fu Manchu*," said the clerk. "That's Sax Rohmer's best."

The house looked like she'd spent the whole afternoon cleaning it. I found her propped up in bed and reading. I held the paperback offering behind me.

"Close your eyes and make a wish," I said.

"What for?"

"Just do as you're told."

She kept right on reading. I went to the bed and gently placed *The Drums of Fu Manchu* on her stomach. She never even glanced at it. She was so engrossed in what she was reading that she didn't even stop to ask how come I'd returned alone or where her husband was. When she did, I would tell her exactly what I'd done. I'd made up my mind to that. I wanted it all out of the way before I brought up Dubrovnik.

"I've read six of them so far," she said.

"Six of what?"

She held up the book she was reading so I could see the cover. It was my collection of short stories.

"They're terrific," she said.

I stood there and counted her blessings. She'd been spared earnestness. She never announced her pains. During all our time together, she'd never mentioned osmosis or credibility. She'd never once said, "Thanks for sharing that with me" or "I feel more secure now." She couldn't tell Brahms from Bach, a Constable from a Wyeth, a piety from a dogma. She could eat a Smitty's Special without doing the drooling, chewing scene from *Tom Jones*. All these were negative blessings, but she had her positive ones, too: her face and her body and her taste in short stories.

She sighed over a sentence she read, one of *my* sentences, and looked up at me as never before. I knew what would happen next. But beyond that there were no certainties. There never were. That's what Hollywood and horse racing were all about. It wasn't even a sure thing that we'd live happily ever after.